GRAVE *of* ANGELS

MICHAEL PRESCOTT BIBLIOGRAPHY

Titles originally published under the name Brian Harper:

Shiver (1992; e-book 2011)

Shudder (1994)

Shatter (1995)

Deadly Pursuit (1996)

Blind Pursuit (1997; e-book 2011)

Mortal Pursuit (1998; e-book 2010)

Titles published under the name Michael Prescott:

Comes the Dark (1999)

Stealing Faces (1999; e-book 2011)

The Shadow Hunter (2000; e-book 2012)

Last Breath (2002; e-book 2011)

Next Victim (2002; e-book 2010)

In Dark Places (2004; e-book 2010)

Dangerous Games (2005; e-book 2010)

Mortal Faults (2006; e-book 2011)

Final Sins (2007; e-book 2012)

Riptide (2010; e-book and print-on-demand)

GRAVE *of* ANGELS

MICHAEL PRESCOTT

THOMAS & MERCER

Text copyright © 2012 by Douglas Borton
All rights reserved.

Printed in the United States of America.

Published by Thomas & Mercer
P.O. Box 400818
Las Vegas, NV 89140

ISBN-13: 9781612183145
ISBN-10: 161218314X

In memory of my mother

1

SWANN sat at a corner table, dressed to be invisible, as he always was on a night when there was killing to be done.

Pulse of hip-hop, flash of bling. Sweaty dancers jerking to the antic beat. A hundred shouted conversations, all going unheard. Most of the patrons were young and stoned. The girls underfed, the boys wiry and hard, showing off piercings, shaved heads, elaborate tats.

He sat away from the dance floor, a glass of melting ice near his hand. No one joined him; he projected an aura that deterred company. He wore a tan jacket over a black T-shirt. A functional outfit, nondescript. No one would look at him or remember him. No one knew that he was on the job, and his job was death.

Swann had a long acquaintance with death. He had taken many lives, for many reasons, and sometimes for not much of a reason at all. The way the world worked, you could suffer, or you could make others suffer. Only a saint or a crazy man—he didn't see much difference—would choose the first alternative.

Swann understood one rule in life, and it was not the Golden Rule.

Know what you want and take it.

He shifted in his chair, tightening his biceps and forearms, enjoying the clench of corded muscle. His body was lean and tough like boiled leather, crisscrossed with ropes of scar tissue. He'd taken a bullet once, been nicked by many blades, but he still had all his parts.

He felt fine. A good hump always left him calm and alert. Only fools practiced celibacy before a big game, and tonight he was playing the biggest game of his life.

Earlier this evening he'd found a whore and brought her to his motel room. The room was a grimy hole, like a thousand others he had known. Pungent odors hung in the stale air. The rug was tracked with wear and stained with unidentifiable spills. The TV got a handful of satellite channels and a decent variety of pay-per-view porn. A mouse lived in the walls; he heard it at night when he lay in bed. It made scrabbling sounds, a small, scurrying thing.

He'd been in worse places. Before long he would be someplace better.

The whore was businesslike and thorough. Only once did she flinch and pull away—when she saw the snake.

As a general rule, he was careful not to give himself any identifying marks. The snake was an exception. It had cost him a lot of pain, because it was inked on the shaft of his cock, a jet-black python that arched and elongated when he got hard. He'd acquired it in a tat parlor in Nogales after gulping enough Viagra to remain erect throughout the application. Later he'd bought a woman and broken in his newly tricked-out equipment. Snaked her, you could say.

Since that day, many women had the met the snake, but none had ever asked what it meant to him. He'd long since stopped expecting the question. People were incurious. They shuffled through life with blinkered eyes, brought every kind of misery on themselves, and never knew how or why. The sleepwalkers, the shambling dead.

Swann wasn't one of them. He was wide awake. He avoided alcohol and heavy meals, drank a great deal of coffee and supplemented it with Adderall and Provigil, brain-boosting meds. He used breath control and mnemonic tricks.

If there was a science of alertness, Swann was its test subject. He was determined never to relax, never to fall into lethargy and complacency. To always be one step, two steps, three steps ahead.

In the kingdom of the blind, the one-eyed man was king. And Jack Swann had both eyes open.

His phone vibrated against his thigh. He knew who it was before answering. Just two people had this number, and only one would be calling tonight.

Impatiently, he listened to the voice on the other end, pressing the phone close to his ear. "I told you," he interrupted, "it's going down. Just chill."

He closed the phone. His employer sounded worried. He ought to be. Things weren't going to work out precisely as agreed.

He stared across the nightclub at the slim, gyrating figure who was, as always, the center of attention. Looking at her, he saw his destiny.

A peculiar thought for him. He didn't believe in portents. Didn't believe in anything he couldn't touch, couldn't see. A realist, he despised all superstitions.

Even so, every time he saw the girl on the dance floor, Swann felt a quickening of his pulse, a tightening in his groin.

Know what you want and take it.

Soon.

2

KATE Malick thought of her as Wednesday's child.

It was crazy, of course. Crazy to look at her with pity—the girl who had it all. The movie star, the tabloid idol. Twenty-one years old, with an estimated worth of fifteen million dollars. She owned a four-million-dollar condo in West Hollywood's Sierra Towers. She rode a chauffeured limousine to A-list parties in Malibu and Bel Air. She vacationed in St. Tropez, bumming rides on private jets because she wouldn't fly commercial. No one could feel sorry for her.

Even so, Kate found the words of the old nursery rhyme running through her head whenever her thoughts turned to Chelsea Brewer.

Wednesday's child is full of woe...

"We need to talk about your daughter," Kate said. She sat on an angular divan, her long legs crossed like the blades of a folding instrument, hands clasped in her lap as she leaned forward into a wedge of lamplight. She owned a dozen copies of the same outfit and wore it always. Double-breasted Michael Kors jacket and skirt. All of it black, jet black, like her boots, her hair.

Sam and Victoria Brewer watched her from matching Eames chairs set wide apart.

"I don't see what could possibly be so urgent," Victoria said. "Whatever it is, it could have waited until tomorrow, I'm sure."

"I'm afraid not. Something happened tonight. About an hour ago, at eight o'clock, a member of Chelsea's entourage got sick."

"That hardly sounds like a critical matter."

"I mean she got sick from an overdose. She mixed alcohol and drugs. Grange called the EMTs, and then he called me."

Like a physical sensation, the memory came back—the high-speed drive through Hollywood, ending in the alley behind the club...

Her car door slamming as she looked around at the sodden squalor, a line of dump bins overspilling plastic garbage bags, one bag split open, its contents bleeding out, and a tide of black insects sweeping over the hill of plastic to gorge themselves on filth. Ahead, a small tableau, three figures posed against the wall, one seated on the asphalt, slumping forward, while another leaned down and the third looked on. The seated figure was a girl, shaking as if to an internal metronome, her high heels beating a ragged tattoo on the pavement. The man leaning over her was Chelsea's bodyguard, Grange, and the onlooker was Chelsea herself. No paramedics. No ambulance.

"Where the hell are the EMTs?" Kate yelled, and Grange glanced up, his broad face red with worry and strain.

"On their way," he said.

"What happened to her?"

"She took something."

"Took what?"

"Nobody knows. Or at least"—he flicked a glance at Chelsea— "nobody's saying."

Kate knelt by the girl, looked her over in the gleam of Grange's pocket flash. She was in her early twenties, or possibly younger and partying with a fake ID. Her pretty face was ashen, and her eyes were jumping everywhere without taking anything in.

"Her name?" Kate asked.

"I don't know."

"Chelsea must know. She's Chelsea's friend, right?"

"Chelsea's in no condition," Grange said simply.

Kate spared a moment to look at Chelsea Brewer, and she saw the vacancy in the girl's expression. Nobody home.

Victoria's voice drilled into the memory: "Was Chelsea involved?"

Kate blinked. "Of course she was involved. It was one of her friends—"

"No, I mean was she involved *officially*? Is this going to get into the media? Police reports?"

"Oh. I see."

She did see, and she couldn't even blame Mrs. Brewer for asking, when the same question had occurred to her as soon as she had arrived.

Bending over the girl, trying to think, balancing needs and priorities. The ambulance would come, bringing with it the paparazzi gathered out front. And there would be police, and if the name Chelsea Brewer were mentioned, there would be media, too—if not here, then at the hospital…

She took a breath and looked at Grange. "All right. I'll stay with this one till the paramedics get here. You take Chelsea back inside. We need…we need to keep her out of this."

Even as she said it, she felt guilty for caring about Chelsea's reputation, her image, when another girl's life was at risk.

"No," she said now, in the civilized quiet of the Brewers' living room, "we shielded her. Though that may have been a mistake."

Victoria's eyebrow arched. "A mistake?"

"It might be better for your daughter if the news did get out. It might help wake her up."

"That doesn't make any sense," Victoria said. She was a small, rail-thin woman, her features masklike after too many facelifts. "Chelsea is perfectly capable of taking care of herself."

Kate felt a stab of anger push through the armor plating of her self-control. "Do you really think so?" she asked evenly.

She wished Victoria could have seen her daughter's face as Grange had led her away, that empty face and those unseeing eyes. Eyes of glass, doll's eyes…

Then she was gone and Kate was alone with the nameless girl. She touched the girl's neck, finding the carotid artery, feeling a rapid, fluttery pulse. When she looked at the girl's face again, she saw the eyelids sliding shut as the pupils rolled up in the sockets.

"No," she snapped. "Stay with me." She grabbed the girl by the shoulders, shaking her weightless body. "Come on, stay with me!"

The girl, flopping passively under Kate's hands, banged her head against the wall behind her. The impact startled her awake. Her eyes drifted into focus.

"That's better," Kate said. "Better. You stay alert, hear me?" But already the eyes were going away again. "Damn it, get up. Get up."

Kate hooked her arms under the girl's armpits and lifted her off the ground, balancing her on two tremulous legs. It wasn't difficult. The girl weighed nothing at all. Anorexic, subsisting on a starvation diet, her rib cage nearly poking through her shirt.

"Walk. Walk it off. Come on."

She made the girl walk. It was like dancing with a life-size marionette, a creature of strings and floppy limbs. Together, they made a circuit of the space between the trash bins, Kate guiding her, the girl's shoes scraping asphalt.

Her head nodded again. Kate shook her back to consciousness.

"You're not sleeping tonight," she hissed, wishing she knew the girl's name. Somehow it would be easier if she just knew her name.

"You're staying with me, and you're going to be okay. You hear me? You're going to be okay."

No reaction, no twitch of interest from the pale face, the distant eyes.

"Is Chelsea all right now?" Victoria asked.

"Your daughter was never in any danger." Kate waited for a question about Chelsea's friend. When it didn't come, she volunteered the information. "The other girl is expected to recover. They pumped her stomach in the ER."

"Well," Victoria said, "that's fine, then."

Another plunge of anger, this one deeper than the last. She felt like shaking Victoria Brewer as she had shaken the nameless girl in the alley. "It's *not* fine," she said. "Chelsea's friend nearly died tonight. If the EMTs had arrived five minutes later, she might not have made it."

Sam Brewer spoke for the first time. "And what does that have to do with us? It's some other girl, some girl we don't even know."

"If Chelsea's friends are doing drugs, you can bet Chelsea is, too."

"That's an outrageous accusation," Victoria said. "Totally groundless."

Kate blinked at her. "Mrs. Brewer, are you aware of how Chelsea spends her nights?"

"I don't follow the tabloids, if that's what you mean. She's twenty-one. Of course she's going to sow some wild oats."

"Her bodyguard has seen things. He's expressed his concerns to me."

Sam crossed his muscular forearms, crowded with purple tats. "So now we're supposed to worry about some glorified bouncer?"

"What I'm worried about," Kate said, "is your daughter's future."

"She's done okay for herself so far, don't you think?" His casual wave encompassed the house, a Frank Lloyd Wright knockoff cantilevered over a chasm. Sunken living room, earth tones in the lavatories, oak paneling in the den—a seventies wet dream bought with Chelsea's money. Victoria served as her daughter's agent and business manager and pocketed 25 percent.

The house was a temple to Chelsea's stardom. Framed magazine covers, arranged in chronological sequence like the stations of the cross, charted her progress from girl next door to vixen to tramp. The point of no return: last year's *Maxim*, Chelsea posing naked, a pair of long-stemmed roses concealing her nipples. "Little Chelsea, All Grown Up," the cover said.

"Chelsea's been partying all night," Kate said, "every night. Often till dawn. She's drinking and using. She has multiple sex partners—"

"For God's sake." Victoria drew a sharp breath. "So she likes doing the club scene. It doesn't make her any less bankable."

"That's not what I—"

"Our publicist says it may even help her image. This is the age of the bad girl."

"I don't give a crap what her handlers say." Kate hailed from New Jersey. She'd lost most of her accent, but a hint of it came out when she was pissed.

"Well, you should," Victoria said airily. "It's their business, not yours, to keep Chelsea on track."

Kate wished she could get through. She felt she was shouting through a soundproofed wall. But where words didn't work, a picture might.

"I want you to look at something." She called up a bookmarked website on her cell phone and handed the phone to Chelsea's mother. Victoria studied the shaky amateur video, then passed it back to Kate with a shrug.

"She's young," Victoria said. "She's having a good time. There's no law against it."

Actually, there *was* a law against dancing topless in a public place. "It doesn't worry you? This kind of behavior?"

"She's a kid," Sam said. "Why've you got a problem with that?" He and Victoria had been divorced for more than a decade, yet he remained a fixture in his ex-wife's life, his presence in the household interrupted only by occasional stints in prison.

He glared at Kate, hating her with a career criminal's instinctive animosity toward someone connected, however obliquely, with law enforcement.

Kate stared him down. "She's not a kid anymore. She's an adult, and she's out of control."

"Come now." Victoria's tongue clucked. "It's perfectly normal to behave that way at Chelsea's age. But you wouldn't know about that, would you? When you were twenty-one, you were a nun."

"For a couple of years. A long time ago." It was no surprise Victoria knew this. Everyone did.

"Well, my daughter is no nun. If you have a problem with that, maybe you should go back to the convent."

"They wouldn't take me. I wasn't a very good nun."

Sam chuckled. "Bad nun." Running some pornographic filmstrip in his head.

Victoria glanced at him, irritated. "My point is, you don't know what it's like to be young and free and to blow off steam."

Kate dug her fingernails into her palms. "I know it can lead to trouble."

"Talk to Chelsea if you're so concerned. You said it yourself. She's an adult."

"And she should start acting like one."

"You're not her mother."

"Are *you*?"

Victoria bristled. "There's no need to get personal. I understand that tonight's…episode has upset you. But it was a one-time thing."

"It wasn't a one-time thing, and you know it."

"What's that supposed to mean?"

"Mila Farris."

Silence for a moment, and a quick exchange of glances between Victoria and Sam.

"I don't know what you're referring to," Victoria said.

"Cut it out, Mrs. Brewer. You know. And so do I, even though you did your best to keep it from me. Which wasn't smart, by the way. I can't be fully effective if you keep me in the dark."

"Whatever you've heard is just a rumor. Mila Farris has nothing to do with…with anything."

"She was one of Chelsea's hangers-on, just like the girl tonight."

"Mila Farris is irrelevant," Victoria said. "And how the hell did you find out about her, anyway?"

"People talk."

"Which people?"

"I'm not answering that," Kate said.

"Then I'm not carrying this conversation any further. It's none of your damn business, any of it. And I understand my own daughter quite well enough, thank you."

"Vicki's a great mom," Sam added, lazily scratching his cheek.

"Just keep the crazies away," Victoria added. "Chelsea's other problems will work themselves out."

Kate took a breath, nodded. She pocketed her cell phone and got up from the divan. On her way out of the living room, she stopped at a corner table.

"There's just one more thing."

She picked up a large glass serving bowl with an ornately scalloped rim. The dish was heavy and solid and when it hit the wall it made a great crash, shattering to pieces.

Victoria Brewer shot upright, her glance ticking from the spray of shards on the tiled floor to Kate's outstretched arm. Kate had slung the bowl underhand, softball style, with her full strength.

"Are you *crazy*?" Victoria gasped. "Are you out of your *mind*?"

"I take it you're upset about losing that item."

"You're goddamned right I'm upset!"

"You can always replace it. But if you lose your daughter, you'll never get her back."

She walked out the front door and down the steps. In the house, Victoria was shouting that the price of the bowl was coming out of her fee, every penny.

"Go to hell," Kate murmured as she slipped behind the wheel of her Jaguar and hit the gas, peeling out of the driveway.

Not a very pious sentiment. But then, she wasn't a nun anymore.

3

MULHOLLAND Drive was a black, coiled serpent riding the ridge of the Hollywood Hills, and Kate took it fast, powering the XK through the sinuous curves, hugging the shoulder as the city swept up at her through breaks in the trees.

She knew she'd blown it. Rather than getting the Brewers on her side, she'd alienated them. But maybe nothing she said could have made them hear. Not if they didn't want to.

She spun the wheel, navigating another S-curve, then clipped on her Bluetooth headset and pulled out her cell phone. She didn't carry a handbag. Too inconvenient. She had lots of pockets.

She speed-dialed Grange. He answered, shouting his name over frantic hip-hop.

"Where are you?" she asked.

"Stiletto."

"She's *still* out partying?"

"Believe it. She's a piece of work, this one. Third club tonight, and it's not even ten."

"Try to keep her there. I'm coming over."

"What for?"

"Just to check on her." And to find out the other girl's name.

She sped on, her fingers light on the wheel, the Jag's aluminum chassis absorbing shocks in the road. Houses flashed past, recessed in roadside hollows. Treetops hooted with owls.

Her phone rang. The ringtone was "Lady Madonna." Nun humor.

She answered without checking the caller ID. It was probably Grange calling back to say Chelsea was moving on. "Yes?"

"Hello, Kate."

Not Grange. *Him.*

"Listen, asshole"—she pressed the rubber earbud tighter into her ear—"I'm getting a little tired of this bullshit."

"You have a dirty mouth. I like it." As always, the voice was electronically distorted. It could have been anyone. Could even have been a woman, but Kate was somehow sure it was a man. A particular man.

"You're not as smart as you think," she said. "My tech guys are closing in on you."

"That's a lie."

It was. His calls had proven untraceable despite Alan's best efforts.

"You're pushing it, friend," she said carefully. "There are laws against stalking. I should know."

"Of course you know. You're the security expert. But, Kate, you need to start worrying about your own security."

"More threats? This is getting old."

"The time for threats is over. It's just about time to get down to business."

"Any place, any time."

"You don't get to choose either the place or the time. It'll be when you least expect it. You'll never know what hit you."

She tried to think of a riposte, but he was already gone. Her cell's LCD screen displayed *Unknown Caller*, as usual.

"Jerk," she muttered.

He'd been calling her for the past two weeks. How he'd obtained her private number, she didn't know. The calls were untraceable, placed from a throwaway cell phone with a calling card, the kind of thing that could be purchased in any drugstore.

At first she'd thought he was a prankster. Lately she was beginning to take him seriously. She even thought she knew who it was. Couldn't prove it. But she had her suspicions.

She caught Laurel Canyon and corkscrewed down, letting the steep grade do the engine's work until she was back on level ground. Sunset Strip slowed her down in a sea of brake lights. She inched past billboards and neon. Waves of bass throbbed from maxed-out car stereos. From somewhere, a scent of night jasmine wafted through the warm September night.

She passed a comedy club with a line outside, everybody on cell phones. Lounging on the sidewalk was a homeless man, too beaten down even to cadge for change. Nobody noticed him. The city bred indifference. When she had been a nun, the sisters had jokingly referred to LA as Sodom.

Or maybe they weren't joking. In Sodom the angels came as visitors and were not recognized. Would they be recognized here?

Up ahead, Stiletto. She eased into the left lane, and her phone rang again. The caller ID said it was Alan, her night dispatcher.

"Hey, chief. Great news. Sal French is on the warpath again."

"Where is he?"

"Philippe's Raw Bar, Century City."

"I know it. I'll get over there as soon as I can. Got another stop to make first."

"Sal's pretty hot under the collar."

"He can wait," Kate said, not giving a damn.

It was ten fifteen when she wheeled into the parking lot behind Stiletto. She killed the engine and got out of the car.

There was a Glock nine in her glove compartment, the compact model known to aficionados as a Baby Glock, an ugly little pug-nosed thing sheathed in a pocket holster. Nun with a gun, that was her. She left it there, knowing the club would have a metal detector at the door. Anyway, Grange would be carrying. His credentials let him take a gun almost anywhere.

A few desultory paparazzi lingered by the club entrance. Bypassing the line of patrons, she walked up to the bouncer. The guy was new and didn't know her. She was about to flash her creds and say she was there on business, but it wasn't necessary. He looked her over, liked what he saw, raised the velvet rope. She passed through the metal detector into the cave of noise and body heat that was Stiletto.

She moved forward, all her senses heightened. High alert—her instinctive reaction to any crowded, busy environment.

Her threat-detection radar wasn't picking up any blips. There was no one who looked out of place, no one studying the crowd with a predator's rapt attention.

Except...

A man sat alone at a table, watching the dance floor where Chelsea could be seen in the rippling crowd. Something about him made her hesitate. Was it her imagination, or was he looking straight at Chelsea?

Through the shifting crush of people, she studied him. She estimated his vitals—better than six feet tall, two hundred pounds, age between forty and fifty. Bald, his scalp gleaming under the lights.

Not having her gun was a problem. But if he'd passed through the metal detector, he wouldn't be armed, either.

She moved nearer, slipping her cell phone out of her pocket. When she was close, she lifted the phone and surreptitiously snapped his picture. For the files.

A trio of inebriated girls slouched past, giggling, blocking her view. Then they were gone—and so was he.

She jostled her way through the crowd and reached his empty chair. Looked in all directions. Chaos, a kaleidoscope of faces and silhouettes.

She struggled through clusters of people, shading her eyes from the downlights, making her way to the front of the club. Outside, she found the bouncer and showed him the photo on her phone's display. "Did this guy just leave?"

"Who's he? Your boyfriend?"

"Just someone I'm looking for."

"We're all looking for somebody."

She cut him off with a hot glare that unmanned him. "Did he leave?"

Shake of his head.

"Don't let him."

"Why not?"

"He's a suspect in a crime."

"You a cop?" he asked uncertainly.

She pressed two twenties into his hand. "Pretend I am."

She plunged back into the maelstrom. Cut down a back hallway, found the fire door. Bold letters across its face: DO NOT OPEN EXCEPT IN CASE OF EMERGENCY. ALARM WILL SOUND.

Would it? She cranked the handle down, pushed. No response. The door was locked.

Safety hazard, fire code violation, but it meant he hadn't gotten out via the front or the rear. He was still in the club. She could track him down.

What was her strategy? Find Grange, have him join the search? No. Couldn't distract him from Chelsea. The girl needed eyes on her. Go it alone, then. Divide the club into sectors, clear one grid at a time.

She was heading back to the dance floor when she felt a breeze.

There was an open casement window seven feet off the floor. Packing crates and pallets were stacked below. She climbed the rickety pile and stuck her head out.

Trash bin beneath her, the lid closed. A man could slip through the window and drop onto the lid. Then it was just a question of getting out of the alley. Brick wall at one end, padlocked gate at the other, but neither would be an obstacle for someone willing to climb.

Finding the open window couldn't have been luck. He must have checked out the club before sitting down, maybe even moved the packing materials into place. He'd prepared an escape route.

He was smart. He was careful.

Someone to worry about.

Definitely.

4

K A T E found Alfonse Grange near the bar, a bottle of Evian smothered in one fist. He wore an open-collared dress shirt and a pin-striped jacket with a cell phone in the front pocket. There was an earpiece in his left ear and a lapel mic by his throat, allowing hands-free operation of the phone once he hit speed dial. All her field ops were outfitted with the same rig. In an emergency they couldn't be fumbling with the phone.

Grange cut an intimidating figure, but at the moment his threat profile was somewhat minimized by the oversized pink handbag cradled in one arm, out of which peeped a round, furry head. Chelsea never went anywhere without her toy poodle, Chanticleer.

"She's got me holding her damn dog now," Grange said as Kate approached him. Despite his complaint, Kate noticed that Grange was petting the poodle, who shivered appreciatively.

"Forget the dog. We just had a situation."

Automatically, Grange looked toward the dance floor, where Chelsea Brewer was flailing around with two guys and another girl in what appeared to be a spastic prelude to group sex. "Do tell."

"I spotted this guy." She showed him the photo on her phone. "He was watching Chelsea, and he booked when I closed in."

"Where was he situated?"

"Table at three o'clock." Kate pointed that way, but the table was invisible behind a mirrored pillar. The man had chosen a seat that allowed him to see Chelsea on the dance floor without being seen by her bodyguard at the bar.

Grange frowned, deep parentheses cupping his mouth. He didn't like missing something. He'd worked personal security his whole life, first for a rock band, then for the CEO of a software firm. "You say he took off?"

"Out a window in the rear hallway, if you can believe it."

"Send the pic to my phone, and I'll show it to the bouncers from now on. With any luck, we can freeze this creep out."

She was already transmitting the photo. "I want you moving around more. Don't stay in one position and let him hide from you."

An eyebrow lifted. "You telling me how to do my job?"

"Obviously. He shows up again, have a talk with him."

A talk with Grange would get anyone's attention. He was 220 pounds of beefy muscle, his bullet head shaved bald, a chrome loop fixed in his left earlobe. He looked like an immensely expanded edition of Andre Agassi, and he covered ground with the same casually aggressive stride.

"You know," Grange grumbled, still stroking the dog, "it would be harder for people to stalk her if she didn't go clubbing every damn night."

Tell me about it, Kate thought.

"She treats me like garbage," Grange added.

"How do you think people treat her?"

He snorted. "Like a star."

"Only fans and hangers-on. How about the people who matter?"

"You asking me to feel sorry for the spoiled little skank?"

"Just providing some perspective."

Grange went silent, his fund of conversation depleted. The bartender asked Kate what she was having. She waved him off. She hadn't had a drink in twenty years, not since the days when she would sit in her one-room apartment and cloud her head with booze and cry. One night something had broken inside her, and with calm deliberation, she had poured the contents of her liquor cabinet down the sink. The next day she had gone to confession and asked about becoming a nun.

"So," Grange said, "you here to talk to her or something?"

"When she's off the dance floor."

"Now's your chance."

She turned. Chelsea and her gal pal weaved toward a side doorway marked *Restrooms*. The friend helped her walk, Chelsea stumbling and reeling as people made way, a sea of commoners parting before royalty.

No one made way for Kate. By the time she elbowed a path to the alcove and pulled the brass handle of the ladies' room door, Chelsea was leaning over a toilet while her companion held her by the hair.

The bathroom was small and smelled of chlorine disinfectant. Two women were washing up at the sinks, but Chelsea and her friend were the only ones in any of the stalls. Kate tapped the girlfriend on the shoulder.

"I'll take care of her," Kate said. "Go back to dancing."

The friend, heavyset and homely, sneered. "Who the fuck are you?"

"I'm her protection. You're in the way. Get lost."

"I'm not going anywhere." She glared up at Kate, squinting. Nearsighted, Kate guessed, and she'd left her glasses at home because she wanted to look pretty.

Chelsea lifted her head. "It's okay, Gabrielle. She works for me."

"I don't like her." The squint deepened.

"I'm crushed," Kate said. "Outta here. Now."

Gabrielle went. The other women headed out also, stealing glances at Chelsea as they left.

Kate helped Chelsea cough up the last of her stomach contents. "How much have you had to drink?" Kate asked as she flushed the filth away.

Chelsea showed a crooked smile, a parody of the lopsided grin that had made her a star on the Family Channel in her teen years. "Hey, you know me. Clean and sober."

Everyone said she was beautiful, and it had to be true because she looked good even here, under the soulless fluorescent lights with flecks of vomit on her blouse.

"Right," Kate said. "So how much?"

"Nothing."

"I can ask Grange."

"Aw, fuck. Couple drinks, is all." She had this little lisp that everyone had found endearing when she was a kid, and sexy now. "Captain 'n' Coke."

"If it was only a couple of drinks, why were you puking?"

"Must've had some bad shrimp."

"Quit screwing around and give me a straight answer. Grange says this is your third club tonight. You must have had at least one drink at each stop. That's three, minimum."

"Wow. Math whiz."

"Probably, you exceeded the minimum, though. So what was it? Six drinks, or more? In addition to whatever the hell you were on when I saw you in that alley at eight o'clock."

"Jeez, what's your deal, lady? Seriously, what do you care?"

"Just tell me how many."

Chelsea heaved a sigh. "Six, I guess. Maybe seven. Shit, maybe eight. I don't exactly keep count. It's not like I pay for 'em."

"Don't you?"

"They're always on the house."

"Because the bartenders all love you so much."

"No." Her face turned serious, and abruptly she looked younger, vulnerable. "Because I'm good for business, is all. They don't love me."

Wednesday's child is full of woe…

Kate almost softened, until she thought of the girl whose stomach had been pumped in the ER. "A friend of yours nearly croaked two and a half hours ago, but I guess a little thing like that doesn't stop the party express from rolling on."

"You think I don't give a shit, right?"

"Is there any reason I shouldn't?"

Chelsea hesitated, then chose defiance. "Nah. No reason."

Kate sighed. "Come on. Let's get you cleaned up."

She led Chelsea to the sink. She wetted two paper towels and blotted up the spatter on Chelsea's blouse.

"I just saw your parents," she said.

"To tell them about Shauna?"

So that was the girl's name. "Exactly."

"I'll bet they didn't care."

You'd win that bet, Kate thought.

"As long as the money keeps coming in," Chelsea went on, "they're not gonna lose any sleep. They don't care about anybody, not even each other."

"They still live together, most of the time. They must feel something for each other."

"My dad feels something. He feels he'd be broke and homeless without my mom to sponge off of. He's quite the bounder, my dad."

"Bounder?" Kate was amused.

"I did a PR tour in the UK. They talk pretty cool over there."

"If all your dad wants is money, he could be bought off."

"That's not *all* he wants." Her eyes flashed. "The green-eyed temptress," the tabloids called her. She'd recently signed a mascara endorsement. "There's the other part, too."

"What other part?"

"Being famous. Being a celebrity." She spat out the word like poison. "That's what they all want, right? That's what everybody wants."

"Is it what you want?" Kate asked gently.

"Oh, abso-fuckin'-lutely." The twisted grin returned, mocking itself. "I'm living the fantasy."

She ran a hand through her ash-blonde hair, dyed two shades darker with sweat. Her bony frame trembled. She was a small girl, achingly thin, her natural curves erased by obsessive dieting. A starved waif.

Kate moistened another towel and wiped the girl's mouth. "If you talked to your mom, maybe you could convince her to get your dad out of the picture."

"I can't *talk* to her." The green-eyed temptress hawked up something shiny and sent it spinning down the drain with a jet of water from the tap. "For me to *talk* to her, she'd have to *listen* to me. Okay? She doesn't listen. Nobody fucking listens."

"I'm listening."

"Go play Dr. Phil with somebody else. I don't need your pity."

"Then try not to be so pitiful," Kate said sharply, losing patience.

"Fuck you. Seriously. You need a hobby? Try shagging Grange."

"Watch your mouth."

"It'll be like fucking a gorilla. Just use protection, 'kay? You don't want that guy's spawn growing in you. Shit, you'd be incubating the missing link, unless you got yourself scraped—"

Kate slapped her.

A light slap, delivered with the palm of her hand, sweeping right to left across Chelsea Brewer's startled face.

There was a moment of astonished silence. Then Chelsea reddened.

"What the *fuck*?"

"Stop swearing."

"You fucking *hit* me."

"I said stop swearing. Or I'll do it again."

Chelsea opened her mouth, shut it. Regarded her with an abused animal's wariness. "You're crazy," she said.

"Grange puts his life on the line for you. Don't badmouth him."

"I didn't know it was such a sensitive area."

"You need to learn some manners."

"Christ, you sound like my mom."

"Do I?"

"Not really. She doesn't care if I talk trash. I could fire you for hitting me."

"You won't."

"Nah, I'll let it slide this time." Chelsea rubbed her cheek. "That hurt like hell."

"Good. So why aren't you at the hospital with Shauna?"

The girl blinked at the change of subject. "Because…because I don't want to be."

"Why not?"

"I figure I'll get there soon enough." She looked down, her voice lowered. "That'll be me someday, in the ER. If I make it that far. Maybe I'll just drop on the spot, game over."

"It doesn't have to be like that."

"Maybe it does. Maybe it's, like, predestined or something. Predestination—that's a religious thing, right?"

"You don't believe that."

"I don't believe in much of anything." Chelsea leaned against the sink, the fall of her hair brushing her reflection in the mirror. "You do, I guess. All that Catholic stuff."

"Yes. All that Catholic stuff."

"The churches are pretty cool. When I was in Paris, I saw Notre Dame. That's Catholic, right?"

"Sure is."

"So what was it like—living in a convent or whatever?"

"I lived in a duplex with seven other sisters. I spent most of my time on the street."

"Like a social worker?"

"In a way." If social workers performed last rites on gang-bangers when they were shot down in the street. "Counseling homeless people, drug users, runaways."

"Turning them on to Jesus?" Chelsea asked skeptically.

"Trying to, sometimes. Or just steering them in the direction of a halfway house."

"So how does a nun slash social worker end up running interference for celebrities?"

Kate smiled. "By the grace of God, of course."

"Yeah? They say the devil's in the details."

That was clever. Chelsea was smart, smarter than the roles she played. Smarter than the role she played in real life, every night, in dives like this.

"There wasn't any master plan," Kate said. "It just worked out that way."

"So you buy into the whole program? God, heaven, angels, all that sh—that stuff?"

"Sometimes I doubt," she said carefully.

"What do you do then?"

"Pray."

"You could be wasting your time praying to something that's not real."

"I could. It's still better than sticking my head in a toilet every night."

"Hey"—that insouciant grin again—"don't knock it till you've tried it."

"I *have* tried it."

The girl tilted her head. "Yeah?"

"We can talk about it sometime. Some of the choices I made."

"You mean, I can learn from your mistakes?"

"Somebody ought to."

Chelsea considered it, twisting a blonde tress around two fingers. "I don't know. You're not turning me into any Jesus freak."

Kate smiled. "I wouldn't dream of it."

She thought she was done here, then remembered the man who'd been watching Chelsea. The spot where he'd been sitting was not only out of Grange's sight line, but angled away from Chelsea as well. Possibly, he'd been afraid the girl would see him. She brought up the photo on her phone.

"Do you know this man?"

Chelsea glanced at the image, then looked harder, her face losing its color. "Where'd you take this?"

"It's not important. You *do* know him."

"I've seen him." Her voice was suddenly throaty. "A long time ago. Back then, he had hair."

"Tell me about him."

"His name is Swann. With two *n*'s. I don't know his first name."

"When was this?"

"When I was with my dad—you know, when I left home."

At age eleven Chelsea had vanished from her mother's house and hitched her way to Colorado Springs, where her father had been living in a trailer. She spent six months there while her parents wrangled listlessly over custody, neither of them too keen on the idea. A court sent Chelsea back to Mama, and soon afterward her acting career took off.

"What was Swann doing with your father?"

"I don't know for sure. It's not like we ever talked about it. But I can guess. My dad never got into any, you know, legitimate business."

"How often did this man come by?"

"Three or four times. Always at night. I never really met him. My dad would push me out of the trailer before he showed up. I was supposed to go over to the neighbors'. But usually I'd hang around, wait for Swann to show. Sometimes I'd look in through a window..."

"What did they talk about?"

"They were planning something, I think. I don't know what."

"I'm surprised you remember Swann after all this time."

"He's not somebody you forget. He scared me. Has he hooked up with my dad again?"

"It's nothing for you to worry about. You're cleaned up now. Get back on the dance floor. Only, cool it with the Cuba libres, okay?"

Chelsea stayed where she was. "Why'd you slap me, really?"

"I told you."

"I trash-talked Grange. That's what you told me. But I don't think so. Something else I said—it got to you."

"Nothing gets to me," Kate said, but she didn't meet the girl's eyes.

5

SKIP Slater, founder and chief executive officer of Celebrity Whack-A-Mole, had come home early with the blonde from the escort service. Now she was dozing on his pillow, and he was restless. He threw on a robe and padded down the hall to the computer room.

Time to look in on the action. There was always action, 24/7, on CWAM.

He'd dreamed up the idea as a sophomore at Tulane, during a late-night drunken bull session in which it was collectively agreed that the Internet had rendered good taste obsolete. A competition ensued to name the crassest possible web ventures. Skip's contribution: a site where people could bet on which celebrity would be next to drop dead.

Luckily, he had the skills necessary to translate inspiration into reality. The enterprise had started small, a sideline he'd pursued while earning a degree in computer science. In the four years since his graduation, the site had taken off. It had been profiled disapprovingly in *People*, disparaged on *Access Hollywood*, panned by *Page Six*. Some of the bluenoses worried that the game cheapened human life, to which Skip replied that the payoffs on his leading contestants were anything but cheap. Other naysayers predicted that some nutball would try to rub out a celeb and score a big prize. Skip pointed to a clause in the users' agreement stating that no money would be paid to anyone convicted of a crime in connection with the deceased.

Truth was, the negative reviews didn't matter. Any PR was good PR. Skip knew that, and the two-faced media vultures knew it, too.

The setup was simple. CWAM tracked nearly a thousand international celebrities. To play, a client predicted which one would kick off next. It was like a horse race, with the various celebrities standing in for the nags on the track. The difference was that the stars, unlike the horses, weren't actually trying to cross the finish line.

Odds were adjusted continually in accord with the betting action. If a star's demise was publicly anticipated, the bets on that person would rise and the odds would drop until the payout was low. On the other hand, sudden, unexpected fatalities could generate a handsome payoff. A lucky wagerer could strike it rich by backing a long shot. While everyone was betting on a B movie Methuselah to be the next DOA, some twentysomething sitcom star could sneak under the wire. Unpredictability made the game fun.

Skip entered the glorified crawl space optimistically dubbed a second bedroom by the Realtor who'd sold him this town house. The entire condo took up only eight hundred square feet. Night and day he heard the clack-clack-clack of footsteps from his upstairs neighbor who wore spiked heels; what made it worse, his neighbor was a guy.

Still, he had a West Hollywood address. It beat living in some shit hole in the Valley.

He squeezed behind his laptop, logged on to the site, and checked the latest updates. Slow day. No deaths. No payouts. Some betting action on a geezer who'd showed up on the news, looking frail while he received his star on the Walk of Fame. He looked about ready to pop. But you could never tell. He might hang on for another two decades. No one knew who was next in line.

The escort girl came shuffling into the room. What was her name? Elke or Ellie? She padded around, poking at his potted plants, all of which were artificial because he was incapable of maintaining any life-form other than himself.

"Wow," Elke or Ellie said, "you've got a ton of books."

"I like to read."

"Who's Hermann Hesse?"

"A deep thinker." He saw her reach for the book. "Don't touch that."

"I was gonna look at it."

"Don't. It's a first edition. Hey, you like TV? Watch TV." He gestured in the direction of his high-def plasma Toshiba.

She found the remote and started flipping through the two hundred channels on his satellite system. That shut her up.

An IM alert chimed. BlitzCraig, his sysop in Sandpoint, Idaho, had a question.

U C the #s on Chelsea Brewer?

Skip frowned. Chelsea Brewer. Though not at the top of the list, she was one of their more interesting commodities. Despite her youth, the little popwreck could conceivably go horizontal at any time. She had convictions for hit-and-run, driving with a suspended license, and something called gross vehicular mischief, which involved driving her Porsche onto the Venice Beach promenade in pursuit of a paparazzo. She was, as the tabloids liked to say, "trashtacular." She lived the lifestyle of the rich and scabrous.

He called up her screen and checked the numbers. There were currently 246 wagers that Chelsea would be the next celebrity to wear a body bag. The betting pool was $22,395. It was one way to measure the value of a life.

He scanned the columns of figures and saw what was worrying BlitzCraig. The average bet was fifty dollars. The largest was ten thousand, and it had been placed fifteen minutes ago by a player with the screen name Loki.

Loki. Norse trickster god. Figure of darkness and treachery.

Ten Gs was a shitload of money to plunk down on any celeb, especially one as young as Chelsea Brewer, even if she was a suicidal nutjob.

Skip felt an icicle prick of fear. *I C it*, he IM'd BlitzCraig. *Expln? IDK. News story?*

That was what Skip was thinking. It was his nightmare, the doomsday scenario.

He IM'd his news monitors. CWAM retained three staff members whose only job was to monitor news updates and the nattering of the blogarazzi. Two of them were on duty at any given time. He could never remember which two.

While waiting for a response, he did some quick math. The odds on Chelsea were currently two hundred to one. If Loki won his wager, he would cash out two million dollars and bust the house.

"Shit," he muttered. The payout on this pop tart would sink him.

"Everything okay?" Elke or Ellie asked from her perch in front of the TV.

"Yeah, no problem."

"There's nothing good on the tube."

"Play a video, then."

His two news monitors responded to his query. No reports on Chelsea Brewer. Nothing on Google News. Nothing on TMZ.

Nothing on Drudge. Nothing anywhere. Which only meant that whatever Loki knew hadn't gone public yet.

Loki could be anybody. A paramedic, a nurse in an ER, some lucky asshole who happened to be at the scene of an accident.

Or a paparazzo. That was Skip's biggest fear. Fucking paps roamed the streets day and night like dog packs. They would be in the lead position to catch a breaking tragedy. If CWAM had been around when Princess Di took a header into that underpass, a fast-thinking pap could have laid down a heavy bet and bankrupted him.

Skip's financial situation was a delicate balancing act not unlike a house of cards. Now the cards might be about to come tumbling down.

What if he didn't pay? It wasn't like Loki could sue him. CWAM was incorporated outside US jurisdiction. He could brazen it out, refuse to honor the transaction. The strategy was problematic. For one thing, Loki might come after him with something more potent than a lawsuit. A sawed-off shotgun, say. Reneging on a seven-figure obligation was the kind of thing that got a person's knee-caps shot off, or worse. Moreover, once word got out that CWAM welshed on a bet, site traffic would collapse. No more eyeballs. No more mind share. No more anything.

He figured he could scrounge together the cash if he liquidated his portfolio and drained CWAM's cash reserves, but after the pay-out, CWAM would be flat busted. There would be no money to pay his tech guys or even to cover his server fees. Without outside financing, he wouldn't be able to keep the site going. And nobody with investment capital would come within five hundred yards of him once CWAM foundered.

Before now, he'd never wanted investors. He'd hoped to keep the operation in-house. All the startup money had been his own, courtesy of an inheritance from Grandma. His parents had begged him to do the sensible thing and invest the seventy-five thousand in a nice mutual fund, but he'd gone for the big score. His gamble had paid off. He wasn't super-rich, but he was comfortable, the site was growing, and lately he'd contemplated branching out into more mainstream web enterprises. It only took one successful site to set the table for a big-time IPO, and he had some ideas…

Correction. He'd *had*. Past tense. Now he had bubkes. He was screwed, blued, and tattooed—if Chelsea Brewer was the next celebrity to die.

There wasn't a lot he could do. But he could try to learn about Loki. Check out his betting history, trace his IP address, maybe uncover his identity. He hunched over his keyboard.

"Get comfortable, Elke or Ellie," he whispered. "This may take a while."

6

PHILIPPE'S Raw Bar smelled of oysters. Or maybe clams. Some sort of mollusks, anyway. Kate caught the scent as she stepped into the restaurant. The smell went with the nautical theme—fishnets strung from the rafters, ship's wheel on the wall. In LA, bad taste became good taste if it was just bad enough.

In a corner booth, snapping his stubby fingers to get her attention, sat Sal French. She strode toward him through a blare of piped-in Paul Anka.

Sal French was a singer himself, specializing in old standards. He was famous for his mellow voice, his artful phrasing, and his temper tantrums. He'd once been surreptitiously recorded chewing out his band members; the remarkably foulmouthed tirade had gone viral on the web.

Up close, he was nearly bald, shorter than he wanted to be, and rheumy-eyed. He stood, assuming the bandy-legged pose of a pugnacious drunk. Sal didn't drink. He was just obnoxious by nature.

"Hey, Sal," she said without enthusiasm. She nodded to Sal's bodyguard, Vincent Di Milo, whom everybody naturally called Venus behind his back.

"You get my message?" Sal asked unnecessarily. "Good. That's good. We have a situation here."

"Involving your security escort?" Kate guessed.

"Right. Yeah. Him." Sal jabbed a thumb into Di Milo's chest, not the most intelligent move, given that Di Milo stood six foot six and could crush a Campbell's soup can in his hand. "And by the way, apropos of nothing, why have I got only one bodyguard?"

"Isn't one enough?"

"You're the expert. You tell me. See that numbnuts over there?"

She followed Sal's finger to a lean figure with salt-and-pepper hair, seated in another corner booth across the room. "Carson Banning," she said.

"That prick just started sporting *two* bodyguards. Not one—*two*. He used to have one, but now he's doubled up. And he's not half as famous as me. Probably doesn't get half the death threats I do, either."

It seemed a dubious thing to brag about. "I'm not responsible for Mr. Banning's security."

"You don't want to be." Sal seated himself with fussy dignity and picked up a breadstick, brandishing it like a weapon. "Guy's a prize dickwad. Over the hill. Not even chasing tail anymore. You never see him with any arm candy. Hey, I ever lose my touch with the ladies, take me out and shoot me, you know what I'm saying?"

Sal was on his fourth marriage, each wife younger than the last. At the rate he was going, his next bride would be in elementary school.

Kate slid onto the banquette opposite him. "I don't think you called me here to discuss a movie star's sex life."

"Movie star." He snorted. "Banning hasn't had a hit in three years. Fucking has-been. Yesterday's news. My last album went double platinum."

Sal's last album had been released a decade ago.

"Can we stick to the subject?"

"Right. I want this asshole replaced." Another jab at Di Milo, poking him in the ribs this time.

Kate waited for the bodyguard to tear off Sal French's arm and beat him to death with it. When that didn't happen, she forced herself to reply. "Mr. Di Milo is one of our very best."

"I don't like him."

"Why is that?"

"He just rubs me the wrong way. No sense of humor."

"You said your last bodyguard was too friendly."

"He was."

"The one before that had a gold tooth you found distasteful."

"He looked like a heavy in a Scorsese flick."

"And now you're dissatisfied with Mr. Di Milo because he's not funny enough?"

"Right. He's got no verve, no life in him. I like a guy that cracks a smile once in a while. So he's gone. Get me a new one."

A slow burn of anger traveled through her. Anger at this smiling turd with a comb-over and bling glittering on his fingers who imagined himself superior to Vince Di Milo. Vince had three daughters of whom he was fiercely proud and a wife he'd nursed through lymphoma.

Calmly she said, "I'm not replacing him."

"You have to. I'm telling you to. I insist on it. I *demand* it."

Kate shrugged. "In that case, you're fired."

Sal nodded, blinked, and did a comical double take. "Huh?"

"I'm through with you. Adios."

"You can't *fire* me. You *work* for me."

"Not anymore."

"God damn it, I'm a paying client. You can't fucking treat me like this."

Kate smiled at him, a smile of knives and razors. "Let me tell you a story," she said. "When I was eighteen years old, I married a guy in Jersey."

"You got married? I thought you were—"

"A nun. That came later. Stay with me, Sal. Back then I was a bit on the wild side. The man I married was twenty years older than me. His name was James. He insisted on being called that, not Jim, *never* Jimmy. He'd inherited some money. He thought it made him a big man. I did too. We decided to move out West, so we drove his Alfa Romeo across country. One night in a Ramada Inn he got drunk and started beating on me. Really worked me over. I'd never seen that side of him before.

"Next day we're driving through the desert in New Mexico when James gets out to take a leak. I floor the gas and take off, leave him jumping up and down, waving his arms and screaming. Not another car in sight. No rest stop for fifty miles. That was the end of our marriage."

She sat there, arms folded.

"So?" Sal said after a puzzled silence. "What's your point?"

"My point is, if I could ditch my own husband that easily, what makes you think I'd have any trouble ditching a washed-up gasbag like you?" She stood. "Vince, take the rest of the night off."

Di Milo, who prized economy of speech, answered with a nod and walked away. Kate moved to follow. Sal was suddenly alone at his table. "Hold on a minute. I'm high and dry here. What am I supposed to do about protection?"

"Wear a rubber."

As she was leaving she looked across the room and caught Carson Banning's eye.

7

THE restaurant was in a Century City shopping plaza with a multilevel parking garage, the kind of place where Deep Throat might turn up. Kate located the limo easily enough, a custom-built Mercedes with tinted windows, parked near the elevator as always. To make a quick getaway, he liked to say.

She waited by the car, assessing the damage she'd done tonight. Already, she'd alienated the Brewers and terminated her relationship with Sal French. At the rate she was going, soon she wouldn't have any clients left.

She missed Barney. He'd had people skills. When she had met him, she'd been a novice working the streets. He'd worked the patrol side of the LAPD for thirty years, never trying to make detective. He retired only when his supervisors made him give up riding a squad car. Riding a desk wasn't for him.

He used to come by the church and drop off canned food. He liked talking to the nuns.

But he worried about Kate. She had a reputation as someone who went looking for trouble. She would meet with street kids in their hangouts, venturing into crack dens and meth houses. Once, she'd had a gun held to her head by a paranoid dealer who swore she was a narc. Another time, she'd received a cut on her arm, the work of a switchblade; it had required sixteen stitches in the ER.

If she insisted on placing herself in harm's way, Barney said, at least she could know how to handle trouble.

He taught her how to outmaneuver an attacker, fend off a knife, spot a concealed weapon. How to know someone was lying. How to shake off a tail. How to use a gun. *It's not always feasible to turn the other cheek*, he said. *Sometimes you gotta kick some ass.*

Now he was gone—dead for two years—and damn, she wished he were still around.

The elevator doors opened and Carson Banning emerged. He swept the area with a glance to be sure they were alone.

"I don't have a lot of time," she said.

"We'll make this quick."

Multiple thumps—the car doors unlocking. She slid into the backseat. He followed, shutting the door. She pushed him down into the leather bench seat and freed him from his trousers. Lifted his wallet from his back pocket, found a condom, inserted it between her lips. Bending to him, she worked the condom into place with her mouth. He was fully erect when he pulled free. She rose, finding herself already wet—pleasant surprise—and settled atop him as he raised her skirt and the car began to rock.

The rocking continued for some unaccountable period of time, driving all thoughts from her mind, erasing all awareness except the intensity of his need and hers, until an electric flash ignited in the pit of her stomach and shivered like a sizzle of voltage, ending in a bloom of white light.

They lay together, side by side, in the tinted-window dimness. "Saw you talking to Sal," he said finally. "You on the clock?"

"It's all work and no play in the security game. Speaking of which, where's your muscle?"

"I thought I'd made that reasonably obvious."

"Not that muscle. The hired kind."

"I told them I was using the bathroom."

"They'll be looking for you by now."

"Not yet. I said I was making number two."

"Wow, too much information."

He smiled, but his face turned pensive when he asked, "Any news?"

About his daughter, he meant. Carson Banning and his ex-wife shared custody of sixteen-year-old Amber. The girl had been staying with her dad when she had sneaked out of the house ten days ago, leaving an angry note. They'd had an argument, and now she was gone, a runaway. Banning had asked Kate to find her, and to keep it quiet. If the tabloids found out, they would turn a family crisis into a media free-for-all.

"If there were," Kate said quietly, "I'd already have told you."

"Right. I know." He checked his watch. "Well…my escorts will be getting antsy."

They got out of the car and parted with a kiss. She walked to the Jag, her footsteps echoing on the concrete, bouncing off the colonnaded pillars.

Sometimes it bothered her that she was willing to meet Banning like this, for a quick, almost wordless encounter. It seemed wrong to need sex that badly. Especially given her background. She had been ready to sign a vow of chastity, after all. Would have done so if she'd remained a nun. And leaving the order hadn't been her choice.

She remembered Barney asking her once if the whole chastity thing didn't seem a little, you know, medieval.

Medieval is what the Church is, she'd answered. *It isn't a dot-com startup. There's a history. You sign on for the whole package.*

But didn't it bother her, he'd pressed, the prospect of being celibate for life?

She'd told him that at that particular point in her life, she hadn't been too interested in having sex again.

Barney'd thought about that. Either she'd had a very bad experience, he'd said, or she was punishing herself for something.

It was a little of both, Kate had said.

In her car, she checked her office voice mail. All Guardian Angel bodyguards were required to leave a message when they moved to a new location. Grange reported that Chelsea Brewer had left Stiletto and progressed to Panic Room.

She thought she might head over there. Could be a good idea to double-team Chelsea for the rest of the night.

Grange wouldn't like it, but it wasn't his call.

8

PANIC Room was smaller than Stiletto, the dancing less frenetic, but still there were stroboscopic downspots dappling the dance floor, a crush of people, the reek of beer. A rock combo on a little stage riffed on speeded-up covers of old C&W tunes. At the front of the club was a lounge with a lower decibel level.

That was where Swann hid the package.

It was a small package, easily concealed under his jacket. In the lounge, he pretended to drop something, stooped to pick it up, and pressed the package against a table leg. The putty on its underside would hold it in place.

Later, when the time was right, he would use the remote control to set it off.

For now, his priority was to get Chelsea Brewer into the bathroom. It wouldn't be hard.

Swann had held many jobs. For a while he had worked as a carnival roustabout. He'd learned the art of misdirection from a carnie named Pistol Pete, who had run a dart-the-balloon scam on the midway. Theoretically, a successful throw would puncture a balloon, revealing a tag that entitled the winner to a lavish gift. In reality, the game was gaffed with underinflated balloons and dull darts, and the prizes were rigged. Pricey gifts like plush toys and clock radios were prominently displayed, but all the tags under the balloons were for cheap "slum"—plastic combs, ballpoint pens, emery boards.

Occasionally a mark would demand to see the unexposed tags. Pete would make a show of revealing valuable gift tags under the remaining balloons. Of course, the tags had never really been there. It was sleight of hand, and when he got drunk, which was often, Pete would show Swann how he palmed the real tag and substituted the phony.

Later, Swann ran a game of three-card monte in the subways of Chicago. The rubes never saw the money card change places with the losing card in the throw. Like the carnival marks, they saw what they expected to see.

He was counting on the same ruse tonight. He knew it would work because people were the same everywhere. They were sound asleep, living in a dream world. He was awake and alert and he could beat them. He'd been beating them all his life.

He waited till there was a break in the music, when Chelsea Brewer got herself a rum and Coke, her invariable cocktail of choice. She chugged most of it, requested a refill, and when a new song started up, left the brimming glass with the bodyguard, next to her handbag with the poodle inside. Then she was back on the dance floor, spazzing around with her ugly gal pal and a half dozen doofuses hoping to score.

Swann stepped up to the other end of the bar, well away from the bodyguard, and exchanged a ten-dollar bill for a Cuba libre.

The bartender, juggling bottles to pad his tips, never noticed when Swann slipped a syringe out of his pocket. The syringe held five grams of GHB, dissolved in ten milliliters of water. His hands hidden, Swann dispensed the solution into the drink.

Holding the glass, he sidled up to Chelsea's yojimbo. The goon recognized him up close. "Bouncer's not doing his job. He was supposed to keep you out."

"That so?" Swann had slipped the bouncer fifty bucks to look the other way. "What's your beef with me?"

"You're harassing our client."

Swann set down his glass near Chelsea's drink. "I'm just clubbing, bro."

"You were at Stiletto."

"So were a lot of people."

The two of them stood measuring each other. The bodyguard was a big man, but in a throwdown, what mattered was quickness, skill—and experience. It was doubtful the yojimbo had ever killed anyone. He would know how to do it, but the knowledge was theoretical. Swann knew in his nerve endings, knew with the deep knowing that predators had.

"Nice dog," Swann said with a glance at the pink handbag. "Yours?"

"Funny man."

Swann reached out to touch the poodle. It growled. "Not too friendly, is he?"

The bodyguard took a step closer. "Dog doesn't like you. I don't like you. Walk away."

"You don't want me near your client, get a restraining order. For now, I want to watch her dance." He flicked a thumb in Chelsea's direction, and reflexively, the bodyguard glanced away.

Swann was sipping a cocktail when the man turned back.

"She's not putting on a show for you. Get going. I won't ask again."

"You didn't exactly *ask* the first time," Swann said, but he moved off.

"I'm watching you," the bodyguard warned.

Not closely enough, Swann thought. He walked away with Chelsea's rum and Coke, leaving the spiked drink on the bar.

When he looked across the dance floor, he saw Chelsea standing frozen. She'd just seen him, recognized him. He was pleased she remembered.

Swann himself had never forgotten. Though he had seen her just once, in Colorado, when she was a little scrap of a thing, and though it was only a glimpse through a window, he'd always remembered her wide eyes and pale, childish face. He had smiled at her, and she had ducked out of sight, and he'd laughed. Sam's daughter, he had guessed, though until then he'd been only vaguely aware that Sam had any family at all.

He wasn't sure why the momentary encounter stuck in his memory. Maybe because he hadn't expected a sewer rat like Sam Brewer to bring anything so wholesome into the world.

In the years since, Chelsea Brewer had become a star, and Swann had occasionally come across her image on magazine covers and in TV ads. He was hardly the sort of person who followed celebrity news, but he was aware that the scared girl from the Colorado trailer park had made a name for herself. It was more than her father had ever done. Swann respected her for it. The planet was crowded with mediocrities who'd been dealt a better hand in life than Chelsea Brewer had, and who'd pissed it away. To fight your way clear of Sam Brewer's negligent upbringing and become a Tinseltown millionaire was a rare accomplishment, the kind Swann could appreciate. He admired anyone who stood out from the bovine herd.

And sometimes he wondered if he'd had anything to do with it. If maybe the flash of fear he'd seen in her face had electrified her into taking chances she might otherwise have missed. If her sight of him, brief though it had been, had opened her up to the possibilities of a larger life.

Probably not. But you never knew about these things, did you?

He threaded his way into the heart of the crowd, watching as the girl separated from her companions and approached the bodyguard. At the bar, her first act was to reach for her cocktail. She threw it back fast. If she noticed a saline aftertaste, she didn't seem to mind.

"You're mine, sugarplum," Swann said softly, the words swallowed by the blare of the band.

9

THIS is a nightmare, Chelsea thought. *Seriously, a literal* nightmare.

One minute she was dancing and then she looked across the room and she was like, *Oh my God, you have got to be kidding me.*

"I want to go," she told Grange at the bar, shouting over the band's cover of "Boulder to Birmingham."

"Because of him?"

"*Yeah,* because of him."

"He's nothing I can't handle."

"You coming with me, or do I go by myself?"

"How about your entourage?"

"Forget them. Seriously, let's just *go.*"

"Fine by me. I hate this rockabilly crap."

They waded into the crowd, Grange gripping her arm above the elbow while she clutched her handbag with Chanticleer inside. Blur of faces, strobe of lights, odor of cigarette smoke, though smoking was illegal in clubs. Usually she didn't mind the smell; she'd been known to sneak a cig herself. Tonight it was curdling the juices in her stomach, and the amped-up noise from the stage wasn't helping. She blinked back a head rush that left her dizzy and uncoordinated.

"You okay?" Grange asked.

"Chugged that cocktail too fast."

But it wasn't the cocktail. It was fear.

Chelsea knew all about fear. She'd been afraid lots of times, starting with those nights when, hiding in her room, she'd listened to her mom and dad. *All parents fight sometimes*, her mom would tell her, but even then, Chelsea knew not all of them fought like *that*.

Then they broke up, and that was worse—her mom alone and crying, holding a pity party every night, and getting wasted on Stoli and pot. She'd been afraid then, too, afraid her mom would lose it and shoot herself with the pearl-handled pistol she kept by her bed.

But her mom's crying jags were nothing compared to the nuttiness of the business. "The business"—that was what everyone called it, like it was the only business around. The business was sick and crazy, and it bred assholes the way dampness bred mold. It wasn't just the horny middle-aged putzes who wanted to get into her pants, the balding clowns with sad little ponytails and Viagra hard-ons. She could handle them. What scared her were the control freaks, the psychos.

Some of them were crazy, really batshit crazy. Like the director of her first TV movie, who slapped her a half dozen times to get her to cry for the camera. When the AD objected, the director knocked him out cold. The slaps hadn't made her cry, but seeing the AD crumple on the soundstage floor had done the trick. They got the shot on the first take.

Yeah, she knew about fear. But of all the things she feared, Mr. Darkness was the worst.

That was how she thought of him. Mr. Darkness. There was this cloud of black hanging over the man. Bad vibes. Sometimes, when he visited her dad's trailer, she would creep to the window and steal a glance through the venetian blinds. Once, Swann caught her looking through the window and turned his gaze on her—his eyes, yellow eyes. And he winked, a friendly wink, but actually not friendly at all.

It was taking forever to get out. Their progress seemed endless, the exit unbearably far away and receding even as they approached. The floor under her feet was weirdly spongy. Each step sank into quicksand. She swayed, her balance faltering, and then she saw him—Swann—standing ahead of them, by the doorway of the lounge.

She stopped. Grange followed the line of her sight and scowled. "You don't have to worry about that putz. Come on."

She shook her head. To go on would mean passing right by him. He would be inches from her. And if he so much as touched her...well, she would drop dead. Seriously. She would just. Drop. Dead.

"He can't do anything here," Grange insisted.

But Grange didn't know. She had seen her dad bow his head before Swann. Her dad, who never bowed to anyone.

"We'll go out the back way," she said.

"The car's out front."

"So we'll walk around and get it. I don't give a fuck."

She pulled him in a circle to face the other direction. It felt like tugging a big, stubborn dog on a leash.

"This is bullshit," Grange complained.

She got it. He didn't want to back off. He wanted a confrontation. Some kind of macho thing. Well, tough on him. He could have his pissing contest some other time. The fear cramping her insides was getting bad, really bad. She needed to be out of here.

They made quicker progress retracing their steps. She looked back, but Swann was already lost in a sea of silhouettes. When she turned her head, the room canted. She stumbled. Grange tightened his grip on her arm.

She was starting to think there was something wrong with her that went beyond fear. One time she'd taken some Ecstasy and had a bad reaction. This was sort of like that. But she would be okay once she got out of the club, away from the press of bodies and the wall of noise…

Someone stepped in front of them, blocking their path—her gal pal Gabrielle, saying, "Hey, *there* you are," as she stood there blinking. She was always blinking because she wouldn't wear glasses and was allergic to contacts or some fucking thing.

"I look away for a minute," Gabby said, "and you're gone. Trying to run out on me?"

She said it lightly, but hurt lay behind the words. She worried constantly about being left behind.

"I just need to get out," Chelsea said.

"She's not feeling so hot," Grange added.

Gabby gave her a sympathetic smile. "Too much happy sauce. Gotta pace yourself, girl."

"Right…right."

Conversation was too hard. She couldn't concentrate on words when the floor kept slipping sideways and her stomach was clenching like a fist. She looked around for some anchor of stability in the shifting room, and then she glimpsed Swann circling around toward the rear exit.

Blink, and he evaporated into the smoky, pulsating haze.

"Uh-oh. I think she's getting ready to hurl." Gabby's voice. Distant, echoey.

"I'll get her into the john." Grange, taking charge. "You stay here."

"I can help," Gabby objected.

"Just stay."

Grange pulled Chelsea off the dance floor, into the hallway that led to the back door. The exit was close, only a few yards to go, when Grange detoured into the bathroom, hustling her inside. She couldn't figure it out. Taking her into the stupid bathroom when she could throw up just as easily outside? Who cared if some asshole with a camera caught her puking? Wouldn't be the first time she'd made TMZ blowing chunks. "Chelsea Spewer," they called her.

The bathroom was empty. Which was kind of weird, considering the mob scene outside, but she didn't have time to think about it. Grange pointed her toward the nearest stall, but her gut twisted and she knew she couldn't make it that far. She staggered to the sink, somehow remembering to hand Grange her purse before she leaned over the steel basin and waited for her stomach to empty.

Nothing happened. She gripped the white countertop and stared at the drain as it spiraled clockwise, the counter rotating with it, and the floor, the whole room, everything spinning while strange, sweet music played in her head and Chanticleer growled.

She lifted her head as the dog barked. In the mirror over the sink, the door of a stall swung open and Mr. Darkness stepped out.

And he was smiling.

10

KATE turned a corner, and Panic Room came up on her left.

Crime scene tape festooned the building. Three black-and-whites were parked on the street, light bars cycling.

Her heart iced over.

She slammed the Jaguar into park alongside a fire hydrant. Stepping out of the car, she speed-dialed Grange. No answer.

Most of the cops and apparently all the clubgoers and paparazzi were around back, but at the front entrance she found a young patrolman in charge of the sign-in sheet. His nametag read *Stengel*.

"What happened here?" she asked.

He looked her over in the wary, judgmental way of all cops. "And you are…?"

She produced her business card. "Chelsea Brewer's personal security."

"Oh yeah. The bouncer told me she was at the club."

"Where is she now?"

"Bouncer saw her leave with her bodyguard. Your guy, I guess."

Relief blew through her. "Thank God."

"They say the man upstairs looks after drunks and fools." Officer Stengel smirked. "I'm guessing your client fits both categories."

"What went down in there?"

"Clubbers heard gunshots, panicked. Turned into a real mob scene. The noise came from the front of the club, so everybody cleared out the back. They're corralled in the rear parking lot now."

"You get the shooter?"

"Wasn't any shooter."

"You just said—"

"People thought they heard shots fired. Turned out to be a sick prank, is all. Bunch of firecrackers."

"Firecrackers?"

"Big ones. Judging from the shrapnel, I'd say they were home-made. PVC pipe and black powder. Not sure how they were set off. Could've been some kinda radio-controlled igniter."

"Doesn't this club have a metal detector at the door?"

"Yeah, but the explosive was just plastic and powder, no metal, and if there was an igniter, it was too small to trigger the detector. This freak worked it all out pretty carefully. We found a bogus out-of-order sign stashed in the ladies' room. Looks like our friend taped it to the door for part of the evening to keep people out."

"Why?"

"My guess, whoever it was wanted a safe location to set off the fireworks and not get flattened in the stampede."

"Sounds like a lot of work for a prank."

"Some people have way too much time on their hands."

"Was anyone hurt?"

"Couple blown eardrums. And there was one guy, got hit by debris. We found him unconscious in the club. He's at the ER now.

Your man may have sustained some facial cuts. There was blood on his face, Eddie said."

"Who's Eddie?"

"Bouncer. Over there."

A few yards away, a blond WWF wannabe stood smoking a cigarette. Kate approached him. "You saw Chelsea Brewer leave?"

Eddie the bouncer expelled a stream of smoke into her face. "Right through this door. Her and her rent-a-goon were the only ones who come out this way. Everybody else, they cleared out the back."

There was a lot of Jersey in his accent. It almost made Kate homesick. "Was this immediately after the gunshots?"

"Nah, it was two, three minutes later. They must've been laying low." He took another drag. "Better 'n getting trampled in a cattle run."

"While all this was happening, you stayed out here?"

"Damn straight."

"Aren't you supposed to provide security for this establishment?"

"Lady, I check IDs, kick loose the losers, let in the hotties. When there's gunfire, I keep my head down like anybody else."

"Very professional."

"You want a hero, call Chuck Norris. 'Sides, this ain't what I really do. I'm up for a part in the next Jason Statham flick."

"When Grange arrived with Chelsea, did he tell you about a guy who's been stalking her? Did he say not to let him in?"

"Yeah, he showed me a picture. But he was wasting his time. The stalker never showed."

Despite his ambitions, Eddie was not a good actor. Swann *had* shown up, and Eddie had let him in, probably for a bribe. But Kate couldn't press the issue without revealing knowledge of the case.

"Okay," she said, "so Chelsea and her bodyguard exited…"

"Yeah, they came out, got into their car. Black Caddy DTS. Nice wheels."

A company car. She had a fleet of them.

"Took off in a hurry," he went on. "Probably wanted to get away before any photogs came back. They all went around to the rear when the shit hit the fan."

"And Chelsea wasn't hurt?"

"No blood on her, but she seemed kinda out of it. Shell-shocked, you know? Probably not so used to being in a war zone." He blew more smoke into her eyes. "Tonight she got a taste of the real world, right?"

"Right," Kate said, and she snatched the cigarette out of his hand and crushed it under her boot.

"Hey, what the hell?"

"I don't like people blowing smoke in my face."

"Yeah? Where should I blow it?"

"Out your ass."

She walked a few yards away and tried Grange's number again. As the phone rang, she tried to figure out what the hell had gone down. Grange should have called as soon as he left the club—unless his injuries were more severe than they'd looked. If he'd passed out, and if Chelsea was stoned again...

The ringing cut off with a click. He'd answered—finally.

"Grange, are you all right?"

"Hello, Miss Malick."

Not Grange. Not any voice she knew.

Her heart slowed down, conserving energy for a coming battle.

"Or should I call you Sister Kate?" he added politely.

"Who is this?"

"My name is Jack Swann. You can call me Jack."

The reply scared her, because he made no effort to keep his identity secret.

"You didn't answer my question," he went on. "How should I address you?"

"Any way you like."

"Then here's the bottom line, Sister Kate. I have Chelsea. Don't worry. She's perfectly all right."

"How did you get Grange's phone? Where is he?"

"I'll let you answer those questions for yourself. Just one hint: People see what they expect to see."

"What does that mean?"

"That's all the help you get."

"Let me talk to Chelsea."

"No can do. Not right now."

"Then how do I know she's unharmed?"

"You think I would hurt her? Why would I do that?"

"You kidnapped her."

"I had my reasons. Good reasons. Have you seen the billboard for her last movie?"

"What about it?"

"I've seen it. I've looked at it plenty of times. And I liked what I saw. I said to myself, there's someone still young and fresh, someone who hasn't been soiled too badly by this shitty world. Not yet. Someone who's still got that glow. Now, why would I want to stamp that out? Why would I want to take that away from the world?"

Because you're crazy, Kate thought. She said nothing.

"Chelsea will be fine. Everything will go smoothly for all of us, as long as you play by my rules. That means you don't contact the police, the FBI, or the media. The only ones who'll know about this situation are you, me, and Chelsea's mom and dad. No outsiders. This is a private party and nobody's crashing. Got it?"

"I've got it."

"I'll call again in two hours with a status report. That gives you plenty of time to brief the parents and set up shop at their house. I've got eyes on the house, and I'll know if you bring in the authorities."

"I won't bring in anybody. Except—I'll need the help of one or two of my associates at the agency."

"So you can trace my next call and track me down?"

"Nothing like that."

Swann made a scolding cluck. "I've heard of a flying nun, but a *lying* nun? Jesus would be so disappointed. But Jesus was a liar, too. The meek shall inherit the earth—that's the biggest lie of all." His voice hardened. "Don't bullshit me again."

"I still want my colleagues on board. You want this done fast and done right? Well, I can't go it entirely alone. Without some assistance, I can't guarantee I'll be able to do everything you need me to do."

"Heh. You're a hardass, aren't you? Okay, bring in one or two of your helper monkeys. But nobody else."

"Fair enough." She tried for a little more cooperation. "You'll have to let me hear Chelsea's voice eventually. Otherwise, how can I trust you?"

"You still don't get it, Sister Kate. I told you, Chelsea's in no danger from me. I'm no ordinary kidnapper. I didn't kidnap her to *hurt* her. I kidnapped her to *save* her."

"What the hell does that mean?"

"It'll be clear soon enough. Believe me, Chelsea has nothing to fear from me. I'm the best friend she ever had."

"What do—"

But he was already gone.

11

KATE shut the phone and stood unmoving. Down the street, the police cruisers' cherry lights were still cycling, and Eddie, the bouncer from New Jersey, was smoking another cigarette. Officer Stengel guarded the perimeter of the cordoned-off crime scene. Traffic flowed on Sunset, decelerating as it passed Panic Room, a river current slowed by a sand bar.

Everything was the same, but nothing was the same. Chelsea had been taken.

But she couldn't have been. She'd left with Grange. The bouncer had seen it.

Wrong. What did he really see? A bald man with a large build and a bloody face, probably wearing Grange's jacket, hustling Chelsea out the door. In the darkness and confusion he wouldn't have noted any details. After all, he'd expected her to be with her bodyguard.

People see what they expect to see.

Chelsea told her Swann used to have long hair. Kate hadn't made the connection, but now it was obvious. He'd shaved his head to pass for Grange. He'd been planning the substitution all along.

A pudgy, moon-faced girl wandered into view, peering everywhere, her head darting like a bird's. Chelsea's gal pal from the restroom—Gabrielle. She squinted in Kate's direction and recognized her. "Do you know where she is?"

Kate hesitated. "She left with her bodyguard. He received some facial cuts. The two of them went to the hospital."

This was partly true. Grange *was* on his way to the ER. He was the unconscious man found in the nightclub. Swann had subdued him, taken his car keys and phone. And Grange's gun and holster, of course. Those items would have raised a red flag if they'd been found by the cops or paramedics.

Gabrielle shook her head. "She wouldn't leave me. She's my ride."

"With everything that happened, she probably forgot."

"She wouldn't just run off. Especially after what happened. She'd want to know I was okay."

"*Are* you okay?" Kate asked, looking closer. There was a minor cut on the girl's cheek and a purplish contusion on her neck.

"Yeah. Shaken up, is all."

"Were you with Chelsea when the craziness started?"

"No, she went to the toilet. She was sick. I wanted to go with her, but Alfonse made me wait outside."

Distantly, Kate was pleased to hear her call Grange by his first name. "Were they in there long?"

"Hardly any time before the gunshots, or whatever it was."

"So you ran out—"

"No *way*. I tried to get to Chels, but with all those people…It was like a riot in there. They just, like, pushed me forward. Like a tidal wave."

That explained the firecrackers. Swann needed a diversion to drive the club patrons out the back, scatter the people waiting on line, and lure the paparazzi into the parking lot, allowing him to make his getaway through the front door with no photographers on his tail.

"I never would've left her if I'd had a choice," the girl added plaintively. "And *she* never would leave *me*. I figured by now she'd be in the parking lot with everyone else. But she's not. And now you're telling me she's left?"

"She had to make sure Grange made it to the hospital."

"She was my ride," Gabrielle said again.

Kate knew it wasn't transportation that had her upset. "She didn't forget you," she said. "Where do you live?"

"Silver Lake."

Kate handed her two twenties. "Call a cab. This'll get you home."

"I should make sure she's okay."

"Go home to your folks. If they hear what happened, they'll be worried about you."

"Right. Um…thanks. Sorry I was a bitch to you at Stiletto."

"You were just looking out for your friend."

She watched Gabrielle walk away. Her story clarified a few details. Grange ordinarily wouldn't accompany Chelsea into the lavatory, but tonight, knowing Swann was stalking her, he would not have let her out of his sight. Swann was counting on that. He had positioned himself for an ambush. Somehow he had known when Chelsea would head for the restroom.

She looked kinda out of it, the bouncer had said. *Shell-shocked.*

Drugged. Probably, Swann spiked her drink with Rohypnol or GHB. He knew the drug's effects would drive her into the bathroom and leave her dazed and compliant afterward.

And the out-of-order sign—he posted it to ensure that there would be no witnesses in the restroom. He must have removed it just before Chelsea entered with Grange.

That much was clear, and so was another thing. She wasn't bringing in the police. She'd made the decision the moment she'd lied to Gabrielle.

She got back into the Jaguar and cruised the neighborhood, looking for the company limo. It was equipped with an OnStar transceiver that allowed its location to be traced via GPS. Swann would know about that. He had almost certainly dumped the car soon after leaving the club. It ought to be parked within a few blocks of Panic Room.

While driving, she called her office number. Alan answered. She filled him in. When she got to the abduction, he cut her off.

"Chief, less than five minutes ago I received an anonymous tip about Chelsea Brewer. The guy said I should check out the action on that celebrity dead-pool site."

"And?"

"Couple hours ago someone placed a significant wager on Chelsea's imminent demise."

A chill passed through her like the onset of the flu. "How significant?"

"Ten Gs." His monotone irritated her. There was such a thing as being too unflappable.

"The creep who runs that site," she asked, "what's his name? Chip something?"

"Skip Slater."

"I need his home address. I know he's local."

"Give me a minute. He's got to be unlisted."

She heard the clicking of a computer keyboard. An unlisted address wouldn't be an obstacle to the online databases Guardian Angel subscribed to.

"Also," Kate said, "I want you to pull in a couple of off-duty bodyguards, send them to check on Grange—and to keep him quiet. We can't let him make an official report. We're handling this ourselves. No police."

"Do you think that's wise?"

"It's our only shot at getting Chelsea back. Now, listen. Swann said he'd call my cell again in two hours. Any way you can trace that call?"

"I'd need some hardware." He slipped into the faraway tone that signaled he was thinking aloud. "Basically, I'd have to connect your cell to an Asterisk box, tweak the configurations to strip out the privacy flags…"

"I don't need the technical rundown."

"Friend of mine has an Asterisk setup. I can borrow his box. If he's home, and not out somewhere trying to get laid."

"Get the box, then go to the Brewers' house."

"You said two hours? I don't know if I can pull it together fast enough, chief."

"Just try."

"Will do. Okay, I've got Slater's residence." He recited the street address and unit number of a condo in West Hollywood. "You going over there?"

"Yes."

"Be careful. Who knows what's up with this guy. He could be part of it."

"If he is, he'll wish he wasn't."

She ended the call. There was a twisting queasiness in her gut. She'd forgotten how much fear felt like hunger.

Ahead, her headlights picked out a black Cadillac DTS parked on Cosmo Street, north of Selma Avenue. Grange's car.

She double-parked alongside it. The Caddy was unlocked. When she opened the door on the driver's side, the dome light came on. She scanned the interior. No large masses on the seats or the floors. She found the trunk latch and popped the lid. The trunk was empty except for a spare tire, a jack, and a first aid kit issued to all her security escorts. Only after she closed the lid could she admit to herself that she'd been looking for Chelsea's body.

She carried out a more careful search of the passenger compartment. On the backseat floor she found Grange's cell phone. No surprise that Swann had abandoned it. His location could have been traced by the GPS signal. Grange's gun and holster were nowhere in sight. Swann had retained those items.

Kate got back into her car, intending to drive on, but for a long moment, she just sat there. Around her neck, under her blouse, she wore a crucifix of carved ironwood. She fumbled it out and rubbed her fingers over its contours. She wanted to say a prayer, if only for the comfort of a familiar routine. But she couldn't remember any words. *Then just pray from your heart.* But she knew she couldn't.

She bit her lip deep enough to draw blood. Tasted its warmth in her mouth. Wounding herself now? Creating stigmata? Maybe next she'd try self-flagellation. Maybe the bite of the lash would bring her, at last, to God.

Stop this.

It was not a thought expressed in words, but a physical tremor of revulsion.

She put the car into gear and began to drive.

To West Hollywood—and the proprietor of Celebrity Whack-A-Mole.

12

S K I P Slater had spent the past two hours in front of his computer, and what he'd learned about Loki had not, repeat *not*, calmed his troubled mind.

Loki was no newbie. He'd played the site for the past three years, placing nearly a hundred bets. He'd won twice and come up dry every other time, his losses far outpacing his winnings. He had no evident system; he seemed to play hunches, and he liked backing long shots. He was, in other words, an addict, the kind of player whose greed and desperation kept CWAM in the black.

All of which should have been reassuring, except that Loki had never wagered this kind of cash before. His previous bets had been for fifty, a hundred dollars a pop. Two fifty, tops, and then only rarely. That was why he had stayed off the radar screen. Tonight he was laying down ten grand.

That was troubling. It suggested he had some special reason to expect success. But if it was a sure thing, why not bet even more?

Maybe he hoped ten grand wouldn't draw any attention. Lay down twenty-five or fifty grand, and you just knew you were going to get noticed. But ten grand, to a person of means, might not seem like a red flag.

And Skip was pretty sure Loki was a person of means. Look at the way his residential address was set up. It was the home of someone with international connections, a world traveler.

Add it all up, and what did you have? A compulsive gambler who was suddenly betting forty times more than he'd ever wagered before. A guy with money and foreign contacts, playing a long-shot bet that could break the house.

An hour ago, Skip sent home Elke or Ellie. No more nookie tonight. No more nookie ever if he lost CWAM and the money it brought in. If he had to rely on his charm and good looks to get women, he would be celibate for life.

The intercom buzzed.

The noise startled him. Until now, he hadn't realized how quiet it was. Even the constant tattoo of footsteps from upstairs had ceased. His tranny neighbor must have taken his high heels out on the town.

Skip rose from his chair, the first time he'd moved his lower body since sitting down at the computer, and hurried into the living room. The intercom buzzed again. Somebody was impatient. He tapped the mic button. "What?"

"Mr. Slater, my name is Kate Malick of Guardian Angel, the personal security firm. I need to speak with you regarding one of my clients."

His heart flipped. He tasted puke at the back of his throat. "Which client?"

"Chelsea Brewer."

He was fucked.

The world's most trashtacular popwreck was deceased, and even if word hadn't reached the media yet, an after-the-fact investigation was already underway. He was about to become another dot-com millionaire with an empty bank account and a wolf pack of creditors on his ass.

"Mr. Slater?"

He thought about turning her away, but it was no use. You couldn't turn away the angel of death.

He buzzed her in. She was at his door twenty seconds later. Must've taken the stairs; the elevator wasn't that fast. He opened up, and damn, she really *was* the angel of death—black skirt, black jacket, black hair, black eyes. She terrified him. She was going to bring his world crashing down.

"Uh, come in."

Kate Malick entered, unsmiling, and stood in the small space the lying Realtor had described as two rooms, a living room and a dining area, when in fact it was all one room—and not a very big room, at that. She kept her hands in her jacket pockets, unwilling to touch anything, as if his very presence rendered the premises unclean. She looked around slowly as if scenting the air.

"You have a problem," Malick said.

"Do I?" He did his best to sound nonchalant. It seemed like the cool thing to do.

"You do. And unless you're an idiot, which I doubt, you already know about it."

He swallowed. "I'm aware someone's put down a sizable chunk of change on your client. I don't see how that's my problem."

"It's your problem because if Chelsea Brewer dies tonight, you'll take a major hit."

If she dies, the woman had said. *If*. Such a beautiful word. Skip had never appreciated its aesthetic qualities until now.

He let out a shaky breath. "Is there any reason to think she might die?"

"She was abducted a half hour ago."

Skip moaned, his reprieve evaporating. "Oh, man, I *knew* shit like this would happen."

"Your concern for Chelsea is touching."

"Hey, I've got nothing to do with this."

"Don't you?" She turned her cold gaze on him. "You've got quite a setup going here. You've found a way to profit from death."

He tried not to be intimidated. It wasn't easy. She was older than he was, and taller, and something in her stride suggested she could kick his ass. "I wouldn't look at it that way. It's a game, that's all."

"It hasn't occurred to you that your game may encourage someone to murder a celebrity for a big payoff?"

"I've got that covered."

"Not well enough, it appears."

"Look, it's not like *I'm* killing anybody. I'm just keeping score."

Kate Malick stared at him. Skip found it kind of fascinating to be in the same room with someone who despised him so completely. Then she turned away, her gaze traveling to the art print on the wall, a reproduction of *Piss Christ*, the Andres Serrano photo of a crucifix in urine. Skip had always found it daring, but now he saw it with her eyes—a bit of childish graffiti, stupidly offensive.

Something about the photograph triggered an association. "Shit. I remember you. You're the nun."

"My personal life isn't relevant to anything."

"You're cool, though. Seriously. They kicked you out of the convent and you just turned around and went entrepreneurial on their ass. Is it true you hired guys off the street to be bodyguards—bums—and you cleaned them up?"

"They cleaned themselves up."

"Personally, I think it was genius. With all the bleeding hearts in this town, you knew you'd get some killer PR. Every celebrity latte drinker would be jonesing to be part of your rehabilitation crusade. Only, it kind of knocks you off your high horse, doesn't it? You exploited the down-and-outers to generate buzz in the community. Then you exploited the do-gooder instincts of the rich and clueless to get yourself a client list. Now that you've hit the big leagues, I'll bet you don't hire street people anymore. But that social activist vibe still clings to you, right?"

"I'm not here to discuss my business practices. I'm here to discuss your culpability in the abduction of Chelsea Brewer."

"Hey, I can't be held responsible for what some mentally unbalanced individual may do. I don't even know that the wager is connected to the kidnapping. Actually, I hope it is. If the bet was placed as part of a criminal conspiracy, I'm not obligated to honor it. No payout."

"So you think you're off the hook?"

"Looks that way."

"I was wrong about you. You *are* an idiot."

"Hey, I'm a pretty tolerant guy, but I won't take an unlimited amount of shit. You're in my house, you know. I can make you leave at any time."

Malick appraised him darkly. "Can you?"

He swallowed. "I don't want to get physical."

"No. You really don't."

She stared him down until he looked away.

"You're not off the hook, Mr. Slater. If my client dies, there will be legal consequences."

"The system can't touch me. My site is licensed through the Canadian Mohawk territory of Kahnawake. The whole operation is outside US jurisdiction."

"But you personally aren't outside US jurisdiction, are you?"

"I haven't done anything illegal."

"It'll make an interesting test case. Care to chance it? Even if you avoid criminal charges, there'll be civil liabilities. Any way you look at it, it's in your interest to keep Chelsea alive."

"And how am I supposed to do that?"

"By giving me the name and address of the person who placed the bet."

"What makes you think I can supply that info?"

"There's a lot of money on the line. You had to be curious."

His shoulders narrowed in a defensive scrunch. "I made an effort to track down the bettor, but I got nowhere. There are layers of anonymity. My clients transfer funds to CWAM via one of several third parties located in places like Costa Rica and the British West Indies. What with the cutouts, I don't know who's playing. All I ever see is a bunch of screen names. The payment processors have the players' real names and contact info, but they don't share their data. They're more secretive than Swiss banks."

"So you've hit a dead end?"

"Right."

"I don't believe you. You're too tech-savvy to get nowhere. And you're a crappy liar." A compliment and an insult in the same breath. She was playing good cop–bad cop all by herself.

"Well…there could possibly be other avenues of investigation. But even if I were to come up with something, I wouldn't hand it over to you." He drew himself up to his full height, which wasn't much. "I don't cooperate with agents of the established social order."

"What are you—an anarchist?"

"Anarcho-libertarian, actually. The state itself is a criminal enterprise—"

"Save it."

"You're not into politics?"

"I'm into saving my client's life. And if you're really an anarchist—"

"Anarcho-libertarian."

"Then you should want to help me. Because I'm not from the government. And if Chelsea dies, people who *are* in the government will be paying you a visit, and they won't be as sociable as I am."

He paused. "That's the first intelligent statement you've made."

"I'm still waiting for yours."

He thought it over. Malick wasn't a cop. She was probably discreet. He just might have to trust her.

"Okay," he said. "I did make some progress tracking down the bettor. I'll walk you through it, and I'll try to keep it nontechnical."

"Let me guess. The money is transferred by the payment processor, but the player logs on to your system from his own terminal. You performed a WHOIS lookup of the player's IP address. Then you ran a traceroute to identify the proximate server."

"Um...yeah." His self-esteem took a hit, but he rallied. "I suppose it *is* pretty obvious."

"But all you'd get via those methods is the name of the player's ISP and a rough idea of his computer's location."

"West LA. That's what came up."

"West LA's a big place. To zoom in any closer, you'd need the cooperation of the ISP. And they wouldn't talk to you without a subpoena."

He fidgeted. "That's where it gets a little dicey."

She got it. "You hacked into the ISP's database." Surprisingly, he thought he saw a hint of admiration in her face.

"It wasn't that hard. They left the back door open. Sloppy."

"So you found the subscriber who matches the IP address. What's his name?"

"I didn't find a person, just a corporation. Consolidated Global Marketing, headquartered in the Cayman Islands. I was trying to run down some info on it—"

"Don't bother. It's a shell."

"That's what I figured. Which means—"

"It means we're dealing with serious people. People who know how to set up a dummy corporation in a foreign country to cover their tracks."

"That's how I see it, yeah."

"Was there a local address?"

"The account owner didn't intend to leave one. All bills go to the Caymans. But…"

"There were service calls."

"One, yeah." Christ, she was sharp. "For a broadband hookup. Details were in the account history—including the address. It's 24012 Cressley Drive, West LA. That's a residential area in Westwood."

"Good enough." She started to go, then turned back. "My office received an anonymous tip about this wager. You didn't call it in, did you?"

"Me? Shit no."

She nodded. "I didn't think you were the public-spirited type."

He mustered a dozen stellar comebacks, but Kate Malick had already left.

13

THE conversation with Skip Slater troubled Kate. She thought about it as she sped into Westwood.

In the beginning she had been sincere in offering a hand to the men she'd met in her ministry.

Background checks eliminated those with criminal records who weren't legally allowed to carry firearms. Personal interviews culled the habitual drug users and the mentally ill. There remained a core of serious candidates.

With a little cajoling, Barney became her partner. He trained the men, armed them, weeded out the incorrigibles.

And she'd had a story to sell, the story of an ex-nun hiring men off the street. The media didn't discover her by chance.

Skip wasn't wrong. She *had* used the men she hired. Probably, she hadn't lived up to the highest ethical standard. But as she told Sam Brewer, she wasn't a very good nun.

She steered the Jag down Wilshire Boulevard and turned onto Cressley, then found the house and parked at the curb two doors down. The Baby Glock in its pocket holster went into the side pocket of her jacket. The holster was essential when carrying concealed; the Glock's safety was part of the trigger and could be released by accident. It wouldn't do to have a tube of lip gloss slide under the trigger guard and blow a hole in her thigh. Just another thing Barney had taught her.

She stepped out of the car into the threatening dark. The Glock felt heavy in her jacket. The neighborhood was very still. It was rare for any part of LA to be this quiet, this empty, even after midnight.

Westwood was an exclusive district of neat little homes with postage-stamp lawns lining the hilly streets like toy houses on folds of bunched-up carpet. Residences went for two million dollars and up, more than her father had earned in a lifetime. It was a neighborhood seemingly cloistered from the horror shows of barrio slayings and gang wars, but the separation was more cosmetic than real. The undergrowth of the urban jungle spread everywhere. Here it might be trimmed back by platoons of gardeners, but if you trod carefully, you could still feel it under your feet.

As if in reminder, every house along the street advertised a burglar alarm system. At 24012 Cressley a red-and-white sign, mounted on a stake in the yard, read, PREMISES PROTECTED BY CARSON HOME SECURITY.

Kate took a long look at the sign. She was familiar with every firm offering residential security services in Los Angeles. Carson Home Security was not one of them. The sign was a bluff.

She approached the house. The windows were dark; she didn't see even the blue flicker of a television set. The attached garage was windowless—impossible to tell if a car was parked inside.

She skirted a drift of azaleas and eased alongside the living room window, directing the long beam of her pocket flashlight through the glass.

Coffee table strewn with magazines. Fireplace with a slate apron. Paintings of sailboats. No clutter, no homey touches. The room might have been a layout in a magazine.

A mockingbird penetrated the silence, riffing on a medley of birdcalls.

She ducked under the branches of a tree bristling with ripe fruit—oranges or lemons, she couldn't tell in the darkness—and crept around to the side of the house. Curtains covered two windows. The third looked in on a bedroom. Nobody in bed. On the walls, more sailboat paintings, as forgettable as hotel room artwork.

In a movie she would have had a set of burglar tools in her back pocket. Lacking these, she hunted around for a rock, wrapped her hand in her jacket sleeve, and smacked the bedroom window. The glass made a soft crunch. It tinkled on the carpet as she swept the window frame clear of shards. The mockingbird, now an abettor, covered the sounds of the break-in with its song.

She hoisted herself up and in, her boots dropping onto a crackling scatter of glass. The sound reminded her of ice splitting. Thin ice—now there was a metaphor for a security consultant who'd just committed B&E.

She listened for any stir of activity, heard nothing. But while the house might be empty now, someone had placed the bet from this address earlier tonight.

Keeping the lights off, she used her flashlight to guide her.

The lavatory was spotless except for a ring of hard water deposits in the toilet. It hadn't been flushed recently. At the sink, she opened the tap and heard a burp of air before a dirty stream squirted out. The water had been standing in the pipes a long time.

The bedroom closet was empty. Dust glazed the television in the den. Beside it sat a Blu-ray player and several stacks of DVDs. No unifying theme to the selections. It was as if somebody had gone to Blockbuster and bought up everything in sight. The books on the shelves looked like random pickings from a library sale.

The kitchen stove was barely used, the drip pans beneath the burners unstained. The refrigerator was empty save for a half dozen gourmet frozen dinners. Only plastic plates and microwavable cookware in the pantry. On the counter, a coffeemaker and a stack of nested Styrofoam cups, the kind of thing she would expect to see in an office, not a home. But this wasn't anyone's home. She wasn't sure what it was.

The house was a blank, a cipher. Fake sign outside, weirdly immaculate decor inside. The company that owned it was a shell, and the house itself felt like one.

She was leaving the kitchen when something stopped her. A smell so obvious and familiar she'd almost overlooked it. The smell of coffee.

She lifted the carafe from the coffee maker and shone her flash through it. Beads of water crisscrossed the sides. Someone had brewed coffee and washed out the pot. Recently.

Reaching into her jacket, she drew the Glock.

She had yet to explore the back hallway. Her flashlight beam guided her past more sailboat paintings to an open door that led to a guest bedroom. The bed was made, the room tidy, but she had the sense that someone had occupied this space not long ago. It took her a moment to know why. No dust anywhere. The bedroom and adjoining bath had been wiped down.

She checked the closet. Empty, but there was a square impression in the carpet, with smaller, deeper dents at two corners. A suitcase with legs or casters had rested there.

Someone had holed up in this room, living out of a suitcase. They had chosen the rear of the house to minimize the risk of being seen from the street. They had covered their tracks when they'd left.

If they'd left.

Into the hall again, moving to the next door, half open. Easing inside, her flashlight revealing a home office. Swivel chair, double-pedestal desk, and on the desk a desktop computer in sleep mode connected to a broadband modem. The LEDs were green, the Internet connection active. The bet must have been placed from this machine.

Her hand had moved to the keyboard when she saw a gleam of light through the crack of a door.

She pushed open the door and entered another room not much larger than a walk-in closet. A row of video monitors stood on a folding table. The room lights were off, but the monitors were on, showing night scope images of rooms and hallways. Bedroom, kitchen, den—the interior of this house.

There was a security system, after all. Hidden surveillance cameras had been watching her the whole time.

On the floor by the table was a small suitcase. Behind her was its owner. She heard low breathing and started to turn.

Something small and cold kissed her left ear. It was a metal circle, and it could have been an object as innocuous as a cigar tube, but she knew it was the muzzle of a gun.

"Don't move, Miss Malick," said a man's voice. "Don't you fucking move."

14

KATE drew a breath. She focused on whom she was dealing with. If she could judge by his voice, he was older than she was. In his fifties, maybe. He sounded nervous, flustered. Not like a practiced criminal. Someone who'd been around a while but was new at this.

And he knew her name.

"Drop your gun." The quaver in his voice worried her. Scared people did reckless things.

She let the gun fall to the floor.

"Kick it away."

The gun skated into a corner.

"Give me the flash."

Raising her arm, she let him pluck the flashlight from her fingers.

"God damn it," he whispered, "what are you doing here?" She felt the hot exhalation of his breath on her ear.

"Tracking you down."

"Me? What do you know about me?"

"I know you placed an online bet on Chelsea Brewer's life. And I know you're working with Jack Swann."

"You can't know that." The flashlight wavered in his hand, the beam briefly slicing into her eye from the side and lighting up the blood vessels at the back of her retina. They flashed across her field of view, a webbed mosaic.

"I know more than that. I know Swann is off the reservation. He's working against you. He wants you caught."

"Bullshit. Why would you say that?"

"Because he's the one who tipped us off."

It was true. Had to be. She had worked it out at some point between leaving her car and entering this room. Worked it out without conscious deliberation.

There couldn't be many people who knew about the threat to Chelsea. Swann was one of the few. And he'd run from her at Stiletto. That was the key. Why had he fled? Because he couldn't have a conversation with her. Couldn't let her hear his voice. He was already planning to call her office later with the tip, and he didn't know who'd be picking up the phone.

"Tipped you off?" The man's words came slowly. She could almost hear him thinking it through, solving it like a puzzle. "That doesn't make sense. Swann works for me. He's my employee—or at least, an independent contractor on my payroll."

Funny way for a gunman to put it. His vocabulary wasn't street. He sounded white collar, a management type.

"Looks like he'd rather go solo," she said.

"He hasn't been fully paid yet. He has no incentive to get me out of the picture."

Incentive—another business term.

"Did Swann tell you he has a prior association with Chelsea's father?"

A pause. "No. He didn't tell me that."

She'd planted doubts. It was something.

He exhaled another breath, tickling her earlobe. "You're just trying to play us off against each other."

"I'm brainstorming. Work with me."

"I'm not letting you mess with my head."

"Was Swann supposed to kill Chelsea at the nightclub? Because he didn't. He took her alive."

The breathing in her ear was ragged now. "What the fuck are you talking about?"

"He created a diversion and spirited her out of there. He's already called me to say Chelsea is unharmed."

"That...that wasn't our arrangement."

"He's playing you. He's got his own plan, and he wants you taken out. He was hoping I'd do it for him."

"Then he miscalculated, didn't he?"

She had no answer to that.

"All right," he said, calmer now, as if a decision had been reached. "Now I want you to turn with me so we're both facing the door."

"We going somewhere?"

"Just do it, Miss Malick."

She managed the turn in a series of sideways steps, like a dance move. He pivoted behind her, remaining out of her sight. If he wouldn't let her see his face, he might be planning to let her live. But she didn't think so. She had a feeling how this was going to end.

"Now, walk," he said.

"I want to know where we're going."

"Just...walk."

The slow deliberation of his words told her what was coming next. Her heart kicked up. She couldn't move. It wasn't stubbornness or brave resistance. Her body simply wouldn't function.

He didn't repeat the order, just pushed her forward into the home office, then into the hall. Flashlight bobbing by her left ear. Gun nudging her neck.

She knew the cliché that in a crisis everything slowed down, but it wasn't working that way for her. If anything, time moved faster than normal, slipping away like a greasy rope that kept squirming out of her grasp. She needed more time and she had too little.

Her perceptions had narrowed to tunnel vision, tunnel hearing. She saw only the blur of her boots carrying her forward across the hallway's carpeted floor, heard only his breathing, rapid and shallow.

A throw of the dice, she thought. *This may all come down to a throw of the dice.*

Ten feet down the hall was a door with a polished brass knob, so shiny she could see blurred fragments of her reflection when the flashlight beam focused on it.

"Open it," he said. The gun bit into the hollow at the base of her skull.

She grasped the knob. It rotated easily, the latch uncoupling. She let the door swing inward. The hinges were clean and new and made no sound.

Before her a flight of stairs plunged into gloom. A cellar.

She got it now. He was taking her into a windowless room below ground, where the pistol's report would be muffled. It was a warm night. The neighbors would have the AC on, windows closed. They wouldn't hear a thing.

"Light switch on your right," he said. "Flip it up."

She groped for the switch and found it, then wagged her index finger against the plate without touching the toggle. "Nothing's happening," she said. "Bulb must be dead."

She worried he might reach past her and try the switch himself, but with the gun in one hand and the flashlight in the other, he couldn't do it. He stood there breathing hard, his respiration fanning her left ear, hot and steady like a pulse.

"Just go down." He beamed the flash at the stairs. "We can see okay."

She took a step onto the staircase. Wood creaked.

"You can just run away," she said. "If you do, I can't stop you."

"You can ID me."

"How? I haven't seen you."

"You've heard my voice. Move."

Another step.

"I can't identify you that way."

"There are other ways."

"What does that mean?"

"Who else knows you're here?"

It took her a second to see the question's implications. The house concerned him. He could be identified through the house. "Several people," she said, descending once more.

He thought about that. "You could be lying. You came here alone. You could have found the place on your own."

"I found it through the bet you placed. I couldn't do it solo. I'm not a computer whiz. If the house is a problem for you, killing me isn't going to solve it."

"It may buy me some time."

"You're not a murderer."

He released a tense little laugh. "I never used to be. But here's a tip for you, Miss Malick. Family is everything. A man can do things he never dreamed of when his family is involved."

"What are you trying to say?"

"Family is everything. That's all."

They were more than halfway down the stairs. There was no getting through to him. No communication. He was not reachable.

Had to fight, then. Her only option. Risk it all on one throw. Now.

She twisted toward the railing and grabbed him by the shirt. A yell of surprise and anger, a stumble, and he nearly lost his balance on the stairs. But somehow he kept his footing as he swung onto the steps directly opposite her.

The gun came up, angled at her face. She ducked and threw herself at his midsection and the gun went off, a crash of noise above her head. She wrapped her arms around his legs and kicked out from the railing, and his knees buckled.

He pitched headlong into the dark, the flashlight flying free and winking out. The gun went off again, another roar and a muzzle flash, purple in the blackness, the shot aimed at nothing, just a reflex of his trigger finger. Then she was sprinting up the stairs, taking them two at a time, crouching low to make a smaller target.

She reached the doorway and darted into the hall just as the gun boomed a third time. Clatter of footsteps. He had recovered. He was giving chase.

She ran into the surveillance room, snatched up her gun, and pivoted, ready to fire, but he wasn't there.

She checked the monitors until she found an angle on the hallway. She saw him exit the basement. The night scope image was grainy, but she could make out his general appearance. White male, tall, dark jacket, button-down shirt open at the collar. Sharp, angular face.

The gun was in his hand, and she wondered if he had the nerve to hunt her down and engage in an exchange of fire. Even as she asked the question she saw him turn to the left, the wrong direction if he meant to come after her. A moment later another camera showed him leaving by a rear door. Its slam echoed through the house. He knew she must have recovered her weapon, and he wouldn't risk combat.

Another screen offered an angle on the backyard, a glimpse of a fleeing figure disappearing through the hedges.

She couldn't catch up with him on foot, but in her car—maybe. She exited the house via the front door and ran to her Jag. Jumped in, started the engine. Took the next corner, flicking on her brights, scanning the shrubbery. She circled the block three times, then tried the adjacent blocks without success.

He'd gotten away.

She stopped the car and sat there, and suddenly she realized she was shaking all over.

It hit her now—only now—the full aftereffects of her encounter. How close she'd come. How incredible that she'd made it out alive.

Through it all, she'd been focused only on survival. Her only objective had been to draw another breath and another. Pure animal instinct. She'd had no thoughts of Chelsea's safety, or Grange's.

And, of course, no thought whatsoever of God. But that fact didn't surprise her. She would have expected nothing else.

She headed in the direction of the Brewers' house in the Hollywood Hills. En route she speed-dialed Alan. He must be out of the office by now, but the call would be forwarded to his cell. He answered at once.

"Chief, what's up?"

"Slater sent me to the location where the bet was placed. I got into a situation."

"What kind of situation? Why do you sound so frazzled?"

"I got jumped, but I'm okay. Contact Di Milo at home and send him to the address I just left. It's 24012 Cressley in Westwood. I left the front door unlocked. Have Di Milo check the surveillance system, see if there are tapes showing the gunman's face."

"The guy was armed?"

"Like I said, I'm okay. He wasn't a pro. The way he talked, I'd say he's a businessman. He said something about his family being involved. I don't know what that means or who he was. Maybe we can identify him through the address."

"I'm on it."

"Listen, the anonymous call that tipped us off about Chelsea—can you trace it?"

"No can do. The guy used a prepaid phone card, so the call was routed through the provider. What showed up on the caller ID was a generic eight-hundred number for AT&T. Anybody could have made the call, from any area code. Why the sudden interest?"

"I think Swann was the caller."

"Yeah? Well, if he uses the same phone card when he makes the ransom call, there's no way we can trace it. All we'll get is the AT&T routing number."

"We have to try anyway. Have you got the...uh...Ampersand box?"

"It's an Asterisk box, and I'm working on it."

"Work fast. Swann will be calling in an hour." There was so little time.

The last thing she asked for was Skip Slater's phone number. She reached him on the first ring.

"Your bettor is definitely mixed up in this. And guess what, Mr. Slater? That means you're involved, too."

"Hey, I want Chelsea back as much as you do."

"Prove it. I want you to go to the Westwood address. One of my men will be there reviewing the security system. You can search the computer's hard drive, see if there's any information that might help us."

"What kind of info?"

"Any kind. Will you do it?"

"I guess, but...isn't this a job for the police?"

"You're the anarcho-libertarian, aren't you? The one who doesn't cooperate with agents of the established social order?"

"True." He didn't seem to catch her irony. "So this is a civilian black op? We're off the grid, running below the radar?"

She rolled her eyes. "Roger that."

When she was done with Slater, she scrolled through her cell phone directory and found the Brewers' home number. She didn't want to say much over the phone, but she could at least confirm that Sam knew Swann.

It took Victoria six rings to pick up. She sounded sleepy and irritated.

"I need to talk to your husband," Kate said.

"At this hour? It's one o'clock in the morning."

"It's important."

"Honestly, I don't know what's gotten into you tonight."

"Just put him on, please."

"He's not even here."

"Where can I find him?"

"Where he always goes to blow off steam. The Ninth Circle."

"What's that? Strip club?"

"It's a video arcade. Hollywood and Western. He'll be easy to spot—the only person over forty."

"Right."

"You know, I wasn't joking about my glassware. That was a very expensive piece, and it's coming directly out of your fee—"

Kate clicked off and drove east, toward Hollywood.

15

HOLLYWOOD and Western was a dicey neighborhood at the intersection of different ethnic territories—Asians to the east, Hispanics to the north, Armenians to the south—a tangle of suspicions and hatreds, pornographic bookstores and loan shark parlors, taquerias and fast-food joints that sold drugs on the side.

Kate eased past a double-parked panel truck whose owner appeared to be burglarizing a TV repair shop. Just beyond the truck was an island of lurid light and animated neon. The Ninth Circle. She found a space at the curb.

She would have loved to carry her Glock, especially after what she'd just been through, but there was a security guard at the arcade entrance and she didn't want him to spot the gun and turn her away. She left the gun in the glove box, trusting the car's customized alarm system to deter all miscreants.

An unnecessary precaution, as it turned out. The guard, engaged in an in-depth exploration of one nostril, didn't glance at her as she went in.

The crowded arcade was a wall of sound. She threaded her way among the game kiosks, reviewing Sam's history. Two juvenile convictions: auto theft and assault. The records were sealed, but people talked. Two felony convictions as an adult and a string of misdemeanors, some pled down from felonies. Burglary, drugs, weapons violations, brawls. He was currently being sued by a paparazzo for breaking the man's jaw.

She passed teenagers jerking joysticks and pumping quarters into slots. A young crowd, Salvadorans mostly. Hard Aztec faces, sullen glares, Gothic letters tattooed on their foreheads, marking them as MS-13 gangstas.

And there was Chelsea's dad, fifty years old, bumping and grinding a video pinball game like he was having rough sex with it.

She waited until the computer-graphics ball dropped through the simulated flippers and out of play. Before he could launch a new ball she thrust an arm across the front of the machine, blocking his view. He pivoted, shoulders hunched in a belligerent stance. His posture didn't relax even after he recognized her.

"What the fuck *you* doing here?"

She didn't have to look far to see where Chelsea had picked up her potty mouth. "I need to talk to you."

He straightened. A bulge under his vinyl jacket printed like a handgun. "About what?"

She flipped open her phone and showed him Swann's photo. "You know this man. Your daughter told me he used to hang with you."

He glanced at the photo, and she saw the heavy swallowing motion of his throat. "Why're you talking to Chelsea about this?"

"Just tell me everything you know about Jack Swann."

He hesitated. "Okay. But not in here. It's too noisy, and this isn't something I want to shout about. Lemme finish my game."

"You're finished."

"Got one round left."

She leaned past him, launched the electronic ball, then delivered a kick to the machine with the side of her foot. The TILT sign lit up, immobilizing the controls. Sam watched helplessly as the ball skipped from one bumper to another in a convincing simulation of gravity before dropping out of sight.

"Shit, lady. Costs a buck fucking fifty per game."

She followed him out of the arcade. Sam had worked with Swann before. There was a chance the two of them had hooked up again, even conspired to pull off the abduction. He could be leading her into a trap.

"Where are we going?" she asked when they stepped onto the sidewalk, past the useless security guard.

Sam pointed to a Lexus RX 330, black and sleek. "My ride."

He unlocked the doors with the remote and got in on the driver's side, letting her climb into the passenger seat. The key, she noted, was jammed in the ignition, and though he hadn't started the engine, he could turn it over in less than a second. If he took off without warning, she might not have time to jump out.

"Tell me about Swann," she said. "Friend of yours?"

He rasped a chuckle. "Friend of nobody."

The Lexus's interior lights dimmed, leaving her and Sam Brewer in the dark. "But you hung out," she said.

"We never hung out. Swann never came by on any social calls."

"Why *did* he come by?"

His hand moved, and she thought he might be reaching for the gun under his jacket. But he only scratched his chin. "How tight are you with the cops?"

"I have contacts in the LAPD and the sheriff's department."

"They help you out, you help them out?"

"Mostly they help me."

"It always goes both ways." Spoken with the weary cynicism of a man who knew only how to use people or be used by them.

"Sometimes they ask me to keep an eye open. Why are we talking about this?"

"If a client of yours—or someone related to a client—admits to a crime," he said slowly, his voice drifting lower, "you'll tell the police."

"It depends."

"On?"

"How serious the crime is. How long ago it happened."

Sam thought about that. "It's not murder or anything."

"Okay."

"It was ten years ago."

"Did anyone get hurt?"

"Not in any significant way."

She wasn't sure what this meant. "And Swann was involved?"

"Swann was more than involved. It was his thing. I was just along for the ride." He turned toward her. "If you're recording this conversation, I'll kill you."

"I'm not recording anything."

"Maybe I should frisk you."

"I'd like to see you try."

He snorted a laugh, then looked away as if satisfied. "It was good, what you did at the house."

"What I did?"

"That glass shit Vicki's always buying. I liked seeing you break it. I'd like to smash all that shit."

"I didn't do it for fun. I did it to make a point."

"Thing is, you *did* it. I like that." He relaxed a little. "Look, the details don't matter, okay? Swann and me pulled off a heist. His plan. I was just the second pair of eyes. We split the take—well, not split, exactly. It was thirty/seventy. You can guess who got the short end of the stick."

"He ripped you off?"

"No, it was our agreement all along."

"Why'd you work for thirty percent?"

"Whole job was his idea."

"That's not a reason."

"You want a reason. Okay, here's a reason. Nobody bargains with Swann. You do what you're told; you take what you get. And you hope he moves out of your life ASAP." He pronounced the acronym one letter at a time, with strange formality.

"And that's why Swann used to visit? So you could do jobs with him?"

"Not *jobs*. Just one job. He stopped by a few times to go over the plan. Then it was done, and he never came back." She saw it again—that slow, viscid swallowing motion of his throat. "Until now."

"You're afraid of him." She expected a denial.

"Goddamn right I am."

"Why? Does he hold some kind of grudge against you?"

"He don't need a grudge."

"What does that mean?"

"It means he don't always have a, you know, rational basis for the shit he does."

"Sam, it's not you he's after. It's Chelsea."

"What makes you think so?"

"This may be hard for you to hear."

"Just say it."

"Swann has your daughter. He abducted her an hour ago. He's already spoken to me on the phone, told me to keep the law out of it. I assume he'll be making a ransom demand when he calls again."

"Huh." The word was flat, toneless. "Does Vicki know?"

"I haven't told her yet. It's the kind of news that has to be delivered face-to-face."

"So…it's got nothing to do with me at all."

In the furtive flicker of his eyes she read relief. "Try not to look so happy about it."

"I'm not happy. Hey, she's my kid."

"She's a meal ticket. That's the only reason you're in her life. That's all she means to you."

"You been listening to Vicki."

"Vicki's the same way. Your daughter's been killing herself and you don't give a damn as long as the checks keep clearing. Now she's been abducted by a psychopath, and you're relieved it's her instead of you."

"I care about Chelsea," he muttered.

"If you do, then help her. Tell me about Swann. Anything that might help me understand him."

"Understand him? You want to *understand* him?"

"Is that so hard?"

"Impossible is what it is. There's nobody like Swann."

"You've known your share of hard cases. What makes this guy so special?"

"I told you. He's not rational. Not right."

"Not right, how?"

He sat silently, breathing, breathing.

"He's polite," Sam said finally.

"What?" Kate thought she hadn't heard correctly.

"It's what makes him…different. He's always polite. Talks real soft. Says *please* and *thank you*."

"And that's a problem?"

"Yeah, it's a problem. Because you never know what's going on inside him. He can be smiling and shaking your hand, calling you his good buddy, and the next thing you know, he's got a knife at your throat. It's just how he is. All charm on the surface, but underneath there's something crazy, and you can't predict it. Because there's nothing he won't do. No kind of pain he won't dish out." He sat quietly. The long speech had exhausted him.

"You're saying he's a sadist," Kate said, thinking of Chelsea.

Sam's mouth twisted. "That's too nice a word. Too civilized for him, for what he does...what he's capable of..."

"Tell me."

"I can't. But I can show you—if you really want to know."

"Of course I do."

"Strap yourself in."

He cranked the ignition key. She made no move to flee. She was no longer afraid of going with him. She was no longer afraid at all.

It was Sam Brewer who was afraid.

16

SAM picked up the eastbound Hollywood Freeway, gliding fast through quicksilver currents of headlights, exiting south of downtown. He parked on a side street in an industrial district, got out of the Lexus, and started walking. Kate followed.

Big warehouses lined the roadside, fed by railroad spurs. Boxcars loomed outside loading bays. A Doberman growled behind a hurricane fence placarded with NO TRESPASSING signs.

"Not a great place to be in the middle of the night," Kate said. "Now I'm actually glad you're carrying."

Sam's eyes ticked toward her. "You saw the piece under my jacket and you still came out here with me?"

"Sure did."

"Balls of steel, lady."

Yards behind them, the Doberman let out a volley of barks. Kate paused, looking back.

"What?" Sam asked.

"I thought I heard footsteps."

They listened. Silence.

"Paranoid," he said, moving on.

———

The goddamned dog nearly gave him away. He bent low in the shadows, breathing slowly, calming himself.

He ought to kill the animal. He had a gun with him, an untraceable black market gun. But it wasn't silenced. Even if it had been, they would hear. The report, though muffled, would carry on a still night.

Anyway, it wasn't the dog he wanted dead. It was Kate.

She was more active than usual tonight. Earlier, she broke into a house in Westwood and a few minutes later came running out, carrying her gun. Then she hooked up with a man he recognized as Chelsea Brewer's deadbeat father, and now they were on a mission together in an industrial wasteland.

But she wouldn't be active much longer.

All he needed was one shot. A clear opportunity. But Westwood had been too quiet, too many people in the houses, and it would take only one night owl to look out a window and identify him. The arcade was too crowded; no way he could maneuver in there.

Now she was in the emptiest part of LA he'd ever seen, a part of town he'd barely even known existed, and it should have been perfect. But Brewer was with her, and the man was a career criminal. Kate was probably still carrying concealed, and Brewer might be, too.

He couldn't chance it. He was a fair shot, but he had no experience hitting live targets. He needed to get close, but the risk was too great.

Hard not to make the move, though. At this distance, he might be able to pull it off. It took all his self-control not to squeeze off four rounds, a double tap on each target from behind. He could picture it: the clouds of blood, the jerking collapse, the shuddering piles of limbs. Maybe Kate would live long enough for him to approach her, show himself. *I warned you,* he would say. *On the phone, remember? I warned you to look out for your own security for a change.*

He could imagine her face, the eyes widening, then clouding over. Maybe he would put one more round into her, a coup de grace to the temple.

Sweet.

He watched them as they walked away. Debated whether or not to follow them. He would have to make his move sometime. He might not get a better chance.

———

Kate walked on with Sam Brewer, passing more warehouses. The soulless industrial buildings reminded her of a day when, at six years old, she had gone with her mother to pick up her dad at work. They had pulled up to a vast, grim structure where ships and trains offloaded goods in huge crates, stacked in great piles by men with aching backs and calloused hands, while a foreman blew a whistle and bellowed orders. It was loud, hot, airless, and it seemed like hell, a place she'd heard about in Sunday school.

Daddy works here, she'd thought, and felt afraid.

She followed Sam across a line of railroad tracks, stepping high over the rails. Past the tracks ran the concrete trough of the Los Angeles River, a trickle of water, oily in the starlight, meandering down its center. Twenty yards north, a railroad bridge spanned the river. On the near side a fire guttered. Beside it crouched a man.

"That's him," Sam said.

"Who?"

"Lazarus. What we call him, anyway. 'Cause he's a dead man walking. It's some shit from the Bible."

"I'm familiar with the reference."

They threaded their way along the embankment, its chalky pallor offset by splotches of graffiti like gray mold. The Broadway bridge lay to the south, groaning with distant traffic.

"Hey, Laz. It's me, Sam."

The man stood up slowly. "You stay the fuck away."

"Just here to talk, bro."

"I'll cut you. Fucking swear I will."

Sam flashed Kate a cocksure smile. "He won't cut nobody. Couldn't, even if he wanted to." He raised his voice. "Come on, Laz, be hospitable."

They stopped a few feet from the man and watched him in the glow of the fire. His hands were what Kate noticed first. Scarred hands, fingers sticking out in all directions like broken straw in a broom.

His face was half slack, the face of a stroke victim, muscles on the left side drooping, left eye unblinking and glassy. He chewed the right corner of his mouth. Drool threaded his beard.

"The lady's come to hear your story," Sam said. "Tell her, Laz. Tell her about Swann."

Lazarus went on chewing his mouth. "That motherfucker."

"Tell her what he did."

"Fucker. Messed me up. My hands…" He nodded and went on nodding like a bobblehead toy. "It hurt."

"What happened to his hands?" Kate asked.

Sam shrugged. "Swann crushed the knuckles to powder, then worked over the fingers with a knife. Cut the tendons one by one."

"Fucked 'em up royal," Lazarus said. He shifted his weight like a restless child. His clothes, pasted to him in layers, gave off a warm cloud of body odor.

"His hands aren't the worst thing. Show her your head, Laz."

Lazarus shuffled his feet, rotating sideways, and brushed back a tuft of hair to reveal a wound above his left ear. In the dancing shadows it trembled like a pale, puckered mouth.

"Swann drove a four-inch nail in there," Sam said. "Pounded it in with his boot. Laid ol' Laz on the floor and just stomped the nail in—wham bam, thank you, ma'am."

"How long ago was this?" Kate asked.

Sam frowned. "More'n ten years."

"Why did Swann do it?"

"That's the wrong question. You're asking that question, it means you still don't get it. There aren't any explanations. Swann does what he likes."

"There must be some reason. An argument between them or something."

"Reason? Sure. Maybe Laz looked at him wrong. Or sneezed, and Swann got to thinking about germs. All that matters is Swann took a dislike. That's how he always says it—*I took a dislike to the man.*"

"Did he get medical attention?"

"Wasn't much the docs could do. Nail's still in there. They can't take it out without doing more damage."

"Fucker," Lazarus murmured.

He shambled closer, his good eye squinting at Kate. It might have been a long time since he'd seen a woman up close. He reached out and let his dead fingers brush her arm. The fingernails were long and soiled, curving like talons.

She didn't flinch. As the sisters had so often reminded her, Jesus touched lepers and rubbed spittle in the eyes of the blind. She could let this sad wreck of a man pat her arm.

"What's your name?" she asked him. "Your *real* name?"

Lazarus said nothing.

Sam answered for him. "Bob Ellis."

"Hello, Bob," Kate said gently.

Lazarus—Bob Ellis—made a mewling sound.

"Still getting the migraines?" Sam asked. "The headaches?"

Lazarus inclined his head. "Hurts like fuck." His head drooped lower until his beard scraped the back of her hand like a steel wool pad.

"All the time, huh?"

"All the time," Lazarus murmured, drawing a deep inhalation of breath. Smelling her skin.

"Yeah, that's rough." Sam smiled at Kate. "I don't know if Swann meant to ice him or what, but I'm guessing when he saw how ol' Laz turned out, he figured it was better than a clean kill."

Kate felt moist pressure on her hand. The touch of his lips. She stood unmoving, trying not to inhale the stink of his sweat or to see the small bright things that crawled in his hair.

"There, there," she whispered. "It's all right, Bob. It's all right."

Sam chuckled. "No use lying to him, Sister Sunshine. He'll never be all right again. And I wouldn't get all weepy about old Bob. It's not like he was any kind of saint. He did plenty of bad shit in his day."

"How did you know he was here?"

"Word gets around. People come and see. Laz here is the dog-faced boy. Everyone wants a peek."

Lazarus continued bowing before her, his mouth on her hand.

"Nobody helps him?"

"He can look out for himself. Okay, show's over. Let's get going."

Gently, she freed her hand. Bob Ellis raised his head, and his mouth warped into a half smile.

"Mary," he whispered.

She glanced at Sam with a silent inquiry.

"Girl he used to go with," Sam explained. "Maybe he thinks you're her."

She looked at the ragged ruin before her and saw yearning, deep and hopeless.

"Mary," Bob Ellis said again. "Love you."

Something broke inside her. She forgot his smell, his sores, and she put her arms around him, rocked him.

"Hell," Sam said in disgust, walking away.

She pulled out some money, tried to press a few bills into his pocket, alms for the poor, but her hand shook and she dropped them on the ground. Kneeling, she started to gather them, but her vision blurred, eyes burning, and she gave up and stood. She rose to follow Sam.

Sam never looked back, but she did, once. She saw Lazarus on his knees, shoveling the bills into a small, precious pile with the heels of his useless hands.

"So that's who we're dealing with," Sam said as they recrossed the tracks. "That's who you want to *understand*."

Yes, Kate thought. She got it now. She saw what Swann was. What he could do.

And he had Chelsea.

17

THE church had fallen into disrepair years ago. Swann had no idea when it had finally been condemned. Since its closure, squatters had come and gone—you could find their leavings strewn among the apsidal chapels and the rectory. Some of them had taken dumps on the floor, like animals. The offal was still there, petrified into glistening coal-black lumps.

Nearly all the furnishings were gone—pews, altar, baptismal font, icons, and crucifixes. But no one had removed the stained glass windows. The lower windows were boarded up, but the higher ones were unobstructed. Saints frowned down, backlit by the rusty glow of streetlights.

Though the church was secured with a perimeter fence, the squatters had found their way in, and Swann had, too, discovering a loose section of fencing that was bent upward, allowing access to anyone willing to crawl. He had first wriggled inside a week ago to ascertain that the place would suit his needs.

Now he and Chelsea Brewer were alone in the church, with only the light of an electric lantern to commemorate the glow of the thousand paschal candles that had been lighted here.

Swann was still coming down from the high that had lifted him ever since he had pulled away from Panic Room in the Guardian Angel limo. He'd carried out the snatch without a single complication.

Euphoria was a dangerous state of mind. There was still much to do. Later, he could celebrate. Later, when it was over.

The girl lay near the chancel, sprawled on the floor, her head propped against the wall, eyes open but unblinking. She had made no sound since their arrival. Swann worried that he'd overdone it with the GHB. She might drift into a coma. But he was prepared. The same dealer who had supplied him with prefilled syringes of GHB had sold him a matching set of syringes containing Naloxone, a GHB antagonist. It might take some experimentation to determine the correct balance, but with luck, he could keep Chelsea in a hazy state, awake but compliant.

He approached Chelsea. She'd gotten dirty when he dragged her under the fence, but the disarray of her clothes and the streaks of dirt on her face made her somehow more appealing, more human than the perfect iconic image on billboards and magazine covers.

The poodle lay beside her, nosing the girl disconsolately. Cute little thing. Its cream-colored head was the exact size of a tennis ball, with a teddy bear face and black-button eyes and a serious, downturned mouth. Swann reached out to pet the dog and gain its trust. The poodle released a volley of yips and snarls.

Not so cute anymore. Irritated, Swann picked up the animal and carried it to a confessional box in a small transept to the left of what had been the main altar. He shut the dog inside the box. Its paws scratched at the door as he walked away.

The confessional box was built into the wall, which must be why it remained when all the other furnishings had been carted off. The wood was old and partly rotten, but still sturdy enough. The lattice that separated the sinner from the priest, the kneeler where the penitent crouched to confess his sins—all of it was still there, overlooked when the church was cleaned out.

He tied off Chelsea's forearm with a rubber tube, then screwed one of the Naloxone syringes into the injector. It held two milligrams of the drug in a saline solution. He uncapped the needle, squirted a few drops, and found a vein, blue like a bruise against the girl's pale skin.

She didn't wince or even blink when the long needle, slender as an eyelash, slid in. He depressed the plunger until the syringe was empty, unscrewed the spent syringe, and flicked it into the shadows. Then he waited. The stuff was supposed to reverse the effects of GHB, and to do it fast.

A minute passed. Abruptly, Chelsea shuddered all over with a hard shock, followed by a series of smaller tremors sweeping through her body and jerking her limbs. Her face twitched. Swann watched her eyes. They still didn't blink, but all of a sudden, they seemed to grow too large for her face, and they stared at him with unnerving intensity.

And then she was screaming.

The screams were torn out of her from some deep hollow of fear and despair. They rang through the church like the pealing of bells.

Shit. Must've misjudged the dose. She was way too lively now.

He seized her by the shoulders, his fingers grinding into the soft flesh under her blouse. She lashed out. He released his grip to ward off her clawing hands. Finally, he got both of her hands in his and squeezed them shut, then forced her arms down.

"Shut up," he said, not loudly, the words enunciated with great clarity. He couldn't have her screaming. Someone outside might hear.

He fixed his eyes on hers. Held her with his stare until her last scream had died in her mouth.

"Quiet now. Hush."

Her throat jerked with a swallow. Another wave of trembling flickered through her, and she was still.

Gently, he let go of her hands. She put them together, clasping them in her lap.

Her first question surprised him. In a raw, spent voice, she asked, "Where's Chanticleer?"

"Who?"

"My dog."

"I'll get him. Sit tight."

He walked to the confessional box and opened the door. The poodle darted out and ran to his mistress, who scooped him up and cradled him in her arms like a baby.

"I didn't hurt him," Swann said.

The girl didn't answer. She seemed to be slipping away again, back into the GHB stupor. She might require another dose of the antidote. He didn't think so, though. He figured it was shock, not the drug, that was deadening her reactions.

The trouble with shock was that if she went in too deep, she might not come out—at least not anytime soon. He needed her alert enough to say a few words over the phone. Sooner or later the nun would have to hear her voice.

He sat down on the floor, facing her, and smiled.

"Chanticleer, eh?" He mimicked her pronunciation: *shon*-ti-clear. "Seems like an awfully big name for such a little dog."

He tried again to pet the poodle, but withdrew his hand when the dog released a yip of warning. Chelsea said nothing.

"That's a French word, I bet. What's it mean?"

No answer.

"Come on, it must mean something."

Finally, she responded. "Rooster," she said dully.

"You named your dog after a rooster?"

"A rooster in a story."

"Tell me the story."

"I don't remember it."

He put on a pouting face. "You just don't want to share."

The first flash of emotion lit up her face. "Why should I share anything with *you*?"

"I'm not such a bad guy."

Already the flash was fading, as quickly as the afterimage of a lightning strike. Her voice dropped lower. "Then why'd you kill Grange?"

"Is that what you think? I didn't kill him."

"I saw you." A whisper now. "You pounded on him, grabbed him from behind—"

"I beat him up. But he's not dead. By now he's probably sitting up in bed in the ER, sipping apple juice."

She tilted her head. "You left him alive?"

"I knocked him out, that's all. Wouldn't have made sense to do anything else. A dead body brings in the police in a big way, and I don't need that." He had her attention now. "Look, I'll be straight with you. I'm not exactly a virgin when it comes to killing. But I don't do it unless it's necessary."

"When's it ever necessary?"

"There are times. Times when you have to kill in self-defense—or for self-respect. A man has to stand up for himself, or he's not a man."

"That's not how you're supposed to act. In the Wild West, maybe, but not in, you know, civilization."

"Civilization's overrated. Civilization makes you soft, weak. Easy prey. In the real world, it's kill or be killed. I didn't make the rules, sugarplum. I just live by them."

"That's really what you think?"

He nodded soberly. "People say the world's a vale of tears. But that's not it. That's saying it wrong. What the world is, what it *really* is…it's blood and craziness. It's an insanity so big that ordinary human craziness doesn't even make a dent in it, doesn't matter a damn. That's the truth, but most people won't face it. They dream up gods and spirits, all that crap, anything so they don't have to see the reality that's staring them right in the face."

"Not like you."

"No, not like me. I'm no fucking dreamer."

"So you kill people."

"Sometimes."

She lifted her head. "How long before you kill me?"

"I won't. You'll be just fine."

"Yeah, right."

He knew she was wearily accustomed to bullshit promises. She'd been used by the users and conned by the con artists until mistrust was second nature to her.

"Hey, kiddo, look at me. Go on, look." He waited until her eyes—green eyes, emerald green—found his face.

She didn't answer.

"I don't believe in cruelty for its own sake. And I won't be cruel to you. Fact is, I've already done you a favor tonight. A big one."

"What favor?"

"Never mind that now. You just have to trust me. You'll live through this. You'll be fine."

"You can't let me go. I've seen your face."

Swann shrugged. "I'm not making any secret about my identity. I've already told Kate Malick my name."

"Why?"

"Because an artist wants to sign his work."

She turned away. "You're lying," she said in a defeated voice. "You'll kill me. I know it."

"You've been doing your best to kill yourself for years, and all of a sudden, you're worried I'm going to do it? Kiddo, you need to figure out what your agenda is."

She made no response, appeared to be drifting off. He wanted to keep her focused.

"You're an actress. How about you do some acting?"

"What?"

"Play a part. Entertain me."

"I don't think so."

"Come on, you've got a captive audience here."

"You're not the one who's a captive."

"Act for me," he said in a crisper tone. "That's an order."

It seemed to dawn on her that he was serious and that she could not refuse. "I don't know any scenes to play."

"All the jobs you've had, all the auditions, and you don't remember any of your lines?"

"Auditions…I memorized a Shakespeare scene once."

"Let's hear it."

"I…I'm not sure I remember."

He cupped her chin. "Try."

She stood up, still cradling the dog. He stood also, to be sure she didn't make a run for it.

"I learned this a long time ago." She seemed self-conscious, almost shy. "It's from *Othello*."

The name meant nothing to Swann, but he nodded anyway.

She took a step back, head lowered, lit by a fall of light from the high stained glass windows. For a long moment she was silent. If she were being obstinate again, he would have to get rough with her.

He was relieved when she lifted her head and began to speak.

"My love doth so approve him that even his stubbornness, his checks, his frowns—prithee, unpin me—have grace and favor in them."

She was playing pantomime with an unseen secondary character. From the way she asked to be unpinned, Swann guessed it was a housemaid.

"Good faith, how foolish are our minds! Lay those sheets I bade you on the bed."

Definitely a maid.

"If I do die before thee, prithee, shroud me in one of those same sheets."

Swann had heard of Shakespeare, but had no exposure to the stuff. If this was what it was like, he hadn't missed much. The words were hard to follow, and the whole thing seemed stupid and fruity.

Now she was saying her mother once had a maid of her own, named Barbara, and this Barbara had been in love with some guy who'd jilted her.

"She had a song of willow; an old thing 'twas, but it expressed her fortune, and she died singing it…"

He wondered how long this would last. He should have had her recite something better.

Then, to his surprise, Chelsea Brewer began to sing.

Her voice was low and sad, crooning tenderly, while her hands went on stroking the poodle, and her gaze was far away.

The poor soul sat sighing by a sycamore tree,
Sing all a green willow;
Her hand on her bosom, her head on her knee,
Sing willow, willow, willow…

The high, sweet song held Swann fascinated.

The fresh streams ran by her, and murmured her moans;
Sing willow, willow, willow;

Her salt tears fell from her, and softened the stones;
Sing willow, willow, willow...

He listened and thought of a creek he'd visited as a boy, a muddy rill reflecting the bleak Missouri sky. He'd liked the aloneness of the place. He would sit and skip stones over the water and watch hawks circle the sun. Sometimes he sat all day, pondering the enigma of his future, imagining great things.

There had not been great things. He grew up on a hardscrabble farm and dropped out of school after ninth grade, having recognized his teachers as fools. Then he wandered, tall for his age, able to pass for eighteen. By twenty-one he had brawled and fucked his way across the continent. He worked construction and oil drilling, spent his wages buying women, got into fights with day laborers who mistook his scrawny build for weakness. He learned how to cap a well, lay a foundation, and kill a man. In an alley in San Antonio he drove a bottleneck into a campesino's throat. He left town in a hurry, afraid the police would be after him. He had to grow up a little more before he understood that some lives were cheaper than others, and a Mexican's life was cheapest of all. No one was looking for him.

His first taste of killing left him hungry for more. It became his livelihood. He was good at it, but rarely did he prosper. When he made money, he wasted it on whores and horse races and cards. Much of his life was spent on the run, sneaking furtively from one hidey-hole to another, always watching his back.

Over the years he learned many things. He knew how to beat a man to death and how to keep him alive long after he wanted to die. He knew how to take a woman from the front, from the rear, and upside down, and how to bring her equal parts of pleasure and pain. He knew Aussie beers were better than American, and German beers were better than both, and Corona tasted like piss.

Above all, he knew how to survive. In the end, he lost his money and his few friends, but he held on to his life and his pride. He told himself he had done as well as he could have hoped.

But hearing the song, remembering the creek, he wondered.

Sing all a green willow must be my garland.
Let nobody blame him; his scorn I approve...

The song trailed away. Swann listened to its fading echo play among the high rafters of the nave. Then there was silence.

"That was beautiful," he said quietly.

She gave him a strange look, then glanced away.

"You should sing all the time. You should do...I don't know... musicals."

"I'm not that good."

"You're better than you know. Best I've ever heard."

She didn't answer. Haloed in the rainbow-colored lights, she could have been a plaster saint, a marble angel.

"Sing me something else."

"I'm really not a singer."

"Sure you are."

"I don't *want* to sing for you!"

She stood facing him, defiance in her posture.

"All right." Swann clapped his hands. "Fine." He grabbed her by the arm, startling a gasp out of her. The dog, spooked by his closeness, jumped free and growled up at him from the floor.

Roughly, he escorted her to the confessional box. It would hold her. He had purchased a padlock and chain for the door. The walls were solid, and even the lattice was sturdy enough to resist attempts at sabotage.

"Inside."

She hesitated. "Why?"

There were all sorts of practical reasons. He had equipment to set up, preparations to make, and he couldn't watch her every minute. But he owed her no explanations. He owed her nothing if she wouldn't sing for him.

"Just get the fuck in," he said.

She obeyed. Before Swann shut the door, the poodle faithfully followed its mistress inside.

18

KATE was quiet during the drive back to Hollywood. She thought about Swann. About Chelsea. She tried not to be afraid.

As Sam pulled up to the curb, Kate turned to him. "I'm guessing you and Bob and Swann worked together. Am I right?"

"What makes you say that?"

"It's obvious you knew him. Come on, we don't have time for any bullshit."

"Yeah, okay. We were a team. The three of us—and a fourth guy, Giovanni."

"This was before or after Colorado Springs?"

"Before."

"How long did you work as a group?"

"Two years. We pulled off a bunch of jobs. Never got busted, either. Made our share of money. Almost as much as we could spend."

"If you were so successful, why'd you split up?"

"You *saw* Bob, right? What Swann did to him? Giovanni and me weren't sticking around after that."

"So you ran off to Colorado. And Swann found you there. Chelsea said you would kick her out of the trailer on nights when Swann showed up."

"I was trying to protect her. I didn't want him to get a look at her."

"She got a look. She was terrified of him. Still is. Now she's his prisoner. And it's your fault. You brought him into her life."

"It's not like I planned it that way."

"No, you never plan anything, do you? Bad things just happen. It's never your intention. Just bad luck."

"I don't need you preaching to me. Save it for those skid row rejects you hire."

"Those men have some excuse for messing up their lives. What's yours? On second thought, don't answer that. I know you have a million excuses."

She got out of the car, resisting the urge to slam the door. "I'm going over to see Victoria. I assume you'll be headed there, too."

"Right behind you. And, Kate, better prepare yourself. She won't take it well."

———

"Is this a joke?"

Victoria Brewer, in nightgown and robe, stood in her well-lit living room between the two Eames chairs, her body canted at an unnatural angle, her face lit up with a ghastly smile. It was the reflexive smile of a proper hostess and it had remained stuck to her face, masklike, while Kate told her the news.

Kate had anticipated many possible reactions, but not this one. She glanced at Sam, waiting in the doorway, and saw his cynical, knowing look.

"Excuse me?" Kate asked.

"It's not very amusing. I suppose this is your infantile way of paying us back for not listening to you before. And I suppose my fun-loving husband is playing along."

"Mrs. Brewer, this is no joke."

"Of course it is. Chelsea hasn't been kidnapped. That's insane."

"It's happened."

"How could it? Grange was there to protect her. That's his job."

"Grange was injured. He's at the hospital."

"Absurd." She looked past Kate and Sam, toward the driveway where their vehicles were parked. "Is Chelsea in your car? Is she out there waiting?"

"Mrs. Brewer—"

Without listening, Victoria stalked out the door, down the steps to the driveway, and began circling the Jaguar, rapping on the windows.

From the foyer, Kate watched her. "She can't possibly believe we're lying to her."

"You don't get it. This is how she deals."

"By *not* dealing?"

"Queen of denial. Didn't you figure that out by now?"

Now Victoria was examining Sam's SUV, stridently calling her daughter's name.

"I guess I did," she said. "But I didn't realize you saw it that way."

"I've been with her for twenty-two years, on and off."

"So when we had our meeting earlier—you knew she was in denial about Chelsea's personal life?"

"Sure."

"But you sided with her, not with me."

He shrugged. "She's the one who signs the checks."

Victoria stormed back in, face flushed. "All right, where is she?"

Kate remained silent, aware that Victoria already knew the truth. It was only a question of waiting until she admitted it to herself.

As Kate watched, Victoria's mouth slowly worked itself into a new smile. "You're not scaring me. This is some sort of insane prank and you're both in on it." She turned from one to the other, her eyes glittering, feral. "Both of you!"

"Vicki…" Sam said, and in the word there was an uncharacteristic tenderness—and a warning.

His tone of voice broke her. The smile stayed fixed on her face while tears abruptly tracked down her cheeks.

"You mean it's true? She's really…? He has her—this man from your past? He has my little girl?"

"I'm sorry," Kate said.

"Oh, God…"

She sagged and Sam caught her. She buried her face in his chest, her shoulders jerking.

"Bring her into the living room," Kate said.

Sam escorted her to the sofa and eased her onto the cushions. "It hurts," Victoria said in a childish whine. "It hurts."

"I know, honey." Sam patted her.

"We'll get her back, Mrs. Brewer."

"Get her back?" Victoria's head lifted. "You're the one who lost her. You let this happen. You were more worried about my daughter's sex life than about her safety."

Kate stood there and took it.

"I'll see you ruined for this." Her head twisted on the stalk of her neck, her eyes seeking Sam. "You were right about her. I never should have trusted her, never…"

"I understand how you feel," Kate began, testing each word to see if it could bear the weight of what she had to say, "but right now we all have to work together. The sooner we come to terms with the situation, the sooner we can bring your daughter home."

"You won't bring her home. You'll get her killed, if she hasn't been killed already." Victoria pushed herself off the sofa, fists clenching and unclenching. "I want you out of here. Out of my house."

"I can't do that, Mrs. Brewer."

"Get the hell out!"

"Swann is going to call me again to arrange the details. I'm part of this. I have to be."

"Where are the police?"

"They don't know anything about the abduction."

"Don't know? What do you mean they don't know?"

"Swann made it clear that if anyone outside the family is brought in, Chelsea's safety will be compromised."

"So he's calling the shots now?"

"Yes, I'm afraid he is."

"That's ridiculous."

"He said if we notify the police, the FBI, or the media, Chelsea would...suffer."

Victoria seized on the words. "The FBI. They're experts in this kind of thing. We have to call the FBI."

She reached for the phone. Kate put a hand on her arm. "Did you hear what I said, Mrs. Brewer?"

"If you think I'm going to let you take charge of this situation after what's already happened—"

"Kate's right," Sam said.

Victoria glanced at him, perplexed. "What?"

"If Swann says to keep law enforcement out of it," Sam said, "we'd better play it his way."

"Ridiculous. I'm calling."

Kate held fast to her arm. "Only if you want your daughter to die."

"You're the ones who're killing her. I'm the only one who gives a damn."

"Swann told me—" Kate began.

"I know what he told you. But they always say that, don't they? It's a bluff. It has to be a bluff."

"Swann doesn't bluff," Sam said.

Victoria ignored him. "He can't possibly know who we call. He's not watching our every move."

"He said he has eyes on the house," Kate told her.

"He's lying." Victoria's voice rose in a hysterical tremolo. "He's a criminal. Criminals lie."

Sam shook his head. "Swann doesn't lie about shit like this."

"Why? Does your friend have a conscience? Is he too honorable to lie?"

"Hell no. But he doesn't make threats he can't cash in. He's got us in his sights, for sure."

"That's nothing but a gut feeling."

"My gut's not usually too far wrong where Swann's concerned."

"Then…you want us to leave Chelsea's fate in *her* hands?" Victoria pointed an accusing finger at Kate.

"I don't see as how there's a whole lot of choice." Sam intoned the words like a judge pronouncing sentence.

Victoria glanced from one to the other. "I still think…the authorities…" Her voice trailed away.

"It's the wrong move, Mrs. Brewer," Kate said softly, "and Chelsea can't afford any wrong moves tonight."

There was silence, broken by the piping tune of her cell phone's ringtone.

It was two a.m., and Swann was calling.

19

KATE wished she'd had more time. Alan still wasn't here, which meant they couldn't try to trace the call. And she hadn't thought the conversation through, wasn't sure what to say.

But the phone was ringing, and she had to answer.

She flipped it open and checked the caller ID. The screen displayed an obviously artificial string of numbers: 000-012-3456.

The phone kept ringing.

"What's the matter with you?" Victoria demanded. "Answer it."

Sam touched her arm, showing a slow smile. "She knows what she's doing."

Kate made Swann wait another few seconds. A petty power play, but it was all she had. On the seventh ring she took the call. "Swann?"

"Call me Jack, Sister Kate. Go on. It won't kill you."

"Hello…Jack."

"Not so painful, was it? I imagine Sam's told you a lot about me."

"He's given me some background."

"Only good things, I hope." Swann's voice fluttered momentarily. Kate prayed this wouldn't be a dropped call.

"I need to hear from Chelsea," she said, "before this goes any further."

"She's fine. Like I told you before, I kidnapped her to save her."

"Explain that."

"There was a plot against her life. You should know about that by now, if you followed up on my tip."

"Yes, I know. But why'd you call my office anonymously? You could have told me directly."

"And you would have assumed I was wasting your time with a phony lead, making you chase your own tail."

"Well...probably. But I still don't understand what the hell's going on."

"I was hired to kill your client. Half the cash up front and half upon completion. I agreed to the deal. But I never intended to go through with it. I've done a lot of killing, but I'm not into killing young girls who've never done me any harm."

"Then why didn't you just say no?"

"Because my employer would have hired someone else. I'm not the only one who can handle this kind of job."

"You could have gone to the police."

He chuckled, a sour sound. "I'm not a going-to-the-police type of guy. And I couldn't have proved anything, anyway. I needed to expose the plot, and the only way to do it was to have my employer place his bet. In the meantime, I needed to get Chelsea out of danger in case he had a backup plan."

"Is that why he hired you—just to make money on a wager?"

"No, he has other reasons. Better reasons. The bet was just a fringe benefit. He doesn't even know I know about it."

"How did you find out?"

"A little bird told me. Have you identified the guy yet?"

"Working on it."

"Well, until he's out of action, I'm holding on to Chelsea—for her own protection. She'll be safer with me than anywhere else." The volume on his end fluctuated again, but she still hadn't lost the connection.

"Why don't you just tell me who this man is and where to find him?"

"Because I'd rather keep you busy tracking him down while Mrs. Brewer makes certain arrangements."

"What sort of arrangements?"

"Not to sound crass, but after all I've done for Chelsea, I'm hopeful that my services will be rewarded."

"So you do want a ransom."

"Not a ransom. A reward. For saving your client and returning her unharmed. I'm a Good Samaritan, just like in the Bible. But even Good Samaritans deserve to get paid."

"How much?"

"I'll send you the details via e-mail. All I need is your private e-mail address."

She gave him the address of a Gmail account she used for personal business.

"Good enough. You'll have the details a minute after I hang up. I'll call back in two hours to make final arrangements. That'll be at four a.m. Have the items ready by then. If you could pack them in a valise for easy transport, I'd appreciate it."

She noted his surreal civility. Sam had told her Swann was polite. "We'll do everything you ask. It's the least we can do, considering your services rendered."

"Nice of you to say so. I knew we'd get along, Sister Kate. I did some background research on you. I could tell you were someone who'd be sensible. Though I still can't factor in the whole God thing. You strike me as too intelligent to fall for that airy-fairy stuff."

"Maybe I'm not as smart as you think."

"Or maybe you really don't believe. Could that be it?"

"I'm afraid not."

He clucked his tongue. "There you go, lying to me again. You have an obvious tell. Your breathing slows down. I heard it just now, when you told me you believe in God."

"I'll have to watch that."

"So when did you lose your faith? Or did you never have any?"

"I'd rather not go into that."

"Fair enough. Though I'd like to hear the story someday. You interest me, and I…wait a minute." His voice changed, hardened. "What *is* this? *What the fuck is this?*"

She gripped the phone. "What's wrong, Jack?"

"You *bitch*. You lying *bitch*."

"What's the matter? What's happened? Talk to me."

"I told you, God damn it, *no police*."

"There aren't any—" But even as she said it, her peripheral vision registered a flicker beyond the living room windows. She turned in that direction and saw the pulsating glow of a squad car's light bar beating against the glass.

"Call the police, and Chelsea will suffer." His voice was ragged over the tattoo of his footsteps. He was in motion, the sound quality deteriorating. "You heard me say that. And you called them anyway. You disobeyed. After all I've done for her, you *disobeyed!*"

A crest of fear broke in her, fear of what he was about to do. "Listen to me, Jack. I didn't call them. I didn't do anything. I wouldn't be that stupid. It's some kind of mistake, but we can fix it. We can work it out—"

"Fuck you. Nothing to work out. We had a deal. You blew it."

She heard a rattling sound. A chain? A padlock?

"You fucked up and Chelsea pays the price!"

"Jack, for God's sake—"

"You wanted to hear from Chelsea? You can hear her now."

Sounds of a scuffle, then a scream.

"You hear her, Kate?"

Chelsea, screaming.

"*You hear her?*"

A sudden percussive roar, and the phone went silent.

"Jack!" Kate shouted, but no one was there. The call was over. And the last sound she'd heard had been a gunshot.

20

K A T E snapped the phone shut. Her hand was shaking.

"What happened?" Victoria stared at her. "What went wrong?"

"The police…he *is* watching the house. He saw the car pull up…"

"What about Chelsea?"

Kate drew a breath. "I don't know."

"Well, what did you hear? What happened?"

"I don't know!" She threw Victoria a furious glare. "Why the hell is there a police car in your driveway? We agreed not to call the police."

Victoria's hands fluttered. "I…I didn't."

"Someone called them. Who else could it be?"

"I didn't do it! I was never out of your sight!"

That was true, of course. Kate would have realized it, if she'd taken a moment to think. But she was rattled. She kept hearing the girl's scream and the gun's report.

She flung down her cell phone and headed for the door, Victoria at her side. Sam had disappeared, absenting himself with a convict's instinctive avoidance of the authorities.

The driveway sloped below street level to form a little clearing ringed by eucalyptus trees. Kate glanced around, uneasily aware that Swann or an accomplice was watching right now. Somehow there were eyes on her. It reminded her of the wildness of these hills, the coyotes and bobcats that still roamed here. Predators with lean, sinewy bodies and iridescent eyes.

In the driveway, two LAPD officers were getting out of their car. They seemed in no hurry. They approached, gun belts clanking, heavy with cuffs and PR-24 batons. The cherry lights on their squad car were still spinning. A dramatic ploy to intimidate the locals, probably. Kate saw none of the urgency of a genuine Code 2 call.

"May I help you?" She scanned their nameplates. Mertone and Berlinski.

"We're looking for Chelsea Brewer," Mertone said. He was the taller of the two, and the more forward.

"She's my daughter," Victoria began, but Kate cut her off.

"What is this about?"

Mertone looked her over. "Are you a family member, ma'am?"

"I'm Kate Malick. My firm provides the Brewers' personal security."

"Then I guess you know what went down at Panic Room tonight. We understand the Brewers' daughter was there. We're interviewing all the witnesses, and since she left the scene before she could be questioned, we're trying to track her down."

Kate made out the division number displayed on the trunk of the car. Number 6—Hollywood Division. The cops were out of their element.

"It seems like a lot of trouble to go to," she said, "just to get a witness statement."

"We try to be thorough." That was the other cop, Berlinski. The smirk on his face irritated her.

"Cut the crap. You don't run all over town, outside your division, just to take a statement when you've already got a hundred witnesses on record."

Mertone answered. "The other witnesses all ran out as soon as the fireworks started. Chelsea Brewer and her bodyguard didn't leave until two, three minutes later. And they took the front exit, when everyone else took the rear."

"So?"

"So it raises a few questions, is all."

Victoria bristled. "Are you implying Chelsea is a suspect?"

Mertone spread his hands. "We're not implying anything, Mrs. Brewer. We'd just like to talk to her. She wasn't at her home, and this residence is listed as an alternate address. Is she here?"

"Yes," Kate said. "But she's asleep. She's had a traumatic night and she needs to rest."

"This won't take long."

"I'm not waking her. You'll have to come back tomorrow."

"That's not your decision to make."

"Unless you have a warrant, it is."

Berlinski looked at Victoria, pointedly ignoring Kate. "Ma'am, may we see your daughter?"

Kate was afraid Victoria would blow it, but the woman had done too many interviews to have any trouble lying. "Miss Malick is right. Chelsea does need her rest. In daytime she'll be more than happy to speak with you."

"It won't be us," Mertone said with a hint of menace. "It'll be detectives next time."

"Fine," Victoria said implacably.

Mertone took a step back, but Berlinski stood pat. Beats of blue and red lit his face from the side. "How about the bodyguard? He need his beauty rest, too?"

"He's in the hospital. He received some facial lacerations. I don't want him disturbed, either."

"Detectives will be having a talk with him as well." Berlinski glowered at her. "And maybe with you."

"Always happy to help out law enforcement."

She and Victoria watched as the squad car pulled away, the roof lights still strobing. They didn't move until the car was out of sight. Then Victoria sagged, releasing a pent-up moan.

"They bought it," Kate said, wrapping an arm around her. "Let's get back inside. Swann is sending me an e-mail with the ransom demand."

Victoria looked at her through a tangle of hair. "You think he'll still send it? After hanging up on you?"

"He'll send it," Kate said, willing it to be so.

21

B U T for ten minutes, he didn't.

Kate turned on the desktop PC in the den, logged in to her Gmail account—and waited. A sick feeling grew in the pit of her belly, and she thought of Swann saying, *Chelsea pays the price.*

But it couldn't be over. Not this way. Not because of a stupid misunderstanding.

As she stared at the screen, a new message appeared in her inbox. The subject line read, *From Swann.*

Her fingers trembled as she moused over the screen and opened the e-mail. The message consisted of three words:

One more chance.

She had to assume Chelsea was alive. In Swann's next call she would insist on hearing the girl's voice. For now, she would go ahead as agreed. And she would try—*try*—to have faith.

As promised, there was an attachment. She opened it, revealing a bitmap file—a scanned document. She magnified it to fill the screen. It was an itemized list headed with the name Victoria Brewer and a policy number.

An insurance list. Kate scrolled through it.

Van Cleef and Arpels white gold necklace with baguette diamonds, $160,000.

Dentelle earrings, white gold and diamonds, $42,000.

A. Lange & Söhne Soiree wristwatch with mother of pearl and eighteen karat white gold, $47,000.

Bulgari sapphire necklace with emeralds and rubies, $78,000.

Cartier diamond pendant, $27,000.

Jeremy Hoye tanzanite ring, $19,000.

Cellini bangle with 18 karat rose diamonds...

Jewelry. At the bottom, the total value was recorded: $2,127,000.

Victoria leaned over her shoulder, studying the screen. "How could he get this?" she whispered.

"Do you recognize this list?"

"Yes, of course. It's on file with my insurance agent, Gregory Niles."

"You'll need to have a talk with him." Kate pressed *print*, then swiveled in the desk chair to face Victoria. "Where do you keep this stuff? In the house?"

"Some of the items are here. But most of them are in my safety deposit box in Beverly Hills."

"We'll have to get them to open up the bank for us."

"But why would he want jewels? Why not cash? Don't they always want cash?"

"It's hard to come up with a lot of cash on short notice, even for someone in your tax bracket. And there's always a risk the bills will be marked, or the serial numbers recorded."

The document printed out, a clean sheet of paper whirring through the inkjet's rollers.

"You're saying it's easier to dispose of jewelry?"

"With the right connections, it can be. Swann can recut the stones, melt down the metals—fence them or even unload some to legitimate dealers. You do still own all these pieces, don't you?"

"The list is up to date."

"Then let's get started." Kate pulled the printout from the tray. "Get hold of the bank manager and have him open the vault."

"I still don't understand how Swann got the list. How could he even know who handles my insurance?"

"So far, there's not a lot he doesn't know."

———

Alan arrived ten minutes after the e-mail came through. He had the Asterisk box, but when he looked at the caller ID information, he said the equipment would do no good. "It was a voice-over-Internet call. That one-two-three numeric string is an identifier for Internet telephony."

"So he's calling from a computer? Is that why I heard drop-offs in volume?"

"Yeah, probably. Data sent over the net is broken up into packets, and some packets get dropped along the way."

"Why would he use a computer to place the call if he has a cell phone with an untraceable card?"

"I don't know, but I'm guessing he's a little paranoid about cell phones. The signal can be intercepted if you have the right gear. A lot of people don't like giving out sensitive information over a cell. Does he seem like a control freak to you?"

"Definitely."

"That's probably it, then. He feels more comfortable using VoIP. Probably, he's hiding behind a firewall and has other security precautions in place. He thinks his message is less likely to be picked up by eavesdroppers, and it's impossible to trace."

"Is he right—about tracing it?"

"As far as I know, there's no way to backtrack an Internet call. Maybe a super-expert could come up with a plan, if you have one of those available."

"As a matter of fact, I do."

She called Di Milo at the Westwood house. He put Skip Slater on the phone.

"There could be a way to trace it," he said thoughtfully. "Here's the thing. The caller ID display only tells us the call was made with VoIP technology. It doesn't tell us which service was used. But there are only a few major providers. So let's say I start with Skype, the biggest name in the business, and assume Swann used that one. Okay? Now these services provide confidentiality but not anonymity. That's something most users don't understand. There's a log of the calls and IP addresses on the company servers. Technically, we can't get that info without a court order. But…well, you remember how I traced the bet."

"You hacked into the server."

"Right. Went through a back door. Maybe I can do it again, with the VoIP provider. Find the call on their log, get the IP addy, run a traceroute—"

"Sounds good. Get to work."

"You understand it's a long shot? He may not have used one of the top providers. Even if he did, I may not be able to gain access—"

"Never know till you try, will you?"

"Right. I'll let Vincent bring you up to speed on the situation here."

"You find out something?" she asked Di Milo when he came back on.

Di Milo wasn't a big talker. He had a way of speaking in sentence fragments to convey maximum information with minimal verbiage. "Checked the cameras. Hooked to a DVR but disabled. Disk erased. No video. Slater checked the PC. Videos on the hard drive. Not current. Surveillance of previous visitors. Sexual encounters. Slater found billing records on the PC. Call girls."

He stopped, as if the data he provided were self-explanatory. Kate took a moment to draw the necessary inference. "It's some kind of corporate lodging, is that right? They let out-of-town guests stay there. Clients. And supply them with party girls—video them surreptitiously for potential blackmail."

"Right."

"Do we know what corporation we're dealing with?"

"House is owned by a shell corporation in the Caymans. Slater couldn't trace it further. But I found brochures, booklets. Corporate propaganda. All for one company. Pulsarix."

The name was familiar, but she couldn't place it. "What's that?"

"Manufacturer of private jets. Headquartered in Burbank."

"Do the brochures list the executives?"

"Sure." She heard a riffling of pages. "The CEO is Daniel Farris. The CFO—"

"Wait. You said Farris?"

"Daniel Farris, yeah."

Kate closed her eyes. She thought of the man with the gun, leading her down the cellar stairs. His voice in her ear: *A man can do things he never dreamed of when his family is involved...*

"Kate? Does that mean something?"

"It means everything," she said.

22

IT was all about family. In the end, family was all that mattered. Family was all there was.

Daniel Farris sat in his parked Mercedes across the street from the church where Swann was holding Chelsea Brewer. He lifted his handgun, feeling its weight and solidity. In the Westwood house he'd fired three shots, but there were still eleven rounds in the magazine, more than enough for the job he was about to do.

He should have used the gun on Kate Malick, of course. Should have killed her immediately. He'd recognized her on the surveillance monitors long before she'd entered the room. But he'd been worried about the noise.

And not only the noise. He could admit it to himself.

He had been afraid when he'd put the gun to Malick's head. He had been afraid when he'd led her down the cellar stairs. He had been afraid of how it would feel to pull the trigger and shatter her skull into fragments.

He had never killed anyone. He had ordered it done, this one time, but never had he done it himself, not up close and personal, by his own hand. He knew he was capable of it—he was capable of anything in circumstances like these—but still he was afraid.

And his fear had given her an opportunity, and now she was alive and he was fucked.

But really, it didn't matter. Malick had probably told the truth about having had help finding the house. Which meant other people knew about it, and killing her would have bought him only a little time.

Besides, Malick wasn't the one who was supposed to die tonight.

He felt it coming on again, the urge to scream, but he forced it down. Blind rage would solve nothing. Only action would make a difference, and action was what he knew best. He had built Pulsarix into a major global player. He'd pummeled the competition, knocking them down and never letting them up again. His philosophy was simple. Hurt your enemy. Show no mercy. Always bring a gun to a knife fight.

Swann had betrayed him, but there was still a way to make things right.

After fleeing the house, cutting through backyards and alleys, he'd returned to Westwood Village, where he'd left his car in a public parking lot. He'd been afraid to park at the house and draw attention to his coming and going. And he couldn't park on the street—if he got a ticket, it would tie him to the neighborhood and spoil his alibi. He was supposed to be at the Biltmore in Santa Barbara, where he had checked in that morning, asking not to be disturbed. After check-in he'd retraced his route down the coast and taken up temporary residence at the corporate lodging.

He shouldn't have placed the bet from that computer. But he'd thought he was safe. He'd been certain the computer couldn't be tied to the house. He still didn't know how Malick had accomplished it.

In the trunk of his car he kept a laptop with a satellite modem. He used it to access the latest headlines. The story leading the local news was a fiasco in Panic Room, a near-riot sparked by apparent gunshots that turned out to be firecrackers. Movie star Chelsea Brewer was among the patrons but left the club without injury...

Without injury.

So Malick was right. Swann had double-crossed him. The bastard broke their agreement and betrayed him to Malick, though how he even could have known about the bet in the first place, Farris couldn't say. And because of that betrayal, Farris was finished.

Oh, he could fly out of the country on one of his corporate jets, lose himself in Europe, where he had contacts and reserves of cash. Run for a while, maybe a long while. Not forever, though. He would be caught eventually, extradited...

Except none of that would happen, because he wasn't flying anywhere. He wasn't going to run. He'd staked his life on this operation and failed, and now he would pay the price. He still had his gun, and he would use it on himself.

But first he would find Swann. And the girl.

Luckily, there were ways of getting it done. Backup plans, contingencies. Farris never took anything for granted, especially when dealing with a man he didn't know.

Although his firm employed people he could trust for minor black bag operations like wiretapping and extortion, none was suitable for a murder-for-hire assignment, especially when the target was someone as high profile as Chelsea Brewer. For that kind of job he had to go outside the loop. He'd gotten nowhere until, serendipitously, a mutual friend had introduced him to Jack Swann.

Swann was the ideal choice, an obvious sociopath with the core competencies Farris was seeking. A man who had lived off the grid for years, who could execute the mission and disappear like smoke.

Even so, Farris didn't entirely trust him. He didn't entirely trust anybody. That was why, before his second meeting with Swann, he tasked one of his most discreet security pros with observing from a distance and tailing Swann when he left. His operative reported that Swann drove a vintage Lincoln Town Car and was staying at a cheap Hollywood motel. When Swann was out, Farris picked the lock on the motel room door and spent some time with Swann's laptop computer. There was no useful information on the hard drive, but there was a built-in webcam Swann didn't use. Farris modified the camera so it would be on whenever the computer was running, with the telltale LED disabled. He installed a program that would send the audiovisual signal to a website, using any available Wi-Fi connection.

Tonight he had been watching that website ever since he'd learned Chelsea was still alive. The site was dark at first, but shortly before two a.m. it came alive. Swann was using his computer at last. The camera picked up scattered glimpses of his activity in a dark location. At two o'clock he sat before the computer, wearing a wireless headset, and made an Internet phone call. Farris heard Swann's end of the conversation. He was talking to Kate Malick, making plans for Chelsea's safe return, boasting of how he'd outwitted his employer and foiled his plans.

The call ended in confusion. Swann, agitated about something, left the computer, though he was still talking over the headset. Distantly, from another room, there came a scream and a gunshot, then childish sobbing.

Chelsea's sobs. Farris had no doubt of that. She really was with him, then.

He might have shot her, but if so, he hadn't killed her. He couldn't kill her until he received his payment. After that, who could say? He might dispose of her, or he might let her go. *Might let her go.*

It was the one outcome Farris couldn't permit.

When the website went dark again, he reviewed the video file of the transmission, automatically saved to his hard drive. He ran through it slowly, looking for any clue to Swann's whereabouts.

He found one when Swann, adjusting the laptop, briefly tilted it up. The camera caught a few frames of something high, colorful, and bright. Image enhancement revealed a stained glass window, illuminated from outside by a streetlight. The design was clear and distinctive.

A person with the right skills could find anything online. Farris found a site devoted to the churches of Los Angeles, with an image gallery of stained glass windows. He scrolled through the images until he found a match. According to the caption, the window was part of a church dating to 1925, which was condemned after sustaining structural damage in the 2008 Chino Hills quake. An address was helpfully provided.

And now he was here.

It was too late to save himself, but he didn't care about that, as long as he could find the justice he'd been denied. Justice for his daughter. Peace for his wife. Vengeance for himself.

Family was everything. A man who didn't defend his family and avenge his precious dead was no man at all.

He raised his head to look at himself in the rearview mirror. His reflection met his eyes in silent agreement, a handshake with his doppelgänger.

He would die tonight. But Chelsea Brewer would die first.

23

T H E Farris house in Beverly Hills was dark. Kate rang the doorbell for a long time before the door eased ajar. Past a security chain, a round-faced woman in a bathrobe peered out.

"Yes?" she said suspiciously, the word rendered *chays* by a heavy Latin American accent.

"I need to speak to Daniel Farris."

"He is not home." The woman frowned. "Is very late."

"I'm aware of the time. This is an emergency—life and death. I need to know if there's any way to get hold of Mr. Farris."

"I no can call him. Is late."

"How about Mrs. Farris? Is she here?"

"She asleep."

"Let me in. I need to talk to her."

"No." The woman braced herself against the door as if fearful Kate would break it down. "Is late. You go away."

"I need to speak to your employer now."

From somewhere in the house, another woman's voice. "What is it, Angelina?"

Kate answered first. "I'm here on urgent business involving Daniel Farris. I need to speak to him or his wife."

The second woman appeared behind the housekeeper. "I'm Louise Farris. But I'm not in the habit of admitting strangers after two a.m."

"I wouldn't be here if it weren't important."

Mrs. Farris studied her. "You're Kate Malick."

"That's right."

"I've seen you interviewed. You..."

Kate knew what she was thinking. "I work for Chelsea Brewer, among others."

Mrs. Farris stood unmoving for a moment, then stepped back. "Let her in, Angelina."

Kate entered the foyer. "Thank you."

Mrs. Farris made no move to invite her any farther into the house. "You said this matter involves my husband?"

"Yes."

"He's not here. He's not in town."

"I saw him in Westwood less than two hours ago."

"No, that's not possible. He's gone to Santa Barbara. He's there overnight."

"That may be what he told you, but it's not true."

Mrs. Farris blinked several times, slowly and deliberately, as if delivering a coded message. "Why would he lie?"

By the sudden fall of her voice Kate knew she already suspected the answer. "I need to speak with him. You don't know where to reach him?"

"If he's not at his hotel..."

"How about a cell phone?"

"Well, yes, he has one, of course."

"May I have the number?"

Mrs. Farris recited it. Kate noticed she didn't insist on knowing what this was all about. It seemed she didn't want to know.

Kate tried the number. The call bounced to voicemail. "He's not answering."

"It's the middle of the night. He's...he's probably asleep."

"He's not asleep. Mrs. Farris, have you ever met a man named Jack Swann?"

"No."

"This man?" She showed Swann's photo on her cell phone.

"I've never seen him. Is he...connected to my husband?"

"Yes."

"And all this has something to do with Chelsea Brewer."

It was not a question, but Kate answered anyway. "Yes."

Mrs. Farris looked away. Kate studied her face. She had been beautiful once—the bone structure was still there, the sharp cheekbones and firm jaw—but she looked beaten down, hollowed out. Her eyes were lusterless, her face creased with perpetual grief. She had the look of a woman who'd wept so long that nothing mattered anymore.

She was what Victoria Brewer would be in a year—if Chelsea didn't survive.

"He's gone and done something crazy, hasn't he?" Louise Farris said.

"Yes."

"I would help you if I could. But I don't know anything. You'll have to believe me." She said it as if she didn't care if anyone believed her or not.

"I believe you."

"Is Chelsea all right?"

"I don't know."

Mrs. Farris nodded, unsurprised by the answer, and too incurious to pursue it further.

Kate turned to go.

"Wait."

She looked back and saw the first glimmer of life in Mrs. Farris's eyes.

"You used to be a nun."

"Years ago."

"Pray with me."

It was the last thing Kate expected. "I...I don't have much time."

"It won't take long. Pray with me, please. Pray for my daughter's soul."

"Of course."

Mrs. Farris led her down the hall. "Angelina, you come too. We'll all pray together."

At the end of the hall was a niche occupied, in better days, by a potted tree or an art object. Now it was a shrine to Mila Farris. Snapshots of the girl were arranged on the wall in a tidy collage, over a small table laden with personal items that must have been hers—a wristwatch, a necklace, a stuffed polar bear.

Mila Farris had been a straight-A college student until last summer, when she had become part of Chelsea Brewer's entourage. She began staying out late, partying with a fake ID, stealing money from her dad's wallet. Her parents worried, but not enough. By the time they realized their daughter was out of control, it was too late. They woke up to find Mila comatose in her bathroom, sprawled on the lime-green tiles, haloed in a puddle of vomit. Serology tests showed high levels of Ecstasy in her bloodstream. The diagnosis was multi-organ failure brought on by an overdose of MDMA ingested sometime in the previous twelve to sixteen hours. Though there was no proof Chelsea had been with her when she took the drug, Mila's parents blamed Chelsea for the overdose. Mila was kept alive for five days on life support, machines breathing for her, until her family consented to pull the plug.

Remarkably, the story never made the news. The Farris family didn't want their daughter's memory despoiled. Victoria and Sam Brewer kept the secret from everyone—even from Kate herself.

But privately, people talked. One of them was Carson Banning, who'd become friendly with Daniel Farris after buying a Pulsarix jet. Banning, in turn, told Kate.

Banning was her source, the source she'd refused to give up to Victoria, because she owed Banning his privacy and owed Victoria nothing.

And now, it seemed, Mila's father had hired Jack Swann to make Chelsea Brewer pay for his daughter's death.

"This is where I pray for her," Mrs. Farris said, and without ceremony, she got down on her knees on the hardwood floor. Angelina dutifully did the same. Kate followed their example.

"I pray she's with Jesus and the angels." Mrs. Farris steepled her hands, eyes shut. "And with her grandparents. All together in heaven."

Mrs. Farris and Angelina bowed their heads. Mrs. Farris's lips moved soundlessly.

Kate did not pray for Mila. She prayed for Chelsea. And for Amber Banning. Prayed that both of them would be recovered unharmed.

She prayed, though she knew there was no God to hear.

24

S H E was driving out of Beverly Hills when her phone rang.

"Hello, Kate."

Him again. The familiar, electronically distorted voice.

She was in no mood. "Aren't you getting tired of this routine?"

"Tired? Things are just getting interesting. You have no idea how close you've already come to being dead."

"Look, I have a lot on my plate right now—"

"Then you shouldn't be wasting your time talking to bums."

He'd seen her with Lazarus. Followed her.

"What would you know about that?" she asked slowly.

"I know everything you've been up to tonight. How you talked with the cop and that other guy outside Panic Room. Your little escapade in Westwood. Then you hooked up with Sam Brewer. What's that all about?"

He'd been on her tail half the night, and she hadn't noticed. Too distracted by events.

"If you want to meet me so badly," she said, "just give me a time and a place."

"I don't want to meet you. I want to kill you. I almost took the shot when you were over by the river. Nice, desolate area. But you weren't alone. And there was that damned dog."

She remembered the barking Doberman. Her sense of being followed. Sam had called her paranoid. "Well, you shouldn't have told me that. Now I'll be on my guard."

"A security pro should always be on guard, Kate. But it won't matter. I've got you in my sights. You're going down tonight."

"Care to tell me what you've got against me?"

"Maybe I don't like nuns."

He clicked off.

Two calls in one night. And he was tailing her and making explicit threats. The situation was escalating. She didn't think he was bluffing.

Well, James had never been the type to bluff.

A stoplight snagged her on Wilshire. She sat there, engine idling, thinking of her ex. She was sure—almost sure—it was him. She hadn't seen him in years, not since their last angry confrontation in LA after he tracked her down. She'd hoped he'd forgotten about her, moved on with his life. But he wasn't the type to forget.

After the calls started coming in, she asked Alan to track down James. It proved impossible. He had dropped off the radar screen. Simply vanished. Last known location—Seattle. That was four years ago, when he was the employee of an import-export firm that was going out of business. Since then, no credit history, no arrests, no tax returns, nothing.

She didn't know with certainty that her stalker was James, but it made sense. He'd always carried a grudge, hated her for abandoning and humiliating him. When he lost his job, he must have started fixating on his ex-wife, security consultant to the stars. The idea that she was flourishing while he failed would have been intolerable. Success had always been important to him. He loved money, loved control. Now he had neither.

And so he'd come after her, disguising his voice electronically so she wouldn't recognize him. And the threats of violence—they fit him, too. He could be physical, even brutal. That was why she'd left him in the first place. She'd never known him to be a gun enthusiast, but a lot could change in twenty years.

As the light cycled to green, her phone rang again. She answered with a snarl. "What now, you son of a bitch?"

"Whoa, chief. What'd I ever do to you?"

"Sorry, Alan. I thought you were our mystery man."

"He harassing you again?"

"Don't worry about it. What's up?"

"I'm afraid there's a problem. Mrs. Brewer got hold of the bank manager at home, but he can't access the safety deposit box with the jewels."

"Why the hell not?"

"The bank vault has a time lock. It can't be opened until seven a.m. There's no override."

"Seven's too late. Let me talk to Mrs. Brewer." Victoria came on the line. "Mrs. Brewer, did you buy most of these items locally?"

"Yes."

"At one particular store?"

"Most of them are from Étagère. It's on Rodeo Drive."

"Call the owner and say you need the store opened now. Get duplicates or near duplicates of everything on the list. Sign an IOU or something, or sign over the deed to your house—whatever it takes to get the merchandise."

"I don't know how to reach the owner." Her voice was plaintive. "What's his name?"

"It's a woman. Rachel Eisenbud."

"Alan can look her up. She's probably unlisted, but he'll get her number. Then you talk to her and make her cooperate. All right?"

"Yes, all right. Thank you. You're…you're keeping a cool head."

Kate didn't feel cool. "Put Alan back on." She told him what they'd worked out. "Get it done."

"Right. Oh, one other thing. I don't know if I should bother you with this right now, but we just got a tip on Amber."

Coming so soon after her prayer, the news felt like a small miracle. "Who from?"

"Volunteer named Georgia at Teen Alliance, a drop-in center at Santa Monica and Las Palmas."

"I know the place."

"It can probably wait."

"No, I'll be headed in that direction on my way back anyway. I'll check it out. It should only take a minute. And we need some good news tonight."

25

S H E ought to be scared. But she didn't feel anything anymore.

Chelsea sat in the padlocked confessional with Chanticleer in her lap. Though she wasn't Catholic, the room seemed oddly familiar. Probably because she'd seen it in the movies—the little bench you were supposed to kneel on, where she was seated now, and the metal grille and the priest in the next compartment listening as you ran through your sins.

Like God cared. Like God gave a shit if you blew some guy or shoplifted a video or took His name in vain. If God cared so fucking much about her, then why was she locked in this room waiting to die?

Kate Malick had talked about God. About prayer. But praying wouldn't stop Swann from doing whatever he wanted. Swann was real, and what he would do to her was real, and all the rest was wishful thinking.

Swann had promised she wouldn't get hurt, but she'd met plenty of liars and he was just one more. Except he wasn't some studio asshole blowing smoke; he was a psycho, mean and malicious, and a stone killer.

Mr. Darkness. The shadow man who haunted her funkiest dreams and now was back, in the flesh, to make her dead.

Whatever he did, she wouldn't fight him. There was no point. If she tried to fight, he would only laugh at her. And if he laughed, she would absolutely lose it. Just absolutely go fucking insane.

She sat rigid, waiting. It was almost like watching herself in a movie. She was on screen and in the audience—in two places at once—part of the story but safely removed from it. Surreal. Maybe dying would be like that. Maybe she would see the bullet enter her heart, watch herself slump to the floor. Dead and not dead. Maybe.

Disconnected memories played in her mind. Swann in the bathroom, emerging from the stall. Chanticleer barking. Grange turning, but not fast enough. The shock of blood as Swann drove Grange's head into the cinder block wall…

The empty club. Swann leading her through the flickering downspots. Then outside, past the bouncer, someone who could help if only she could talk or scream, but her throat wouldn't work. She was drifting in a dream and nothing was real…

Into a car, then another car, then dragged under a gap below a fence and hauled into a church. Everything so bright all around her, and yet blurry, bleary, like the world was melting, melting in the rain, acid rain, was she on acid, tripping, bad trip, nothing made sense, she must be asleep, asleep and dreaming…

Then a needle in her arm, a hard shock of alertness, and Swann was leaning over her and it was real. *It was real.*

She shook her head, didn't want to relive it. Didn't want to think about it or about anything. Wanted to turn off her brain, but her thoughts kept coming with a will of their own.

Her head hurt. She never got headaches or hangovers, but tonight she had something. Probably whatever Swann had drugged her with was still causing side effects. But the headache wouldn't kill her. Swann would.

She stroked Chanticleer's belly and breathed in, out, in, out. It was all she could do, just pet the dog and breathe. And soon she wouldn't be breathing anymore.

But she didn't care. Like Swann said, she'd been trying to off herself for years. She was ready to die.

"So come on," she whispered, "just kill me, get it over with, shoot me, blow my fucking brains out."

It would be a goddamned relief, a blessing. Sure it would.

Except that wasn't true. It was only another lie, like everything else in her stupid, pointless life. Her friends were lies; they only wanted to hang out with her to share her spotlight. Her mom was a lie, faking love when all she cared about was the next paycheck and her 25 percent cut. Her career was a lie—pretending to be other people on screen, wearing a mask, living a fantasy.

All bullshit. Nothing real about any of it. Every minute of her life had been a fucking joke. Now it was over and all she could say was that it had been a big, dumb waste of time.

Even so, she didn't want to die. She'd never realized that fact until just now, when it was too late to matter.

She shut her eyes and for some reason began to sing the willow song. The sound of her own voice was comforting in the darkness, like the reassuring touch of a friend. As long as she could breathe and sing, she wasn't dead. She held onto that thought. She wasn't dead.

Footsteps.

She heard their slow approach and broke off the song.

Swann was coming back.

She shuddered. Silent now, forgetting even to pet the dog, she waited.

The footsteps stopped outside the confessional, and she heard the creak of the door to the other compartment. Light filtered into the priest's cell. Through the grille, she saw a man's face.

Not Swann.

"Mr. Farris," she said, her voice hushed. "What are you doing here?"

Daniel Farris stared at her through the grille, an unsmiling confessor. He raised his hand, and in it gleamed a gun.

"I'm an old-fashioned guy when it comes to my family, Chelsea. I believe in an eye for an eye…and a life for life."

26

TEEN Alliance smelled of Lysol. Inspirational posters checkered the cinder block walls. Fluorescent tubes buzzed overhead, behind plastic casings spotted with insect carapaces. It was the kind of place Kate's father would have disapproved of. *You can't help people who won't help themselves,* he would have said. Yet her mother would sneak dollar bills into the poor box when he wasn't looking. Or had he only pretended not to look?

Kate looked over the few people who occupied the place, mostly kids lounging in plastic chairs, watching a wall-mounted TV. Some of them glanced her way, sizing her up.

They were just like the kids she'd ministered to. The same unlined faces and wary, hooded eyes. The boys, sullen, leaning forward with bunched fists, sending every signal of challenge. The girls, brazen in their tight, unbuttoned shirts, marketing bodies that were bruised, scabby, and wasting away.

They wanted so badly to be men and women of the world, but they were children. Lost children. Some would make it and some wouldn't. Survival of the fittest, according to the hard logic of the modern mind.

Only one volunteer was on duty. Georgia was a heavyset woman whose milky Southern drawl fit her name. Her desk was littered with pamphlets and chits for soup kitchens. A corkboard displayed handwritten letters, expressions of gratitude from parents and kids. Success stories. There weren't many.

"She was in here earlier tonight," Georgia said. "But it wasn't till later that I saw the flyer. I was shuffling through papers and came across it."

"You're sure it was her?"

"I heard her friends call her Skeeter."

"Her street name," Kate said.

"Yes. Like on the flyer."

"Did she look okay?"

"Tired." She rendered the word as one long syllable, honey-smooth. "But they all look tired, don't they? Otherwise, I'd say she's in good shape. Holding up better than a lot of them do."

"Did she say anything?"

"She asked about meal vouchers for herself and her friends, that's all."

"Any idea where she hangs out?"

"You know the Western Avenue overpass above the 101 Freeway? She and her friends crash there sometimes, I'm told."

"I'll check it out. Listen, if I don't find her, and she comes back here…"

Kate took out a business card embossed with the words *Guardian Angel, Inc.*, a halo askew over the capital A. She wrote a number on the back. "Here's my personal cell phone number. You can call me anytime, night or day."

"Don't you ever sleep?"

"I had a good night's sleep once. Back in 1985, I think."

Georgia took the card. Her hands were older than her face, age-spotted hands with blue protruding veins and bitten finger-nails. "You're taking quite an interest in this girl."

"I'm a friend of the family."

"And they wish to remain nameless? Is that why there's no last name on the flyer?" Georgia didn't expect an answer. She smiled, a kind smile marred by a dead tooth turning brown. "Whoever she is, I have a feeling you'll find her. Things have a way of working out."

"I hope so." Kate thought of Mila Farris. "Not every story has a happy ending."

"You just need a little faith."

Kate managed a smile.

She headed to the overpass, thinking of Amber Banning.

By now the girl must know how badly she'd screwed up, but she hadn't phoned home, and Kate knew why. It wasn't stubborn-ness. It was the deep, crushing certainty that an irreparable mis-take had been made.

Kate understood that feeling. She knew what it was like to fall down a steep precipice, to fall so far you were sure you could never climb back up.

She parked the Jag on Western. Before leaving her car, she rummaged in the glove compartment and found a spare flashlight to replace the one she'd lost in Westwood.

She stepped to the edge of the grassy hillside that declined steeply to the freeway below. In this part of LA the surface streets, belying their name, were elevated above the freeways. She stood, looking around at the dark street. If her secret admirer was still fol-lowing her, this was a place he might choose for an ambush. It was no less deserted than the industrial area near the river. She'd been with Sam then. Now she was alone.

Easing the Glock out of its pocket holster, she placed her finger over the trigger guard. A concrete wall ran along the verge of the incline, but she easily hoisted herself over. She made her way down the hill, her flashlight beam picking out soda cans and beer bottles that threatened her footing.

This side of the overpass was supported by a colonnade of round pillars. Between the pillars and the hillside was a triangular gap, an artificial cave large enough to serve as shelter. That was where Amber and her friends would be camping, if they were here.

She saw no flashlights, no candles or trashcan fires. But that didn't mean the place was empty. She approached with caution. At the threshold of the cave, she paused, beaming her flash inside. There was more litter, the leavings of a group of people. The stuff had been here for a long time, the residue of many nights spent under the roadway, barely protected from the elements, subsisting off the urban wild like the coyotes in the hills. But at least coyotes had some quiet. Here there was always the thrum of traffic overhead and the louder rush of vehicles on the freeway directly alongside the embankment. Even now, at nearly three a.m., headlights flashed past in an inconstant stream, flickering through gaps in the pillars, their glare brighter than her flashlight but less steady. A ceaseless strobing sidelight, reminding her of the pulsing lights in Stiletto.

She ignored the flicker and focused her attention on the cave as she stepped inside. Makeshift accommodations had been added. A ripped-up, badly stained mattress, probably rescued from a curbside refuse pile, lay draped in ragged blankets. Bottles and cigarette butts and spent matches and a few needles. The pillars and reachable parts of the roof were embellished with tangled skeins of taggers' marks and obscene doodles and spray-painted obscenities. From her days as a novice she remembered the omnipresence of graffiti in the world of the street people; it was everywhere, a constant backdrop, dirtying every gas station restroom and motel stairwell, every fence and alley wall, even the tree trunks and boulders in public parks. It was inescapable, like the beat of rap and hip-hop.

The thought of Banning's daughter in that environment doused her caution. "Amber?" she called out, the cry bouncing among the pillars before vanishing in the traffic noise. "Amber, are you here?"

No answer. No one was here. Her flashlight had swept the area, finding only garbage and a few sad comforts—a sleeping bag, a hardcover book with waterlogged pages and a broken spine, a cracked CD featuring the British pop singer Adele.

Did Amber like Adele? Kate didn't know. She'd never met the girl. Banning, keeping their affair on the down low, hadn't let Kate into his home. But maybe that was just as well. If—when—Kate did catch up with the girl, she might be able to approach without scaring her off.

She turned to go, her flashlight lowered again to check out her footing. The beam passed over something shiny in the dirt. Kate stooped and picked it up. A charm bracelet.

Banning had said his daughter always wore a charm bracelet. Had been wearing it the night she disappeared.

Something rattled in the dark, the noise echoing. A plastic bottle, perhaps. It could have been disturbed by a scurrying rodent or by the wind.

Or by a footstep.

She slipped her finger inside the Glock's trigger guard and turned slowly in the direction of the sound. It had come from the far end of the tunnel. If someone had followed her here, he might have descended the hill on the other side of the overpass, paralleling her movements while staying out of sight. She stood unmoving, tense in the shadows. Traffic sounds surrounded her, the hum of tires overhead, the whoosh of vehicles on the freeway at the bottom of the hill. The flicker of headlights passing between the columns made the tunnel a stroboscopic dance floor.

He could be there, yards away, concealed in darkness, drawing a bead on her.

Another faint, echoing clatter. Something metal. Closer than the noise she'd heard before.

He was coming.

She crouched low and moved to the nearest column, taking cover. She debated her options. Run for it, and he could gun her down. Once on the hillside, she would be exposed. She couldn't make it to the top before he took her out.

Stay put? If she did, he could work his way back up the hill and descend on the nearer side, taking her from behind. Or he could simply wait her out. She couldn't hide all night. And he was patient. He'd already proven that.

Right now the advantages were with him. He must have a good idea of where she was, while he could be anywhere. If she could trick him into revealing his position, she might have a chance.

"James?" she called, hoping the sound of his own name would startle a reaction out of him.

Her shout came back at her in an eddy of echoes. There was no other reply.

"James, I know it's you!"

More echoes. And something else. Muffled and indistinct.

Laughter.

He was laughing at her. Laughing in the dark.

She tried to pinpoint the sound. No use. It was too soft, and the maddening acoustics distributed it everywhere, an ambient noise blending with the traffic thrum.

"Show yourself, you son of a bitch!"

The laughter stopped. Now there was only the road noise and the dimming echoes of her own cry.

He was going to make his move. She felt sure of it. If he hadn't known where she was, he did now. And if she tried to move to new cover, she risked exposure.

Her best bet might be to retreat out of the tunnel, crawling through the dirt. Get outside and take up a position near the entrance, and she could nail him when he followed.

If she made it that far.

She began easing down onto her belly, and then the tunnel lit up in a shaft of white light, fanning through the gap in the pillars. A searchlight from a patrol car easing to a stop in the right lane of the freeway, cherry lights flashing to warn off traffic.

Saved.

She pocketed the gun and emerged from hiding, then tramped the rest of the way down the hill, holding her hands well away from her body so as not to make a threatening silhouette. She prayed the cops weren't Mertone and Berlinski from the Brewers' house.

They weren't. She'd never seen this pair. The cop on the passenger side looked at her through the open window. "Hello, ma'am. Got a reason to be here?" He wore rimless glasses that caught reflections of the passing glare.

"Looking for a runaway. Was tipped off that she and her friends might be camping here. But they're gone."

The cop nodded, his gaze fixed on the bulge in her pocket. "You carrying?"

"I have a permit. I'm a security professional."

The driver leaned forward in the seat. "I know you. Malick, right? Guardian Angel?"

"That's me."

"You came by the station when Joey Puck got picked up on a D 'n' D."

"You'll have to narrow it down," Kate said, and they all smiled. Puck was a client, a stand-up comic with a wild hair for booze, drugs, and fistfights. He'd been detained many times, but somehow charges were never pressed. The rules really were different for celebrities—at least in this town.

The cop riding shotgun let his gaze slide past her, up the hillside, where the beam of light continued to probe.

"There a problem?" Kate asked him.

"Thought we saw someone moving around in there. Not you. Someone else."

"Somebody was in there. I heard him."

The cop shrugged. "A vagrant."

She didn't argue the point. If she told them she was being stalked, she would be tied up in questioning. Besides, nothing had happened, really. Already, she doubted whether the man in the dark had been James or just some drunken derelict.

"It's not good to go nosing around in places like this in the dark," he added. "Some real nutcases wandering around."

"That's why I need to find this girl."

"Well, if she was here, you just missed her. We came by about an hour ago and a whole bunch of kids took off running."

"Why? Are they in trouble?"

"Nah, they always run. They know if we bust 'em for loitering, we'll run 'em through missing persons, and they'll be sent home."

"Why'd you roust them?"

"Sometimes they set fires to stay warm. Dry as it's been lately, fire is a hazard. We've been told to keep the grassy areas clear."

The driver studied her. "Why would Guardian Angel be looking for a runaway?" he asked.

"It's just personal. Favor for a friend."

"Well, if you have a picture of the kid you're looking for…"

Kate unfolded a flyer from her pocket and handed it over. "Her name's Amber."

"We'll keep an eye out," the driver promised.

"Thanks. One more favor. Could you keep that light on me till I get back up the hill? Just in case that man is still hanging around."

"You got it."

She ascended the slope, the beam spotlighting her all the way to the top. When she reached her Jag, the light winked out, and the radio car eased back onto the freeway. Kate slipped behind the wheel, the charm bracelet in her hand.

An hour, she was thinking. *Just one hour sooner, and Amber would have been found.*

27

"Y O U mean," Chelsea Brewer said, "*you're* working with Swann?"

Farris pushed the gun's muzzle through the grille, centering it on her chest. "To be accurate, he was working *for* me. But he didn't carry out his instructions. So I'm here to get the job done." He liked the sound of those words and repeated them. "To get the job done."

It was easier to think of it that way, as simply a job to be carried out. No different from firing an unsatisfactory employee. A different kind of termination, that's all.

"Because of Mila," Chelsea said, grasping it at last.

"Of course, because of Mila. Nobody fucks with me and mine."

He waited for her to whine and plead and say it wasn't her fault. He would enjoy putting a bullet in her while she said that.

Instead, she simply lifted the poodle off her lap and set it down gently on the floor, taking it out of the line of fire. The dog never stirred. Farris looked closer and saw a gleam of wetness in the fur.

"Is that dog…?"

She nodded. "Dead." She said it without emotion, but her eyes lowered, the lids fluttering. "Swann shot him."

"Why?"

"I don't know. He opened the door and grabbed Chanti and…" Her shoulders lifted, fell. "Then he locked me in again. He's still around. He'll kill me, if you don't."

"Killing you is my job. I'm exchanging your life for Mila's. You took her away from me, took *everything* away, destroyed my family, and I hate you for it."

Now was the time for her to make excuses, but she only said, "I know."

This wasn't the answer he wanted. "And you didn't even come to her funeral." Distantly, he was surprised to be explaining himself.

"My mother made me stay away. She didn't want me linked to it."

"Because it would hurt your career."

"Yes, I guess that's right." She sounded sorry, ashamed.

He felt a touch of sympathy and brushed it aside. "You know what I did after she was buried? I came home and checked the blogs that follow celebrities around town. You were out dancing. I followed your progress all night. You went from club to club."

"That's true, I guess."

"You never gave a damn about Mila."

"You're right. I didn't think about her."

"I guess you're proud of that," he said, though there had been no pride in her voice.

"I'm not proud. I just…put it out of my mind. Like I couldn't deal with it. I didn't want to know."

"Were you with her when she took Ecstasy that night?"

"No."

"You're lying." He wanted her to be lying. It would be easier for him if she'd been with Mila, if she'd supplied the drug herself.

"I wasn't with her. But if I had been, it wouldn't have made any difference. I would've taken it, too."

"Then maybe you'd be dead."

"Maybe I would."

"You should be dead. You deserve to be."

"Probably."

"Give me one reason why I shouldn't pull the trigger." Still hoping to make her beg or bargain.

"I can't. Except...I don't think Mila would want you to."

"It's not about what she would want. It's about what I want. About what you did. You have to pay. You *have* to."

"Then do it."

No challenge. If she had shown even a hint of defiance, he would have fired. But there was only resignation and blank despair.

He had come this far. Just one last step to take. He could do this thing. Of course he could.

It was only—he'd never noticed before—she looked like Mila. Something in the tilt of her head, the set of her mouth. How could he shoot her if she looked like Mila? How could he kill his own daughter?

Crazy thought. His daughter was dead, and this girl, this lying brat, had killed her. It should be easy to hate her. He'd hated her for months.

If only she would flinch or cry. If only she wouldn't sit there primly, as if posing for a picture, her head tilted in that familiar way...

The decision was reached by his body before his mind had processed it. He saw his hand lower the gun. Saw his finger flick the safety on. Only when the gun was pointed uselessly at the floor did he allow himself to know that it was over, and conscience or cowardice had won.

"You goddamned bitch," he whispered. "I wish…I wish…"

He stumbled out of the confessional. He looked up at the high stained glass windows, the colorful saints blurring in his tears.

He turned away from the windows, and Swann was there, watching him from yards away, a half smile on his face.

"Not so easy, is it?" Swann said.

Then all his hate found its object, and Farris raised the gun, released the safety, and fired twice at Swann, missing both times, and a purple cloud erupted in the darkness, a muzzle flare from the gun in Swann's hand, and suddenly, he was weak, confused, and when he looked at his shirt, he saw something black and tacky like tar.

He went down on one knee. He tried to lift his gun again, but his arm wouldn't operate. Then Swann was beside him, plucking the gun away and pushing him onto his back to stare down in triumph.

"You killed me," Farris said, amazed.

Swann's smile bloomed white and cruel. "Not yet."

28

KATE called Carson Banning's home number as she drove. It was a number she'd never dialed before, but she kept it stored in her phone just in case.

Four rings, five, and Banning's voice came over her earpiece. "Yes?"

He sounded groggy, a man dragged out of sleep.

"Carson, I'm sorry to wake you, but I'd like to stop by."

"Stop by?"

"Something's come up."

"Is it Amber?"

She caught the flash of panic in his voice. "Nothing's happened. It's not bad news. It's just…I found something that might belong to her, and I need you to look at it."

"Oh. Okay. You know where I live?"

"Yes. Ten minutes."

She arrived at the house in Bel Air at three a.m. Though she had never been there, she knew the address. She didn't even need to call Alan and have him look it up.

The house was gated, the upstairs dark, the ground floor glimmering with a few lights in the front windows. She was about to buzz the intercom when the gate retracted with a whir of gears.

He'd been watching for her. She wondered if he was nervous about having her there. Going to his home, after all, was a violation of their arrangement's unspoken rules.

She had been seeing Banning on the down low for the past six weeks. She'd met him at a private gun range, where he had been learning to shoot an Uzi for an upcoming action picture that later fell through when the studio opted for a younger, up-and-coming star. The issue of protecting him had never come up. She tried not to mix business with her personal life.

Banning's career might be headed in the wrong direction, but his face remained one of the most recognizable in America. And that made him a prime target of the paps. Their obsessive stalking had broken up his last two romances. He'd vowed to keep this relationship secret. It meant impromptu liaisons in slightly sordid places like the Century City garage. That was okay with Kate. There was something appealing about a clandestine affair.

He was standing on the front steps when she got out of her car. He wore a blue terry cloth robe and slippers. This was the first time she'd ever seen him in something other than a sport jacket.

She reached him and felt suddenly unsure how they should greet each other, with a kiss or a hug or nothing at all. He solved the problem by pulling her toward him and giving her a light kiss on her cheek. "Come on in."

He led her into his living room, more spacious than the Brewers' and more tastefully decorated. No framed magazine covers on the walls, no ostentatious tributes to success. Instead, there were model ships with elaborate rigging, a photo of a World

War II rifle company posing indifferently—the caption read *101st Airborne*—and another photo, autographed, of Mickey Mantle and Ted Williams. She hadn't known he was a baseball fan. There was so much she didn't know.

"I got a tip to her possible whereabouts," Kate said. "When I got there, the place was deserted. But I found this." She showed him the charm bracelet.

Banning's eyes gave her the answer. They were suddenly too wide and too clear, his gaze fixed on the bracelet.

"Oh," he said, and nothing more, but there was a lifetime of heartbreak in that single syllable.

He reached for the bracelet, the gesture disarmingly tentative, as if he were afraid it would evanesce into thin air at the first contact. She handed it over and he let it lie lightly on his palm, turning his wrist slightly from side to side, watching the metal charms catch the light.

"This is a good thing, Carson. It means we're close."

"Or it could mean…"

"What?"

His voice was husky, hollow. "It could mean she's dead."

"Why would you say that?"

"Because she always wears this. Never takes it off. So why isn't she wearing it now?"

She explained about the cops, how they'd rousted the runaways from their hiding place. "The kids all ran. She probably lost it in the scramble."

He raised his eyes to her face. There was a different light in them now, a cold gleam of purpose. "Where?" he asked simply.

"I don't think I should tell you that."

"I'm not going to go looking. I just need to know where it was. Where she was."

"Hollywood. Beneath an overpass. That's all I'm going to say."

"How the hell did you trace her there?"

"She was spotted earlier tonight at a place called Teen Alliance. A volunteer there set me on her trail."

"An overpass." He shut his eyes. "Living under a goddamned bridge."

"With other kids. There's safety in numbers." This, she knew, was not always true. A gang of runaways could turn on each other or single out one member for abuse. There was a practice called hunching—the boys encircled a lone female and forced her to submit to each of them in turn.

She wondered how much Banning knew about life on the streets. In his gated enclave, sheltered from the rawness of the city, he could have no clear idea of what life for a runaway was like. Amber hadn't known, either. Probably, she'd imagined something glamorous and free, and now she was scrounging for meals, cadging change, shoplifting, and squatting, a hunted thing.

The girl wouldn't survive for long on her own. She was too innocent and ill-equipped. The city would consume her. Only in promotional brochures was Los Angeles the City of Angels. To those who knew it, really knew it, it was not a city, but a vast, open grave swallowing up young lives.

Banning stared past her, out the window into the dark. "I can't stand knowing she's out there and I'm not doing anything."

"There's nothing you can do."

"If this were a movie, I'd track her down myself."

"If you tried, you'd just scare her off. She'd run farther."

"Run from me," he whispered. Moisture glimmered in his eyes. "My little girl."

Kate touched his arm. "We'll get her back, Carson."

"You keep saying that, but there's no way to know."

She remembered Georgia's words and tried them here. "You just have to have faith."

He managed a smile. "Easy for you to say."

She wished it were.

"Lady Madonna" piped in the room, the cheerful tune inappropriate, laughter at a funeral. Kate turned away and took the call, hearing Skip Slater's voice.

"Okay, I did it."

It took her a moment to realize he'd traced Swann's call. "You located him?"

"I located where he was when he called you. Can't say if he's still there now. He was using Skype. I got into their system and checked their logs. IP address belongs to a coffee shop in Koreatown. According to their website, they're open all night and they're a Wi-Fi hotspot."

Kate kept her voice low so Banning wouldn't hear. "He couldn't have called from a public place."

"He was probably piggybacking off the signal from nearby. Someplace close, say within a three-hundred-foot radius."

"Give me the coffee shop's address."

Skip recited it. "You shouldn't go there alone."

"This can't wait. And I'm not far." From Bel Air to Koreatown was a short trip at this hour, with no traffic on the streets. "But you'd better send Di Milo to back me up. And hey, Skip—good job. Really good."

"Starting to warm up to me, aren't you?"

"Not as much as you think." She clicked off and turned back to Banning. He was watching her with open curiosity.

"Something big going on?" he asked. "Sounded serious, from your tone of voice."

"It is."

"You'll handle it. You always do."

She hoped he was right about that.

29

KATE reached the Buzz Café at Seventh and Berendo ten minutes later, after a fast ride during which she violated all speed limits and blew through several red lights. The café had a small parking lot off the side, mostly empty at this hour. She parked and went in, carrying the Glock in its pocket holster.

It was a small, homey place with dim lighting and a pervasive odor of cigarette smoke. The windows were open and a fan was blowing, but the smoky aroma hung in the air, a permanent feature. A pockmarked kid with a laptop sat in a corner with his knees braced against the table, and a woman who looked lost sat at the window sipping green tea and staring into the night. Everyone in the place was Korean.

She approached a waitress, showed her the cell phone photo. "Have you seen this man?"

The waitress shook her head. "No English."

Kate tried the man behind the counter, who was removing stale pastries from a display case.

"I not see him," the man said in answer to her question.

She hadn't really expected Swann to come in here. Before leaving, she asked the counterman, "Has anything unusual happened in the neighborhood tonight?"

It was a stab in the dark, but the man took the inquiry seriously. He put down his pastries and scratched his chin. "Noises. Bangs."

"Like gunshots?"

"Could be. Or car backfire."

"When?"

"Half hour, maybe."

"Where?"

"Couldn't tell. The bangs were, um, muzzled."

"Muffled?"

He nodded. "Could be alley. Or down street. Or inside building. Maybe church."

Kate had noticed the condemned church next door, fenced off, dark. A place for Swann to hide, perhaps.

"You didn't call the police?" she asked.

He shrugged. "Just bangs."

Gunfire in this neighborhood probably wasn't out of the ordinary. Locals preferred to mind their own business.

She thanked him. As she moved away, she noticed the waitress eyeing her with hostility. Because she was white? Because she drove a Jag? Because she asked too many questions?

All of the above, Kate decided.

"Someone just left."

The words came from the woman at the window. She wasn't looking at Kate, might have been talking to herself, but Kate stopped anyway. "Excuse me?"

"From behind the church. A car came out right before you got here." Her English was better than the counterman's.

"Did you see the driver?"

"A man with no hair."

"This man?" Showing the phone again.

"Could be," the woman said after a brief but studious look.

"Do you know what kind of car it was?"

"Lincoln Town Car. Big and old. From the eighties." The woman showed a shy smile. "I worked in a dealership. I know cars."

"Color?"

"Dark."

"Which way was it headed?"

"That way."

East on Seventh. Kate ran to the Jag.

Normally there would be no hope of catching up, but at this time of night traffic was minimal, and if the Lincoln stayed on Seventh and got caught by a few lights...

She might have a chance.

30

NOTHING could be this bad. There had never been anything like this anywhere, ever in the universe. She'd thought she knew terror, knew craziness, but everything she knew was crap. She'd never been afraid in her life before now. Whatever she'd thought of as fear was something different, something trivial. This, right here, right now, *this* was fear, and it was nothing she'd ever felt before.

Chelsea tasted the sour tang of vomit in her mouth and choked it down. If she threw up in Swann's car, he would probably kill her. Not that he wouldn't kill her anyway. Killing was what he did.

You could ask Mr. Farris about that. Except you couldn't because he was dead, and not from the gunshot. Oh, the gunshot might have killed him eventually, but Swann didn't let him die that way. Swann wanted to inflict more pain. And he was good at it. She listened from the confessional, unable to see what was happening, and not wanting to see, but hearing the long, drawn-out groans from Mr. Farris as Swann asked him the same question over and over. *How'd you find me?* It took Mr. Farris a long time to answer him. Chelsea didn't think he was being stubborn or heroic. He just couldn't force out the words past the pain. If anything, Swann was making it harder for him to speak. But then maybe Swann didn't know what mattered to him more—to make Mr. Farris talk or to make him hurt.

There were other sounds. Wet, crackling noises like when a tree branch snapped in a rainstorm, the same kind of awful splintery sound. She knew it was Mr. Farris's bones breaking. Many bones, each one broken slowly, with an artist's exquisite touch. Finally, he told Swann the answer. Something about having a man follow him and, later, breaking into Swann's room to tamper with his computer.

Swann must have been satisfied with the answer. He said only, "Then it was my fault. I shouldn't have let your man tail me. Mea fucking culpa."

After that, he let Mr. Farris die.

Then there was silence, and somehow the silence was worse than the sounds had been. From another part of the church she heard Swann talking in low, urgent tones. Talking to himself, probably. Why not? He was a fucking psychopath.

And suddenly, he was back, pulling her out of the confessional, dragging her past the twisted body on the floor. She noticed he didn't take the computer, just left it behind. Probably, he didn't trust it anymore because of what Mr. Farris had said.

He'd forced her out of the church and into his car—a big old Lincoln, a relic from before she was born—and now they were going somewhere else, a new hiding place where the nightmare could go on.

But it couldn't go on. She couldn't take any more of it. She kept hearing those groans and those snapping bones and Mr. Farris's hoarse, whispery voice when he got the words out at last. The voice of a dead man. A corpse's voice.

And the thought came to her very simply and clearly: *That's how he'll do me.*

With that thought, her fear seemed to recede into an insignificant corner of her mind, and she was suddenly calm. Her head cleared, her heart slowed, and she knew without doubt that she could not stay in this car, could not let him take her to another prison.

Swann was pushing the Lincoln in a straight shot down a long urban corridor lined with strip malls and sickly, graffiti-scarred palm trees. There was almost nobody on the road and Swann was moving fast, his fists clutching the wheel, the knuckles squeezed white. His head was thrust forward in profile, his jaw set hard, a muscle in his cheek twitching. He hadn't spoken a word to her. He seemed barely aware that she was even there.

She wasn't belted to her seat and her door wasn't locked. She could pull the handle and throw it open and fling herself out onto the street rushing past. It might kill her, but it might not. If she hit the asphalt just right, rolled just right, she might survive. It was a chance, anyway. By the time he realized what she'd done, she could be running down an alley, hiding in shadows, free.

There were fewer strip malls with every passing block, and more boxy, windowless buildings. Warehouses or something. An industrial area, deserted, lifeless. She'd never been here, had never seen this part of LA, had scarcely known that places like this existed. For her, LA was the clubs and the backlots and Melrose and Malibu, not scuzzy brick buildings with signs reading Bronson Machine Parts and Central Produce Suppliers.

No traffic, and no one on foot, no one anywhere. She and Swann were alone in the world and there was no help for her. But she could help herself.

She slid her right hand toward the car door. How fast were they going? At least forty-five. Too fast. But he had to slow down sometime. And when he did—

"Shit," Swann muttered.

She glanced at him. His gaze was fixed on the rearview mirror.

Looking behind her, she saw a car moving up fast.

Swann reached for his gun, and why would he do that unless the other car meant trouble?

Someone chasing them. A rescuer.

He was turning in his seat, poised to lean out the open window on the driver's side and take a shot at his pursuer. He had murdered Mr. Farris and now he would murder her last hope and then he would murder her.

Chelsea threw herself across the front seat and spun the steering wheel hard to the right.

———

Kate caught up with the Lincoln as it crossed Hoover, heading into Pico-Union. Swann had stayed on Seventh, and his car was distinctive enough to stand out on the lonely streets.

She came up on her quarry too fast, tried at the last moment to slow down before he spotted her…

Too late. He'd seen her. She knew he had.

She was trying to decide on her next move when she saw a flicker of movement in the Lincoln's front compartment, a struggle, and the car went sideways, hopping the curb.

Chelsea was fighting him, fighting for control of the car.

Kate didn't think about what she did next. It was instinct.

She punched the gas and closed the gap with the Lincoln, and just as her quarry skidded back onto the street, she rammed it hard, sinking the Jag's front end into the bigger car's side panel, throwing up pinwheels of sparks.

Through the Lincoln's window, she glimpsed Swann, his face a knot of rage.

He shoved Chelsea away and plowed the wheel hard to the left, trying to use the Lincoln's greater mass to force her back.

Kate bore down harder, the Jag nosing deeper into the Lincoln's side, crunching metal like a shark crunching bone. Her car was smaller, but she had momentum and the engine's power on her side, and she forced the Lincoln up onto the curb again and then the Lincoln was on the sidewalk, bumping raggedly as she forced it to slow down.

Swann manhandled the wheel to his right, ripping free of the Jag.

A mistake.

The Lincoln was abruptly angled away from the street, hurtling toward a wall of brick that reared up out of the dark.

It was the windowless facade of a warehouse, and Swann hit it head-on at thirty miles an hour.

Kate spun away to the right and slammed to a stop before the same building.

She turned in her seat and saw the Town Car wrecked against the wall, the long, rectangular hood crumpled like a sheet of paper, the windshield deformed, crumbs of safety glass everywhere, the horn sounding long and monotonous and then cutting off.

The car was still. Too still. No movement inside.

Chelsea…

Kate threw open the door of the Jag and staggered out, just as the Lincoln's passenger door flew wide.

Chelsea stumbled into view, dazed, unaware of her surroundings, until she saw Kate. Her face lit up, amazement and gratitude and relief all competing for expression, and suddenly, she was running to Kate, reaching her, wrapping her in a deep hug while her slight body shook with hiccupping sobs.

"You…" she said in a choked voice. "You…you…"

You came for me. That was what she wanted to say. Kate heard the unspoken words and held her tight.

"It's all right now," she whispered. "It's all right."

But it wasn't.

The Lincoln opened up on the driver's side, and there was Swann, looming huge, his face bloodied, his arm rising.

Kate knew that movement, knew he had a gun in his hand and was about to fire.

She tore herself free of Chelsea and shoved the girl into the parking lot next to the building and screamed, "Run!"

Chelsea glanced back and saw Swann, and she let out another sob, a strangled sound.

The gun boomed in Swann's hand, but Kate was already running with Chelsea, the two of them sprinting side by side past empty parking spaces.

She drew her Glock as she ran. There was no cover anywhere. If the lot was fenced in, she would have to turn and fight.

She didn't want a shootout. She wanted to find a safe place to hide, a place where Swann couldn't find them.

When she looked back, she saw him enter the lot, but he was moving slowly, injured, limping. He couldn't catch them. They had a chance at a clean escape if the lot offered a way out.

It did. An opening ahead led them into a wide alley that paralleled Seventh. They plunged down the alley, running east, past dump bins and piles of industrial trash, and emerged on the sidewalk of a smaller side street, a mix of commercial and residential structures.

"Is he…?" Chelsea gasped.

"He's still behind us." Kate knew it without looking. Swann had been slowed by his injuries, but he hadn't been stopped.

She scanned the street. A few doors down was a long-faded apartment complex sagging under a sign that read Palm Shores. There were neither palms nor shores in evidence, but there was a light in one of the ground-floor windows and a small, curious face peeping out.

"Come on." Kate ran to the door and battered at it. "Let us in, please let us in!"

She threw quick glances over her shoulder, knowing Swann would emerge from the alley at any moment, and then they would be caught in the open. She would have to gun him down, if she could. If she could hit him before he got her...

The door opened, an old, tiny, dark-complected man gaping at them, and Kate rushed out a thank-you and pushed Chelsea inside, following, slamming the door, locking it, praying Swann hadn't seen them.

She found the lamp by the window and turned it off, and the three of them waited in the dark, Chelsea slumping against Kate, Kate hugging the wall, and the old man silent, understanding that it was dangerous to speak, to risk being heard.

There was a grandfather clock in the room, and it ticked loudly, each tick like a hard, solid clunk, counting time.

Ten seconds. Thirty.

"I lied to you," Chelsea whispered suddenly.

"About what?"

"About not caring if I live or die."

"I think you were lying to yourself," Kate said gently.

"And you knew it."

"I've told myself the same lie. You and I—we have a lot to talk about."

"Okay." A small voice, childish and obedient.

"First we'll get you to a hospital, call your folks, then—"

A slam against the door and a scream of rage. Swann's scream.

Chelsea screamed too, as if in sympathy, and Kate hustled her away, yelling to the old man to hide himself, but the man didn't move. Kate left him, pulling Chelsea into the bedroom.

Make a stand here? No, she wanted Chelsea out of the line of fire. Through the open window, then.

She punched out the screen and hoisted Chelsea over the sill and followed.

They were in another alley, a narrow space between this building and the one next door. From the apartment, they heard the crash of the door and the report of a gun.

The old man, their Good Samaritan—she'd gotten him killed.

Now there was nothing to do but get Chelsea into the clear, then stand and fight.

"Go that way," Kate ordered, pointing her toward the side street they'd been on before. "Go and flag down a car, do it!"

The girl clung to her, afraid of abandonment, tears still bright on her face.

Ruthlessly, Kate shoved her away. "*Go!*"

Chelsea broke into a run, heading for the street.

Kate retreated into the shadows of the alley, aiming the Glock at the window, ready to fire when Swann showed his head.

She would have one chance. One glimpse of his face, before he knew she was there. She would have to squeeze the trigger fast, take him out with the first shot. Don't think about it, just do it. As soon as he showed his face.

But he didn't.

She counted off thirty long seconds under her breath. Nothing.

She risked emerging from hiding. Approached the window, alert for an ambush.

He could be drawing her near for an easy shot. She could picture it—the gun snaking out of the window, the muzzle in her face, the crash of a report at point-blank range.

Jesus be with me, she thought in reflexive supplication, and she went up to the window and looked in.

The room was empty.

Swann wasn't there. No one was there.

It didn't make sense—until Chelsea screamed.

31

CHELSEA ran out of the alley into the street and looked around helplessly. Flag down a car, Kate had told her, but there were no cars. The neighborhood was deserted, though a few lights in residential windows had flicked on, the occupants awakened by the noise.

She was trying to decide what to do when headlights appeared in the darkness. A Hyundai hatchback had turned onto the street.

Salvation.

She stepped boldly into the middle of the avenue and waved her arms. The Hyundai pulled closer, pinning her in its headlights, and for a moment, she thought the driver might run her down rather than stop.

Then the car eased to a halt and a man leaned out the window on the driver's side. Chelsea ran to him.

"Please...I need your help."

He was a middle-aged guy with a squashed nose and sleepy eyes that widened in sudden recognition.

"Holy shit," he said. "You're *her*, aren't you?"

Though it was incredibly dumb, she couldn't help feeling pleased to be recognized.

"I'm in real trouble," she said. "Can you give me a lift? Me and my friend?"

"Sure." The man looked flabbergasted and stunned, and she knew he would be dining out on this story forever. The night he rescued Chelsea Brewer…

She turned toward the alley, hoping to draw Kate's attention, and then she screamed.

Swann hadn't taken the alley. He'd left the apartment through the front door, and he was crossing the street in an ungainly lope, one leg stiff and halting, and the gun was up and Chelsea jumped away from the car as Swann fired and fired and fired…

He must have hit her, couldn't have missed, but she wasn't bleeding, wasn't wounded. She didn't understand until she looked at the driver, the guy who'd recognized her, and saw him shaking in his seat, a bloody mass, his face half gone and red bubbles boiling out of his open mouth.

Then Swann was beside her, throwing her to her knees on the pavement, kicking her so she stayed down, and he hauled the half-conscious man out of the car and threw him to the ground. He yanked her to her feet and slapped her and slapped her again and the gun was in her face and she was screaming.

———

Kate ran out of the alley and took it all in at once—the stopped car, the fallen driver, Swann manhandling Chelsea in the middle of the street. He had his gun out and he was crazed, and Kate was sure, just sure, he was about to shoot and kill.

She was exposed, no cover, and no time to find any. She couldn't fire on Swann without hitting the girl. But she could draw his attention.

"Swann!"

Her shout echoed through the desolate block.

He spun to face her, the gun raised, Chelsea still blocking her shot. The look on his face—pure rage.

She ducked back into the alley as his gun cracked. Chips of brick scattered near her face. She dared another look into the street, expecting a new assault, but Swann was already packing Chelsea into the car and jamming himself behind the wheel.

He didn't want a shootout. He wanted to take his prize and flee.

And she couldn't stop him. Chelsea, in the passenger seat, was still in the way.

Helplessly, Kate watched as the car tore forward, skirting the unconscious man in the street. Kate caught a last glimpse of Chelsea, her face pressed to the window, eyes big with shock.

Then the girl was swallowed by shadows and night.

Gone.

32

SWANN took the corner so fast Chelsea thought the car might tip over, and he came up on Seventh and cut east, passing the wrecked Lincoln and the abandoned Jaguar and speeding on.

Blocks away from the scene of the crash, he swerved to the curb and slammed the car into park. He turned in his seat, breathing fast and shallow, staring at her from inches away.

"So you thought you could run from me?"

With his left hand, he slapped her face, stunning her. Her vision doubled.

"You don't run. You don't disobey. You do what I want."

"I will."

He smacked her again. "What I want. Only what I want!"

"I will, I promise, I swear..."

"You don't fuck with me anymore. You understand that?"

She nodded.

He backhanded her a third time. "Say it!"

"I understand."

"All right then. All right." He was still staring at her, but there was a different light in his gaze. The same look she'd seen after singing the willow song. "We're together now, okay? You're with me—all the way."

"Yes," she whispered.

"I'm sorry I lost my temper, sugarplum. I didn't mean to hurt you."

He dug in his jacket and pulled something out. It flashed between his fingers. A needle.

"I've got something that'll calm you down. Take your fears away."

"You don't have to do that."

"Sorry, have to." He screwed the needle into a larger mechanism, a cylinder with a plunger. "Can't have you running out on me again. You can see how worked up it gets me—the thought of losing you."

"Please...I said I'd be good."

"I know what you said." He squirted a few drops from the needle. "But I still don't trust you."

"Look, just leave me alone and I...I can be good to you. I can... do things...things you'll like. I can get you off."

"I'll just bet you can. But there'll be time for that later. A lot of time."

He took her arm, not roughly, and before she could react, he slid the needle under her skin and depressed the plunger. She watched as the contents of the syringe drained into her body.

"What the hell is that? What are you giving me?"

"Same stuff you took in the club, only an injection works faster. GHB. It didn't make you feel so bad last time, did it?"

"Why don't you just give me an OD and get it over with?"

"Hush. Don't talk like that. Everything will be okay."

"Right. And you'll let me go. Sure you will."

He looked honestly puzzled. "When did I ever promise to let you go?"

"You said...you told me..."

"Letting you go—that was never in the cards."

"But...what...?"

The question died in a sudden haze fogging her mind. She felt warm and strange, and though she knew it was the drug taking effect, she didn't care.

Swann withdrew the needle and carefully put it into his pocket. "You think I'm all about the money, but that's only part of it. The least important part." He shifted into drive and got the Hyundai moving again. "I don't want just money out of you, little girl. I want...well, I want all kinds of things."

She sat back in her seat, her eyes half shut, her mind frozen. Dimly, she was aware that Swann was smiling.

"You and I are going to be together for the long haul. For a lifetime, sugarplum."

33

KATE reached the Jaguar as sirens were drawing near. She only hoped she could get the car going again. The key was still in the ignition, but the motor was off. She cranked the ignition.

Finally, the engine turned over. She nursed the gas and eased the car off the apron of pavement in front of the warehouse, onto the street. The car was making some questionable noises under the hood, but it was running, and that was all she cared about.

She flipped a U-turn on Seventh and headed west. Swann had said he would call at four a.m. to arrange the ransom drop. After the events of the past ten minutes, the call might be delayed or it might not come at all—but if it did, she would be ready. And this time she would insist on hearing Chelsea's voice.

Regret stabbed her, and she briefly shut her eyes.

She'd *had* her. She'd embraced the girl. Huddled with her in the apartment. Had almost felt her beating heart.

And now Chelsea was lost to her again.

The memory of how the girl had clung to her, unwilling to run to the imagined safety of the street, came back to her and hit her hard.

I forced her into that street, she thought, *and Swann anticipated it. If she dies, I sent her to her death.*

"I'll get you back," Kate breathed. "I swear I will."

Now there was work to do. She got out her phone, speed-dialing Di Milo. Before he answered, her phone started beeping. Low battery. Damn, she'd forgotten to charge it.

"Vince, you at the location yet?" She spoke fast, cramming in as much conversation as possible while the battery lasted.

"I'm at the coffeehouse. Counterman told me you were here and left in a hurry."

"I went after Swann, but it didn't work out. He was inside the abandoned church before he took off. There's got to be a way in, probably around back. Find it. I'll be there in five minutes."

Di Milo started to answer, then went silent. The battery had failed.

"At least nothing else can go wrong," she muttered.

But she was pretty sure that wasn't true.

———

It took her ten minutes to reach the church, coaxing the wounded Jag down every block. She found Di Milo's beat-up Buick Skylark parked in the coffeehouse lot. By now he must be inside the church, having made a thorough inspection of the premises.

A squeal of tires made her turn. A bright-yellow Mazda RX-8 whipped into the lot and slant-parked across three spaces. Skip Slater climbed out from behind the wheel.

"What are you doing here?" she asked, unaccountably peeved.

"Making a delivery." He nodded toward the passenger side of the car, where Grange was stepping out. His bald head was bandaged.

"Vic. You're supposed to be in the ER."

"I left."

"They let you go?"

"Sure. I'm fine."

"He's not fine," Skip said. "He left AMA—against medical advice. Your guy Alan sent me to pick him up. Like I'm an errand boy."

Kate frowned. "Alan was supposed to send a couple of bodyguards to look after you at the hospital."

"He did. I told them to get lost. I don't need babysitters."

"No, just a chauffeur," Skip groused.

Kate ignored him. "Why come here?" she asked Grange.

He shrugged. "Chelsea's my responsibility. I lost her. I'll help get her back."

"No one's blaming you. Besides, you don't even like her. Didn't you call her a spoiled little skank?"

"She's that, all right. But...I don't want her getting hurt."

"Neither do I," Kate said, wondering if it was already too late.

A perimeter fence sealed off the church from intruders. Exploring it with her flashlight, she picked out a gap under the fence that showed signs of trespass—long smears in the dirt left by crawling bodies and bits of cloth caught on the sharp edges of the bottom of the fence.

"They got in this way," she said. "By now, Di Milo's in there, too." She turned to Grange. "You'd better stay outside and stand post. Just in case Swann comes back."

Looking past Grange, down the alley that led to the back of the church, she saw a flicker of movement.

Di Milo? He might have heard their arrival. But he would show himself plainly. He wouldn't sink back into the shadows. Hiding. Watching…

Him.

He'd been tailing her all night, and now somehow he was here.

Impulsively, she broke into a run. She had been stalked by this son of a bitch for too long. She hadn't saved Chelsea. She hadn't stopped Swann. But she could catch this man and put him away.

The alley intersected with another one running east along the rear of the café. That was where he'd gone. She followed, fumbling the Glock out of her pocket, hoping she had a chance to use it.

He was a dozen yards ahead, sprinting hard. Behind her, footsteps. Grange, pursuing also.

At the end of the alley stood a chain-link fence, screening it from the street. She had time to think; she'd cornered the bastard. And then he jumped onto the fence and climbed.

She wanted to shoot him, but he was still too far away.

He reached the top of the fence and swung over, dropping down heavily. She hoped he'd shattered an ankle, incapacitated himself, but no such luck. He took off running again, up the sidewalk.

By the time she reached the fence he was gone.

Only now did she realize the risk she'd taken. If he hadn't panicked, if he'd turned and taken aim, he might have cut her down in the middle of the alley.

She still didn't care. She *wanted* him. She wanted something to go right tonight.

Then Grange was beside her. "Who the hell was that?"

"Somebody who was watching us."

"You see his face?"

"No."

"Might have been nothing. A vagrant, maybe."

"He wasn't a vagrant."

"You think it was Swann?"

"No. Not Swann."

She headed back to the church, saying nothing more.

Skip was waiting there, unsure what had happened. "False alarm," Kate said smoothly, then lay flat and wriggled through the gap under the fence. She dusted herself off and moved toward the church, looking for a way into the building itself.

A crunch of footsteps behind her made her turn. Skip had followed.

"You don't have to accompany me, Mr. Slater."

He showed her an insouciant grin. "I have a taste for adventure."

It was easier to let him shadow her than to argue about it.

"Do you spell your last name with a c-k, or just a k?" he asked as they retreated along the rear of the building.

"C-k."

"I'm just wondering because Malik, without the c, is the name of an angel."

"I'm no angel."

"Well, actually, Malik is more of a demon. In Islamic tradition he supervises hell."

"I'm not a demon, either."

"Maybe not, but you do look after a passel of celebrities. That's gotta be hell."

She had to give him that.

A few yards away, she found a rear door that had been pried ajar.

She opened it and entered the church. Irrationally, she felt like an intruder here.

"Vince?" she called, and her own voice came back at her in a volley of echoes.

"Coming." Di Milo appeared out of the dimness, holding a thin, rectangular object in one hand. "You were right about Swann. He cleared out. But he left this."

He held it up. A laptop. Kate nodded to Skip, who took it eagerly, pleased as a child. He flipped open the lid, and the screen cast a blue glow on his face. The glow shifted as he clicked rapidly through a series of screens, balancing the computer on one knee.

"He's got a camera on the Brewers' house," he said suddenly, turning the computer so Kate could see. "Live feed from a webcam."

"He said he had eyes on the place. I assume the feed is uploaded to a web server."

"Yeah. And by stealing the Wi-Fi signal next door he could access the site anytime." He squinted at the image. "Looks like the camera's across the street, probably wired into a utility pole. I can find it and shut it down."

Kate shook her head. "Even without the laptop, Swann must have some way to monitor the signal—a backup computer or his cell phone. If the video goes dark, he'll terminate communication and we'll never get Chelsea back."

An icicle of fear pierced her stomach as she said the last words. She wished she hadn't spoken them aloud. It felt too much like uttering a prophecy.

"You think so?" Skip asked dubiously.

"I'm sure of it. This man is all about control."

"Then why'd he leave his equipment behind?"

"I don't know."

"Swann left something else behind," Di Milo said quietly. From his tone of voice, Kate knew it was nothing good.

She followed him into what must have been the sanctuary, where the main altar had been. In the transept on the left, electric light from outside glimmered through high stained glass windows, throwing a dim pool of color on the body that lay on the floor.

"Jesus," Skip breathed.

Kate approached the corpse. It was a middle-aged man, trim and tall, almost familiar. He'd been shot—she saw the gunshot wound in his gut—and then tortured, his arms and legs broken, bent at impossible angles, like a smashed stick figure.

She thought of Lazarus's smashed knuckles and broken fingers. Swann liked cracking bone.

"You check his ID?" she asked Di Milo.

"Didn't have to. Recognized him from the brochures in the Westwood house. Daniel Farris."

A wave of weakness passed through her as she remembered the slow descent down the cellar stairs.

She tried to understand how it had happened. Farris hired Swann. Swann didn't follow the game plan. Farris had it out with him and lost the argument. That was the essence of it, anyway.

When she looked away from the body, she caught Skip staring down at it, his face pale.

She couldn't resist a jab. "Squeamish, Mr. Slater? I'm surprised. Death is your livelihood, isn't it?"

"It's not so real when it's just pixels," he said softly.

"No, it's equally real. You just don't have to see it. Well, you're seeing it now." She focused her flashlight on the corpse. "Take a look. Take a good look."

Skip swallowed slowly. He had no smart comebacks.

"Farris tried to defend himself, it looks like." Di Milo pointed at a pistol lying a few yards away from the body.

Kate glanced at it. A Sig Sauer 9. The gun Farris must have held to her head in Westwood. The gun that had nearly ended her life.

She fanned her flashlight beam across the floor and saw a pair of shell casings. "Two rounds expended."

"Swann must be a better shot," Di Milo said.

"Farris was probably scared. He was scared in Westwood, too." Fear could throw off even the best shooter's aim.

Her flashlight probed farther and found a discarded syringe, empty.

"Think Swann used drugs on Farris?" Di Milo asked.

"No. He drugged Chelsea in the club. He's still using drugs to control her. She must have been right here." The flashlight picked out the door to the confessional, ajar. Something small and cream colored lay inside.

She moved toward it. The beam illuminated Chanticleer, dead, the pallid fur stained purple in patches with drying blood.

"Hell," Di Milo said.

"Entry wound," Kate said, leaning over the small body.

"He shot the dog?" Skip was appalled.

"He's done a lot of shooting tonight," Kate said, thinking of the old man who'd given them refuge in his apartment. "Let's go."

"What do we do about him?" Skip pointed at Daniel Farris's corpse.

Kate turned away. "We leave him. Let the dead bury their dead."

34

SWANN felt it in his palms. The itch.

He knew the feeling. It had come on him before. Always, it led to the same conclusion.

He drove east, taking side streets in case the police were looking for the stolen Hyundai. The car was a zippy little thing, unpretentious but serviceable. His left knee ached; he'd banged it up pretty good in the wreck. But the pain didn't matter. He'd known pain before, plenty of it. He almost enjoyed it. It kept him alert, heightened his awareness, staved off complacency.

That was why he'd made the whore cut him tonight. After she'd done her job, he'd given her a straight razor. "Cut me," he'd said, his legs spread, exposing the web of thin, pale scars on his thighs.

Her hand had trembled, and he had seen she wanted to refuse but didn't dare. She'd taken the razor by its handle, chosen a clean spot among the nest of scars, and pushed the blade down, breaking the skin, raising a slim line of blood, then guided the razor in an unsteady course, slicing flesh.

He'd released a deep, slow groan of pleasure and pain. She'd done the job well, adding a fine new notch to his belt. Any deeper and she might have nicked the femoral artery. The wound still burned a little when he shifted his legs. The electric current traveling up his groin made him feel alive and free.

Free, despite the nun's best efforts.

The nun. Though his mind ought to be on his next move, he couldn't stop thinking about her.

He could have killed her in Stiletto, of course. If he'd waited in the back room instead of clearing out, she never would have stood a chance. But he hadn't wanted her dead just then. Someone would have found the body. There would have been a commotion. His plans for Chelsea would have been jeopardized. Under the circumstances, he'd shown admirable self-restraint.

But now he wanted her dead. Or if not her, then somebody. In a city of millions, there had to be someone he could kill.

Then he remembered. And smiled.

At a stoplight, he turned to the girl, cupping her chin and staring into her eyes. She gazed back blankly. The drug had done its job.

"Mind if we make a detour? You won't give me any more trouble, will you?"

Chelsea didn't answer.

"I mean, you won't run away or start screaming or pull any other stupid shit, right?"

Mutely, she nodded.

"Good girl."

The light cycled to green. He punched the gas.

The itch was still there, gnawing at him, but he didn't mind it now.

Kate had pushed the damaged Jag as far as it would go. She left it in the diner's parking lot next to the church and rode back to the Brewer house with Di Milo. She was thinking hard. Thinking about James.

She was sure he'd been watching her in the alley. But how could he have known where to find her? She was sure he hadn't followed her from the scene of the crash. It was almost as if he'd been at the church before she was, waiting for her, but that didn't make any sense…

Di Milo's phone chimed—no cutesy ringtone for him—and after answering, he handed it to her. "Alan," he said in explanation.

"Another problem," Alan said as soon as she took the phone. "Got a call from Barry Larrison."

"Oh, hell." Larrison was an attorney-turned-reporter with his own tabloid TV show and a regular gig on *Good Morning America*.

"He knows something's up, and I couldn't put him off. I said you'd call him."

"Give me his number."

She punched it in and waited.

"Larrison," a chirpy voice answered.

She identified herself.

He cut her off. "Right, your guy said you'd call. Here's the deal, Kate. I know what's up and I'm gonna run with it."

She didn't know him and disliked his smarmy familiarity. "Nothing's up, Barry. You've been misinformed."

"Nice try. I have a source at the hospital who confirms that Chelsea Brewer's bodyguard was brought in tonight, sans Chelsea. Your client didn't leave Panic Room with her security guy."

"That's correct. She left with someone else."

"I'll bet she did."

"What's that supposed to mean?"

"It means Chelsea's mom just bought up a truckload of jewelry on Rodeo Drive in the middle of the night."

"I don't know anything about Mrs. Brewer's shopping habits."

"Kate, you're starting to piss me off. And that's something you don't wanna do."

She shut her eyes. Lying to him was pointless. He'd already guessed most of it.

"All right," she said. "Chelsea's been abducted. Her mother is obtaining valuables to use as ransom. The kidnapper has made it clear that if word gets out to the media, all bets are off. So you can't run the story, Barry. If you do, Chelsea will die."

"You don't know that. The guy could be bluffing."

"He's not bluffing. Look, we can get her back. We *will* get her back. Unless you blow it for us."

"It's too big a story to sit on."

"If you put this out there, it'll kill Chelsea. Is that what you want?"

"Hell, she's been doing a pretty good job of killing herself."

She hated this man. It took an effort to keep the contempt out of her voice. "She's one of the most popular celebrities in the world. If she doesn't make it, I'll publicize the fact that your irresponsible pursuit of a scoop cost Chelsea her life."

"No one says 'scoop' anymore."

"You know you have to keep this quiet, Barry."

There was a beat of silence. "What time is the ransom exchange?"

"Soon."

"How soon? Give me a window."

"Within the next three hours."

"Fine. At seven a.m., I break the story. I do it live on the West Coast edition of *GMA*. I'm passing up the East Coast time slot for this," he added in an aggrieved tone.

"I appreciate it, Barry." The words tasted like poison in her mouth. "It's the right thing to do."

"Yeah, yeah, I'm a saint. Look, if I get word someone else is about to break the story, I'm going on live no matter what time it is."

"No one else knows about this."

"You didn't know *I* knew till I called your office."

"Nobody's going to break this story without calling me first, and you're the only one who's called."

"So far. One more thing. When this is over, I want an interview with Chelsea. An exclusive sit-down—one hour, minimum—full details of her ordeal."

"She can do that."

"If she's still around. If not, I get an exclusive with the grieving mom."

Kate resisted the urge to fling the phone out the window. "All right."

"I'm doing you a solid, Kate. You owe me one."

"Of course I do, Barry." *I owe you a slap in the face*, she added silently.

With luck, she would have a chance to make good on that obligation. She looked forward to it.

35

SWANN crossed the railroad tracks, tugging the girl along. Their shoes crunched on chunks of gray gravel between the wooden ties. Yards away, a sheet of newspaper blew across the tracks like a tumbleweed, folding and unfolding itself as it fell end over end.

The sky overhead was crisscrossed with high-tension cables and crowded with stars. Swann had been all over the country, and the stars were the one thing that never changed. People said they were giant balls of heat and light millions of miles away. He didn't know about that. He cared only about facts he could use. Something unimaginably far off, something he couldn't touch or taste, steal or sell, meant nothing to him.

He did like to look at them, though. The stars.

Together, he and Chelsea approached the fire under the bridge and the tattered vagrant warming himself by the flames. His face was changed now, overgrown with a mountain man's beard. But the crippled hands told the story.

"Hey, Bob," Swann said with a slow smile. "Long time no see."

Bob Ellis got to his feet, shoulders hunched. His eyes stared up like the eyes of a dog awaiting punishment. He seemed to want to speak, but no speech came.

"This is my friend Chelsea. She's promised not to make trouble. She knows it'll go hard for her if she acts up. Isn't that right, Chelsea?"

Mechanically, she nodded.

"Good girl. Sit down."

She huddled close to the fire as if she were cold.

Swann watched her until he was sure she wasn't going anywhere. Then he took a step toward Bob. The homeless man backed up against the stone pillar and reached out with a pleading gesture. Swann waved him off.

"Hey, hey, no need to be scared of me. Our little misunderstanding is all in the past. We're buddies now. Come over where it's warm, and we'll shoot the shit."

He took a fistful of Bob's woolen coat and escorted him to the fire, exerting gentle downward pressure. Bob sat, facing the girl across the flames. His stink was something awful, but she didn't seem to notice.

Before seating himself, Swann rummaged through a sack of Bob's trash pickings and came up with an unopened can of peaches. He could use the sugar hit. "May I?"

There was no answer.

"I mean," Swann added, "it's not like you'll be eating 'em. You couldn't even get the can open with those messed-up paws of yours."

He sat down beside Bob, crowding him, and produced a pocketknife. He pried open the rusty pull-tab and popped the lid, then speared a chunk of peach with the knife and put it in his mouth.

"Juicy." He patted Bob on the shoulder. "Almost makes up for stealing my sandwich that time."

A sound like a sob escaped Bob's throat. Swann pretended not to notice. He looked past the fire and smiled at the girl.

"See Bob's hands? And his face—how fucked up it is? I did that. You might be wondering why."

He paused for the question, but it didn't come. He answered it anyway.

"I had this deli sandwich, roast beef and mayo, no lettuce, no tomato, on a hard roll. Was keeping it in the fridge. Bob ate it. I don't like people eating my food. It got my dander up. I took a dislike to him."

Bob shivered. Swann continued to look at Chelsea, and she continued to watch the flames, her eyes empty.

"I know my reaction may appear extreme. But here's something I learned a long time ago. Violence is the only thing men respect, the only thing that matters. Men of violence made every damn thing there is. History is a chronicle of violent men. So's the nightly news. You know how the Romans maintained their empire? They crushed every rebellion. They smashed every rival. They crucified thousands of people and burned whole cities and salted the earth. In this world, you got to stand up for yourself, even if it's only over a sandwich."

Bob wept.

"But like I said"—Swann speared another slice of peach— "that's all in the past."

He swallowed the peach with a noisy slurp and turned to the man next to him.

"Feels like old times, doesn't it, Bob? Us having a talk, sharing a meal. Want to know a secret? My gal here is a movie star. I abducted her. She's my captive." He said the word with satisfaction, liking the sound of it. "I've moved on from those small-time jobs we used to pull. I'm into something big. You know that movie, *I*

Am Legend? That's going to be me, Bob. By this time tomorrow, I'll be a goddamned legend."

He leaned in, wrapping one arm around Bob's shoulder. The shock of contact startled a single word out of the man. "Fuck."

"Fuck is right." Swann paused with a chunk of peach in midair, trembling on the tip of his knife. "Hey, you remember my snake, don't you, buddy? You saw me in the buff enough times when we were on the run, camping out and bathing in the river. But did I ever tell you why I got that ink? What it means to me? Because of course it means something. A man doesn't put himself through that kind of pain for no reason. See, it's not just any snake. It's a python."

The bit of peach went into his mouth.

"And a python has a special way of killing. He hypnotizes you with his eyes. He charms you. And when he's got you sleepy and smiling, he wraps himself around you and then he starts to squeeze. Gently at first, then harder, but so gradually you almost don't notice. Until you try to suck air and your rib cage won't expand. Then you know you've drawn your last breath, and you never even put up a fight."

He ate the last peach and tipped the can to his mouth, draining the syrup, then wiped his mouth with the back of his hand.

"People talk about sharks and panthers, but for my money, the python is your perfect killing machine. Because he kills you and he makes you like it. He makes you cooperate in your own death. And that's more than instinct. That's genius. A man who could kill like a python would be king of the fucking world. And that's me, Bob. I'm the king, and soon the world is going to know it."

Swann had surprised himself with this little speech. These were thoughts he hadn't shared before. He hoped Bob appreciated the rare privilege of being taken into his confidence.

He pitched the can away in a lazy overhand toss. It hit the concrete embankment and clattered down, coming to rest in the riverbed among the other trash.

Then there was a long silence except for the crackle of the fire. The girl didn't move, hardly breathed, but her eyes seemed bigger than before.

"Pretty soon, princess over there is going to get a look at my artwork. Up close and personal. I got this place down in Baja, on the coast in a little village where nobody speaks English and people mind their own business. That's where we'll be living, the two of us. I'll have changed my look, and she won't get out much. But I'll keep her plenty busy at home." He patted his groin and smiled at Chelsea. "I'm going to snake you, sugarplum. Snake you good."

Her face showed no expression, but a slow shudder moved through her thin body.

"Know what you want," Swann said, "and take it. That's how it is for me. That's my Golden Rule." He checked his watch. "Hate to eat and run, Bob. But I've got miles to go, and all that shit."

His grip on Bob's shoulder tightened just a little.

"Hope there's no hard feelings," he said, smiling, and slowly, tentatively, Bob smiled back, half his mouth lifting in a lopsided grin.

The python's victim. Mesmerized. Trusting.

"But before I go," Swann added in a casual tone, "there's just one more thing."

Just a touch more pressure on Bob's shoulder.

"I never did finish the job I started on you, did I?" Swann's smile bloomed in its full radiance, and Bob tried to shrink away. "What do you say I finish it now?"

A snap of his right hand and the gun was up, quick trigger pull, Bob Ellis's face disappearing in a mist of blood.

Swann watched him fall sideways like a bag of laundry. He looked at the girl and saw her blink once and shiver.

"Not like the movies, is it, princess? A little more graphic in real life."

Swann leaned over Bob Ellis and found the nail buried in the side of his head. He made a quick incision, opening up the scar tissue, and forced his knife under the misshapen nail head. He got some leverage and jerked the nail from side to side, extracting it in fits and starts, the metal slippery with blood. When the nail was halfway out, Swann took hold of it between his fingers and wrenched it free.

Slowly, he stood and released a deep exhalation. His palms didn't itch anymore.

"Guess I should've let him keep this." Swann twirled the nail. It gleamed, black with blood. "But I believe I'll have a use for it before long."

He put the nail in his pocket and began to laugh, and the funny thing was, once he got started, he just couldn't stop.

36

KATE had no idea how Victoria would react upon learning that her daughter had been found and then lost again. She imagined a variety of responses ranging from grief to rage, but Victoria took the news blankly.

She merely nodded once, as if confirming something to herself, and said, "All right."

She seemed to be off in another place, zoned out. Kate wondered if she'd taken something.

Probably not. Probably, it was shock.

Victoria had done her job, though. She'd obtained all the necessary jewelry from the shop on Rodeo Drive and, with Sam's help, packed it in a valise. Kate hefted the bag. Two million dollars didn't weigh very much.

"And I know how Swann got ahold of the list," Victoria said, her voice flat. "The only person who had it, other than myself, was

Gregory Niles, my insurance agent. I called him on the way to the store. He told me there was a break-in at his office last week. The place was vandalized. Papers strewn everywhere. All the files in disarray. He's still trying to restore order."

"And your file was missing?"

"Not all of it. Just the asset inventory."

"He didn't tell you?"

"He didn't know. Not until I told him I had reason to believe the inventory had been taken. He went over and checked. I got his call as I was driving back. That one page is gone."

"That explains it, then," Kate said. She didn't mention that there was still the mystery of how Swann had known the identity of Victoria's insurance agent in the first place.

Victoria seated herself in one of the Eames chairs, and Sam took up a matching position in the other one, nursing a drink. Ice water, Kate thought at first, but when she drew near, she smelled a faint acrid odor. Scotch. The ice clinked with each slow swallow. He seemed unperturbed, indifferent to his daughter's fate. Kate found herself hating him.

Skip and Grange arrived a moment later. Alan installed Kate's SIM card into a spare cell phone so the phone would receive her calls. Skip watched with a bland smile of approval.

Her gaze traveled toward Sam again. The ice clinked in his glass as he took another swallow. She could almost taste the slow burn of alcohol, like liquid fire. It was the first swallow she liked best, the warm shock of hard liquor on her tongue, then sliding down her throat and singeing the delicate membranes, then settling into the stomach, the gut, and simmering there, a bonfire that cast long, vaporous tendrils of heat throughout her body, into her bones, along her spine…

She tried not to look at the drink in his hand, the cocktail glass, the melting ice, the slosh of clear liquid, the fatal temptation. Not one drink in seventeen years. She'd broken the addiction by willpower. No support group, no sponsor, no twelve steps. She'd done it herself, and she would not undo it now.

But damn, it sure would taste good.

Four o'clock came. The phone didn't ring.

"What makes you think he'll call?" Victoria asked at 4:02. "You chased him down, wrecked his car. You made him angry."

"Angry or not, he'll call. He wants his payment."

Victoria looked at her ex-husband. "What do you think?"

Sam scratched his chin. "The sensible thing is to call."

"Will he do the sensible thing?"

"That's just it. I don't know. There's no telling with Swann."

"He wants his payment," Kate said again, repeating the words like a mantra.

"He does," Sam agreed. "But he can't always keep ahold of himself. If he gets worked up…"

"You mean he could have killed Chelsea," Victoria said, not asking a question. "He could have gotten so angry he did something crazy."

"It's been known to happen." Sam looked at Kate, and she knew he was thinking of Lazarus, with his broken hands and a nail in his skull.

Another minute ticked by. The cell phone didn't ring.

"He's not calling," Victoria said.

Kate held her voice steady. "He will."

Suddenly, Victoria was on her feet, shaking like a taut wire, her hands squeezed into fists at her sides. "He won't. He killed her. *He killed her!*"

"We don't know that, Mrs. Brewer."

"*I* know it. I can feel it. In here." She thumped her chest with a small white fist. "She's gone. My baby's *gone.*"

Kate moved toward her. "Take it easy, now."

"I won't take it easy. She's my only child and I've lost her."

"Mrs. Brewer—" Kate reached out.

Victoria brushed her hand away. "Don't touch me. Don't pretend to understand. You've never been a mother, have you? So you don't know. You *can't.*"

She spun and fled the room, retreating down the hall and disappearing behind a slammed door.

Sam began to rise. "I'd better go talk to her."

"No," Kate said. "Let me."

He looked at her skeptically. "Your funeral."

"Give me a shout when the phone rings," she said as she left the room.

37

KATE went down the hall to the closed door and tested the knob. It turned freely. She pushed it open and stepped into a bedroom.

Chelsea's bedroom. That was obvious from the furnishings and decor. The girl had her own place now, a condo in an exclusive West Hollywood high-rise, but her mother had left her bedroom unchanged and untouched, a vault of memories.

Victoria lay curled on the bed, her knees pulled high and her head buried in her arms, a childlike pose. Above her hung a framed poster advertising Chelsea's first feature film four years ago, the girl's seventeen-year-old face smiling down.

Softly, Kate closed the door, then sat on the edge of the bed.

"Go away," Victoria murmured.

Kate extended an arm and laid her hand on Victoria's ankle, resting it there gently, just to establish contact.

"You're wrong." Her throat was tight and the words came with difficulty.

Victoria didn't answer.

"I don't know what you're going through. I can't. But I do know something about loss."

Victoria made a dark, dismissive sound.

"I was married once. I was very young. He abused me, and I abandoned him. Stole his car, actually." She managed a smile at the memory. "I drove that car to LA, and when I got here, I was alone and broke, and too proud to go back to New Jersey. And then…"

She swallowed. This was the hard part.

"Then I found out I was pregnant."

The words dropped into the stillness of the room like coins down a deep well, with no splash and no echo.

"That was when I really panicked. I had no money, no job. I was living in a cheap hotel. I was scared to death. And so I went to a clinic and—they took it out of me. For some reason, I wanted to see it, but they wouldn't let me. They wouldn't tell me if it was a boy or girl. They said it was better not to know."

Victoria lifted her head, watching her.

"But in my heart, I always felt it was a little girl. It just felt that way to me. And this will sound stupid, irrational, but…I loved her. I know I didn't have any right to love her. But I did. I do."

"Yes," Victoria said with a strange new inflection, which was simple kindness.

"After it happened, I got some jobs and made a little money, enough to live in a crummy apartment by an alley, with crackheads down the street. But I couldn't stop thinking about her. I would cry all night, and sometimes I'd drink too much. Eventually, I was drinking nearly all the time. I didn't have a job anymore. I didn't have anything. I thought about suicide."

"How old were you?"

"Nineteen."

"That's very young."

"I didn't feel young. I felt a million years old. I felt worn out and ready to die."

"Yet you survived."

"Not on my own. I had help. I joined the order. I became a postulant with the Sisters of Mercy. They saved me. I didn't save myself."

"So your faith in God pulled you through?"

Kate shook her head. "I never had any faith. I joined because I needed a home. Needed a purpose. But I never believed. I pretended. I knelt with the others. I said the same prayers. But I never believed."

"They took you in anyway? Despite all that?"

"They didn't know."

"About your lack of faith or...?"

"About any of it. I lied to them. Lied about everything. I said I loved God. I never told them I'd been married—in fact, technically, I was still married. I hadn't gotten a divorce. And of course they didn't know about...her." She shook her head. "I was a nun under false pretenses. Not very holy, was I?"

"Were you happy as a nun?"

"I was happy."

"Then why did you leave?"

"Because my past caught up with me. It took two years, but James tracked me down. I think he wanted his car back, not me. Tough luck. I'd sold it long before. Altered the registration and sold it for cash."

"And he told them about the marriage?"

"Sure."

"Why?"

"To hurt me. To get back at me for hurting him. He's the type who carries a grudge." *Carries it for a long time*, she added silently, thinking of the taunting phone calls, the laughter beneath the overpass. "He knew I loved the order. But a married woman can't be a nun. Or a divorced woman, either. And besides"—she bit her lip—"when that part of the story came out, I made a full confession. I told it all to the mother superior. And she cast me out."

"And you lost everything."

"Yes." She and the sisters had roomed together, cooked and cleaned together, shared stories and jokes, prayed the divine office twice a day—and then it was over, and she was shunned, a pariah. "But I deserved it, didn't I?"

"Did you? You're not the first one to make a mistake. We've all done things we're not proud of. Some of us, a lot more recently." Victoria sat up on the bed. "Kate…how old would your daughter be now?"

"Seventeen."

"Just a few years younger than Chelsea. Is that why you care so much about her personal life, the choices she makes?"

Kate wanted to deny it, but there was no point. "I know she's not my daughter, obviously. Not my responsibility. But when I see her making mistakes—dumb mistakes, mistakes that can ruin your life—"

"Like the mistakes you made."

"You should have listened to me," Kate said simply.

"I'll start. If there's still time."

"There is."

There had to be.

Through the closed the door, Alan's voice rang out from the living room. "Incoming call!"

Kate leaped up, glancing at her watch. The time was four thirty. Swann had made them wait an extra half hour. Made them sweat.

But he was calling now.

38

KATE forced herself not to run. Swann had kept her waiting, and now it was his turn to wait for her.

Her new cell phone rested on the coffee table in the center of the room. Alan and Skip sat on the divan. Skip's face was white with tension.

The caller ID showed a number with an out-of-state area code. Swann must have been using the AT&T phone card again.

She took a breath before pressing the phone's *talk* button. She wanted to sound calm. "Hello, Jack."

"How's it hanging, Sister Kate?"

"Everything's copacetic, Jack."

"Yeah, right. Sure it is. Sure it fucking is."

His voice had a new, halting quality. It was the voice of a man finding it hard to hold himself together. The strain had to be getting to him, especially after he'd come so close to losing everything in the car crash.

She paced, making tight circles on the carpet. "I need to hear Chelsea's voice."

"After the shit you pulled, I'm not doing you any favors. You have the jewelry?"

"Yes, it's all ready. But first I have to hear Chelsea's voice."

"I told you, no favors."

"It's not a favor. It's business. The last time I saw her, she was in a car with you, and you'd just taken a shot at me. I have no way of knowing what you did next. Put her on, or I'm hanging up this phone."

"You're not hanging up anything, and you know it."

"Okay then. Put her on, or else waste the next twenty minutes arguing with me about it."

He hesitated, thinking it over, then let out a sigh. "Fuck, you're a pain in the ass. Hold on."

A beat of silence, then Chelsea came on the line. "Kate?" Her voice was strangely subdued. A lost soul's voice.

"Chelsea, are you okay?"

"I guess so." The words were faraway and hollow. "I saw him shoot at you. Couldn't tell if he hit you…"

"He didn't. Don't worry about me. Listen, we're going to bring you home, we just—"

The phone was snatched from her hand and Victoria was shouting into it, pressing her ear to the small speaker. "Chelsea? *Chelsea?*" Then her face changed, turning dark with rage, and she screamed into the phone, "You let her go! You crazy son of a bitch, *let her go!*"

Kate pried the phone from her grasp and pushed Victoria away.

"Who the fuck was that?" Swann asked, his voice ragged. "Her mommy?"

"Yes."

"It's you I'm supposed to be talking to. No one else. Just *you*."

"She wanted to hear her daughter's voice."

"Fucking bitch screaming at me, giving me orders. Nobody gives me orders." He was breathing hard, like a man who'd just run a mile. "Keep her the fuck off the phone, you hear me? You *hear* me?"

"Yes, Jack."

"I don't want to hear her again. I'm not interested in dealing with hysterical women."

"Is that why you drugged Chelsea again?"

"I had to give her a booster shot. So what?"

"What's she on, Jack?"

"Nothing that's dangerous in the right dosage. Don't fret. She's doing fine. I've got enough drugs to last a good long while, and there's more where they came from."

A chill flickered through her. "Why would you need enough to last a long while?"

"Well, let's suppose I don't get paid. Then I go to plan B."

"Which is?"

"Chelsea stays with me. She'll be my female companion. After enough time has passed, I won't even need the meds anymore."

She lowered her voice, hoping Victoria couldn't hear. "I thought you were looking out for her best interests."

"Altruism only goes so far. Besides, I'm not talking about killing her. She'll be perfectly okay."

Sure she will, Kate thought, *a drugged sex slave*. "Is that really what you want for her?"

"Maybe it is. Or maybe I'll sell her. There's a thriving market in such commodities. A movie star would fetch a fair price."

"You don't want to do that, Jack."

"Don't tell me what I fucking want. You don't get it, Kate. You don't *see*. You used to pray, didn't you? Pray to God?"

"Yes."

"And who's God? The man in charge, right? Well, that's me. I'm in charge. I hold Chelsea's fate in my hands. I can do whatever I want with her. I can give her back, or I can keep her, or I can sell her, or I can kill her. Anything. Do you see?"

"Yes, Jack, I see."

"*I'm* your God now. You bow down to me. You pray to *me*."

"All right."

"I've saved your client's life, you stupid bitch. I think I deserve some fucking gratitude. Some fucking respect."

"I'm sorry if I offended you."

He hitched in a sharp breath, like a gulp. "You have the jewelry?"

She'd already told him so. Repeating the question was another sign of his deteriorating condition. "Packed in a valise, as you asked."

"That's good, Sister Kate. But since you distrusted me and interfered, I think I'm entitled to additional compensation. There's some fine artwork in the Brewers' house. An Ellenshaw in the master bedroom, a William Wendt in the den. And don't forget the Wyeth."

She didn't ask how he knew so much about the household decor. More information from the insurance files. "Those items may be difficult to transport."

"Not if you remove the frames and roll up the paintings one inside the other."

"It'll take some time to get that done."

"I'll give you an extra twenty minutes. This little milk run doesn't have to get underway till five a.m. But no later. Remember, I'm still watching the house."

"Where do you want me to bring the stuff?"

"*You* don't bring it anywhere. You're not the messenger. Sam Brewer makes the delivery."

Kate was glad Sam couldn't hear Swann's end of the conversation. "He's not going to like that idea," she said quietly.

"It's Sam or it's nobody. I know him. I've worked with him. He's the one I want. He puts the valise in his SUV, the black Lexus. And he takes his cell phone. That way I can call him once he gets started. I'll instruct him where to go after he's on the road."

"You'll need his number."

"Already know it. I'm always three steps ahead, Sister Kate. Always."

You weren't three steps ahead when I plowed my Jag into your Town Car, she thought. "Yes, you are."

He laughed, a crazed sound like a hyena's bark. "I like the way you said that. So nice and humble. You must've been a good nun, all docile and timid. A sad little virgin married to Christ—that was you, wasn't it?"

"Yes."

"There's that tell again. Liar, liar. So you weren't a virgin? You were a fucking whore even way back then?"

She didn't like his voice in her ear. It was too much like being inside his head, thinking his sick thoughts.

"But you pretended to be a virgin, didn't you? You faked it. Why not? Religion's all bullshit, just a way to keep the sheep in line. Isn't that right? Most people are sheep. And then there are men like me. Ask Chelsea if any God would let a man like me do the things I've done."

"What things have you done, Jack?"

"More than you want to know, Sister Kate. Put Sam in his car and on the road. Have him take Mulholland to Beverly Glen into the Valley, then work his way over to San Fernando Road, northwest bound. You writing this down?"

"I'm recording the call."

"Of course you are." Another bark of laughter. "I'll call him when he's underway. He has to be alone. Got that? Just him in the car. And nobody follows him."

"Right."

"You tried fucking with me once tonight. I don't want any more surprises."

"When will we get—"

Get Chelsea back, she meant to ask, but the click in her ear told her the call was over.

It didn't matter. Whatever answer she might have received would have been a lie. His tone of voice when he talked about plan B had not been speculative. It was the tone of a man who'd imagined that scenario many times and relished the prospect.

She was starting to think plan B had been Swann's real plan all along.

39

KATE summarized the conversation, watching Sam's face when she mentioned his role in the drop-off. His eyes flickered, and he shifted in his chair. That was all.

"So we'll collect the artwork and put it in the valise," Victoria said. "We'll give him what he wants, and he'll let Chelsea go."

Kate pursed her lips. "I'm not so sure about that."

"What do you mean? He has no reason to hurt her if we follow his instructions."

"I don't know. Some of the things he said…" She didn't want to repeat what she'd heard.

"You're saying he'll kill Chelsea?"

"No. I think he wants her alive. With him. I think…I think he's going to run off with her."

"Run off?"

"I could be wrong. But his control is starting to slip, and he may have said more than he intended."

"Then what can we do?"

The answer came to her without thought, but instinctively, she knew it was right. "We need to apprehend him. The drop site is our one opportunity."

"But if you do that," Victoria said, "he could panic and…" She didn't need to finish.

Kate nodded slowly. "It's a risk. Everything we do from this point forward is a risk. If we play the game his way, he may disappear with Chelsea for good. Or he may eliminate her once he doesn't need her anymore. If we move in on him and try to take him down, he could sacrifice Chelsea, or she could be hit in the crossfire. There's no risk-free option. I'm sorry."

"We need time…there has to be more time…so we can think…"

"There is no time. We have to decide now."

"Oh God." Victoria shut her eyes. "You think this is the best way? You really do?"

"Yes, Mrs. Brewer."

"All right then. All right." She said it firmly, but tears ran from beneath her closed eyelids.

Kate turned to Alan. "We'll have to track Sam on the road."

"Easy. His cell phone has GPS. There are online services that allow real-time tracking." He glanced at Skip like a student eager to impress the teacher with a good answer.

Kate wasn't satisfied. "What if Swann takes the Lexus before we can intercept him? Is there some way to track the car itself?"

"It has Safety Connect," Victoria said. "It's like OnStar. If the car is stolen, it can be located."

"No good." Alan had the faraway look he got when he was deep in thought. "Those security systems can't be utilized until an official police report has been filed. And even then, the info would go to the authorities, not to us."

"Let's say we modify the system"—Kate was thinking aloud—"hack into it or something."

Alan shook his head. "The proprietary software in automobile computers is designed to prevent third-party alterations. A hack like that just isn't possible."

"I can do it," Skip said simply. He allowed himself a small smile of triumph, leaning back with his hands behind his head.

Alan blinked at him, irritated. "No way."

"Yes way. Safety Connect is an ATX-based telematics system. When it's activated, it basically makes a cell phone call to the ATX call center. I can reprogram it so it calls a different number, and the information will show up on any computer screen."

"I'd like to see that," Alan said skeptically.

"Watch and learn."

"Swann has a camera on this house," Kate pointed out. "If you start fooling around with the car, he'll know something's up."

"I don't think so." Skip flipped open Swann's laptop. "I'm looking at the webcam feed right now. The camera doesn't have a good angle on the Lexus. The car's half hidden by shrubbery. I can slip inside and do my thing, and Big Brother will be none the wiser."

"You really believe you can make this work?" Kate asked.

"Belief has nothing to do with it. When it comes to this stuff, I've got mad skills."

"Then do it." She ushered them out the door, then looked at the others. "Di Milo and Grange will wait here until after Sam leaves, then follow in Vince's personal car, the Buick. They'll stay at least a mile behind at all times." She frowned, seeing the bandage on Grange's head. "Alfonse, do you think you're up to it?"

"I'd love another crack at that son of a bitch."

"Okay, then it's set. You two will hang back until Sam reaches the drop site and Swann shows up. Then you'll move in and take him. I'll drive a separate vehicle and close in from another direction to cut off escape."

The two bodyguards exchanged a glance.

"I don't think so, boss," Grange said. "It's not a good idea, you being there. You're too personally involved."

"As if you two aren't?"

"Not the same way. I've seen how you talk about Chelsea. You've got an emotional connection to the case that could...um... impair your judgment in a crisis situation."

She turned away. "Bullshit."

"They're right, Kate." It was Victoria. "Remember what you told me? You *know* they're right."

"Anyway," Grange said, "someone needs to monitor the computer and call the shots."

"So I'm a desk jockey now?" Kate heard the bitterness in her voice. "Just because I care about my client?"

"Because you care too much," Di Milo said.

She stifled a retort. It could be true. She was tired, stressed out, maybe not thinking clearly.

Of course, she could override their objections, insist on going along. But then she would be creating friction, serving as a distraction. The last thing she wanted to do.

"Guess I won't be needing these," she said softly. She handed her Glock and a spare clip to Grange, who'd come unarmed from the hospital.

Grange nodded. "It's the right call, boss."

"Just make sure you get her back. Make damn sure."

"Count on it."

"It's really great how you're all in agreement on this fine strategy you've come up with," Sam Brewer said. "There's only one hitch. I'm not doing it."

Silence in the room. Sam stood up slowly, staring at the ring of faces.

"You have to," Victoria said without heat or rancor, as if stating the self-evident.

"Don't gotta do nothing. Ain't gonna do this."

"But…" Victoria stopped, at a loss. "But *Chelsea*."

Sam's face was set, his eyes cold. "We'll have to work it some other way."

"There is no other way," Kate said. "You're the one who's always saying Swann is all about control. If anybody else is driving that car, the deal won't go through."

"I don't know about that. I only know I'm not your delivery boy."

Victoria took a step toward him, then paused, oddly hesitant, as if approaching an unfamiliar specimen of wildlife. "You can't be saying this," she whispered.

Sam was silent.

"She's your daughter, too." A note of pleading entered Victoria's voice. "Don't you care about her?"

"Sure I do," he said without a trace of feeling.

"That man will kill her. Or take her away forever."

"If I go to him, it's me who'll get killed."

"That's ridiculous. You worked with him. He knows you. That's why he wants you to make the delivery. He trusts you."

"Swann trusts nobody."

"I'm not saying you're best friends—"

Sam let out a snort of laughter.

"But he's got no reason to hurt you."

"Swann don't need a reason."

"Sam," Kate said carefully. "You and Swann were a team, years ago. Probably, he's got nothing against you."

"Right." Sam smiled, a crooked smile that touched only half his face, reminding her uncannily of Lazarus. "Maybe he just wants to get together and talk over old times."

"All you have to do is hand him the valise and go."

"He'll never let me go."

"Why are you so certain of that? What's between you and Swann?"

"Nothing."

"We don't have time for games. What are you afraid of?"

He set his teeth in a stubborn look, but his resistance lasted only a moment. "Shit, I'll tell you. It's not like you'll think any less of me. I snitched on Swann."

Kate stared at him. She couldn't imagine what mixture of misguided self-interest and perverse self-destruction would prompt a move like that. "When?" she asked slowly.

"Last time I was arrested. That was…what…a year and a half ago. Some small-time shit, but with my record, they could've put me away for years. And I couldn't go back inside. Didn't think I'd make it out alive this time. When they find out you're Chelsea's dad, they all want a piece of you, and they get pissed if you can't pay. And I can't fight back as good as I used to…"

"So you made a deal," Kate said, moving the story along. "You gave the police information in exchange for a reduced sentence."

"You guessed it. I got off with community service, and they got a description of some old jobs I pulled with Swann and an agreement that I'd testify against him if he ever came to trial."

"Why the hell would you ever agree to that?"

"To save my ass, like I said."

"You weren't scared of what Swann might do?"

"Fuck, lady. Of course I was scared."

Di Milo spoke up. "You could've dished dirt on one of your other buddies. Why Swann?"

"He's the one they wanted."

"Why?"

Sam managed another smile, one that covered his whole face this time. "This guy don't say much, but when he talks, he asks the right questions."

"So give him some answers," Kate said.

"The law's been chasing Swann for years. He's like a bogeyman to them. His name has turned up in connection with so much bad shit he's like a fucking urban legend."

"What kind of bad shit?"

"Well, there's the drug wars, for one thing. Back in the nineties, Swann was a hit man. Got hired by a drug cartel to take out the competition. This was in Miami. Then the guys who hired Swann started getting whacked. Turned out"—Sam actually chuckled—"Swann sold his services to both sides. He was doing both sets of hits."

"Risky game," Kate said.

"Yeah, but he made his money. Spent it all, or lost it, like he always does. But he had his fun."

"The cartels ever find out he was playing both ends against the middle?"

"Sure, but by then it was too late. He'd skipped town. The feds found out, too. That's when he became a priority. DEA was hot for him. Still are."

"And with the cartels and DEA looking for him, he's stayed alive and out of prison all this time?"

Sam shrugged. "I wouldn't have believed it myself. But the guy has discipline. He lives below the radar, totally off the grid. No paper trail. Never stays long in one place. He's like a damn cockroach, adaptable. And damn near indestructible."

"Why didn't you say any of this before?"

"Didn't figure it mattered. I told you what Swann's all about. Hell, I even *showed* you. Bob Ellis is worth a thousand words, right?"

"Who's Bob Ellis?" Victoria asked, but Kate and Sam ignored her.

"Even if you did give this information to the police," Kate said, "there's no reason to think Swann knows about it. He got this job because Farris hired him, not for any personal reason."

"I'm not sure I buy that. Swann always works more than one angle. He's already double-crossed Farris, hasn't he? Nobody can buy him. He's got his own agenda, always."

"You don't know he's out for revenge against you. For all we know, he just thinks of you as an old acquaintance."

"Maybe. But I'm not ready to start singing 'Auld Lang Syne.' Word could've reached him about what I done. If he knows, he'll want payback."

"It's a risk," Kate conceded. "But it's one you'll have to take."

"I don't think so."

"Then there's no hope for Chelsea."

Sam looked at her, then looked hard at his ex-wife. "*C'est la* fucking *vie*."

He started to walk off. Amazingly, he held his head high, his shoulders straight. Conscious of the eyes on him, he would show no weakness.

He was almost out of the room when Victoria said, "Hold on."

With insolent slowness, he turned to her. "Something to say?"

"Yes, God damn it, I have something to say. You're not thinking very clearly right now, are you?"

"How so?"

"You've been mooching off me for years—off me and Chelsea. You've been riding the gravy train, and it's been a damned smooth ride, hasn't it? But not anymore. Turn your back on Chelsea now, and it's over. You're on your own."

The cynical smile clung to Sam's face, but the light in his eyes was dimming.

"You'll be flat broke. You'll be a bum on the street. You can sling hash in a diner, like you used to. Minimum wage. Enough to get you a rented room in some shit hole."

"You wouldn't do that, baby," Sam said, his tone suddenly ingratiating. "You can see I'm only looking out for myself."

"You've always looked out for yourself. Tonight you're looking out for Chelsea, or you're all done. You can rot in a housing project until you get desperate enough to start pulling jobs again. Then you can rot in jail."

"We're a team, Vicki," Sam said, still wheedling.

"Not anymore. I'm pulling the plug. Unless you deliver that bag, you're out of my life for good."

She said it coldly, without hysteria or tears. Maybe that was what convinced Sam she meant it. Kate watched his face as it ran through a series of expressions, from fury to panic to acceptance.

Victoria had beaten him. She'd played her hole card, and played it well.

"All right," Sam said quietly. "Get the shit ready. I'll do it."

Kate stared at Sam's back as he retreated down the hall.

I'll do it, he'd said.

She wished she could believe him.

40

I T took Skip twenty minutes to modify the Lexus's onboard computer. Kate was beginning to worry he'd promised more than he could deliver. She couldn't check on his progress without the risk of being seen by Swann's hidden camera.

Her phone rang. It might be Swann, but no. The caller ID showed a number with a local area code.

"Miss Malick?" Georgia from Teen Alliance. "Sorry to call at this hour, but…"

"It's fine. I never sleep. What's up?"

"I just wanted to say your secret's safe. I swear."

"My…secret?"

"About Amber. Who her father is. I won't breathe a word."

"How do you know…?"

"Well, he was here. He said you sent him."

"He was at Teen Alliance? Amber's dad?"

"Yes." She lowered her voice. "Carson Banning himself. Is he a client of yours?"

"Just a friend."

"Well, I can see why you're keeping it quiet. It would be a tragedy if word got out. The press are so mean to him as it is. They never let the poor man be."

"When did he see you?"

"Why, not half an hour ago. Can you imagine what that was like? Him, walking in out of the blue like that?"

"Was he alone?"

"I'm afraid so. I told him it wasn't safe, wandering in this neighborhood at such an hour. Such a distinguished-looking man, so well dressed. He's bound to attract the wrong sort of attention."

Kate was barely listening. She knew how Banning had found Teen Alliance, of course. She'd mentioned it to him at his house. A mistake on her part, but she hadn't thought he would follow up. He'd promised not to. She shouldn't have believed him.

Banning must have sent his bodyguards home long ago and hadn't called them back on duty. He was looking for Amber on his own.

Stupid. But a desperate father would do stupid things. She should have known that.

"Anyway," Georgia was saying, "I just wanted you to know I'll keep it under my hat. Amber's identity, I mean. I'm sorry the overpass was a dead end, but I'm still trying to track her down. I'm asking everyone who comes in."

"I appreciate that."

"Carson Banning's my very favorite. I couldn't believe I actually met him. People say he's washed up, but I see every movie he's in. Some of them twice."

"I'll tell him you said so."

"Actually"—a nervous laugh—"I told him myself. He gave me his autograph."

"That was nice of him. Mr. Banning gave you his phone number, too, I imagine."

"Why, yes, he did. In case I come up with anything."

"Georgia, I have to ask you not to call him. He means well, but he really shouldn't be out looking for his daughter. If he tries to approach her, he may just scare her off."

"If you feel that way, why did you send him here?"

"Well…"

"Oh, I get it. You didn't send him."

"He can be a bit impulsive."

"I understand." She sighed, disappointed. "All right, I'll call you and only you."

"Thank you. It's for the best."

"We'll find his little girl, Miss Malick. Don't fret. I'm on the case."

Kate had no doubt that she was. What worried her was that Carson was on the case, too.

She didn't have time to think about it. Skip had appeared in the living room, trailed by Alan.

"That was awesome," Alan said.

Skip shrugged off the praise.

"You got it reprogrammed?" Kate asked.

"Without breaking a sweat. Like I said, mad skills."

"Isn't it refreshing to use your powers for good instead of evil?"

"Yeah, but it's not as remunerative."

"There's more to life than money."

"True. There's sex. But I kind of need money for that, too. By the way," he added in a louder voice, "I tweaked the system so it's permanently activated. It's like the panic button has been pressed, and there's no off switch. So if by any chance Swann decides to take Mr. Brewer's car, we can still track him. There's no way Swann or anybody else can kill the signal."

He said this with a glance toward the Eames chair where Sam sat nursing another scotch.

Kate got it. It wasn't Swann he was worried about. He thought Sam might try to make a run for it. Skip didn't trust Sam Brewer any more than she did.

"Good to know," she said. "Okay, Victoria's got the paintings out of their frames and rolled up. So I guess we're ready to get started."

Alan spoke. "Just one more thing. I need to outfit Mr. Brewer with a headset so he can receive our transmissions without tying up his phone. If he keeps his cell on speaker, we'll be able to hear Swann when he calls." He produced a small transceiver with an earbud and stalk microphone dangling from it. "I rigged it up while Skip was doing his thing."

The smile on his face showed that he was still looking for an apple from his teacher.

Sam eyed him suspiciously. "You want me to wear that thing?"

"Right. You talk into the mike and listen through the earpiece."

"I know how to use a headset, jerkoff. But Swann'll kill me if he knows I'm wearing a wire."

"You'll take it off before you meet him. Obviously."

"What if he's watching me and he sees that thing on my head?"

"He'll assume it's a standard hands-free kit."

Sam gave in. "Fuck, I'll wear it. What the hell, I'm a fucking lamb to the slaughter anyhow." He snatched up the headset and slipped it on, then grabbed his cell phone and stuffed it into his pocket as he rose from his chair. "Let's do it."

He was trying for an air of bravado, but the tremor in his voice spoiled the effect.

Victoria had been staring out the window all this time. Now she turned to the man who had been her husband. "You're doing the right thing. You know you are."

"Guess I don't have much choice."

"You're saving our daughter."

"If she's still alive to be saved."

He said it casually, but Kate saw how Victoria flinched from the words.

"She'll come back to us," Victoria said quietly. "To both of us. You're going to be all right."

"Sure I am. Swann wouldn't hurt me. He wouldn't hurt a fucking fly." Sam pulled on his jacket. From its weight, Kate knew the gun was still inside. She thought about ordering him to leave it behind; Swann wouldn't be happy if the messenger showed up armed. But if she pressed the point, Sam might not go at all.

"You'll be all right," Victoria said again, as if willing him to believe it.

He ignored her. "Where's that satchel?"

Victoria gave him the valise, crowded with jewelry and the tight cylinder of paintings. Sam took it from her without a word.

"Remember, he wants you to get on San Fernando Road, heading northwest," Kate said. "Then he'll call with new instructions."

"Been over that. Don't need a refresher course."

"Vince and Alfonse will be a mile behind you." Kate knew he was aware of this also, but she thought he could use the reassurance. "They can catch up in a minute if they have to."

"A lot can happen in a minute," Sam said, not looking back.

He went out the door.

"Good luck," Victoria called out, but the door was already swinging shut and he didn't answer. Kate saw him glance up at the sky as if searching for something. Swann's hidden camera, probably. It was out there somewhere and no doubt Sam Brewer could feel it. Could feel Swann's eyes on him.

She wondered if she had just sent a man to his death.

41

CHELSEA wasn't herself.

She knew that much. Her head was light as a balloon and her fingertips were a million miles away. The brightness was too bright and the ceiling was too high. Some kind of major weirdness was going on.

She even knew why it was happening. She just couldn't remember right now. But she was sure it had to do with Mr. Darkness.

She stood in a corner of the kitchen, shifting her weight from side to side, watching him. The kitchen was large and cluttered with saucepans and big pots, racks of spoons and spices, piles of dinner plates in a giant aluminum sink. Fans were mounted in the ceiling to blow smoke and steam into ventilation ducts. A big stand-alone freezer hummed against the wall.

It was the kitchen of a restaurant—something Trattoria. The aromas of tomato sauce and basil hung in the air, and would have made her hungry if she'd been there to notice.

Swann had driven into the alley behind the building and let her in through the rear door, using a key. She had no idea where he'd gotten the key. Maybe he'd produced it by magic, out of thin air, presto.

He'd made a call on his cell phone, punching in a long string of numbers before he dialed. Chelsea had listened to his side of the conversation without interest. Even the part about what he might do with her didn't seem important. It was all just words.

Hearing Kate's voice was nice. And her mom. She'd hoped she might get to talk to them again, but Mr. Darkness had closed the phone and pocketed it.

Now he was checking his gun and whistling. It was the first time she'd heard him whistle. She didn't like it. There was nothing cheerful about it.

He wasn't looking at her. His attention was fixed on the gun as he checked the clip. He didn't look up when she moved toward him, holding the knife casually down at her side, the blade tucked behind her.

It was a medium-sized steak knife, and she'd seen it lying among the dirty dishes in the sink. It had been hidden under her blouse throughout the phone call. She would have used it then, if he'd given her any chance, but his eyes had been on her the whole time. His scary yellow eyes.

God, she would love to put out the light in those eyes.

She didn't dare think of it. In a movie, sure, she could spring the knife on him and jam it into his heart. In real life, she knew it wouldn't work that way. He was fast and strong and wily. She couldn't kill him—at least not quickly enough to save herself. Even if she got in a good deep stab, he would have the strength and the rage to kill her before he collapsed.

But he would have to do it fast. That was what she was counting on. He couldn't let her linger, not if she hurt him badly enough.

He would kill her, but it would be quick. He wouldn't get to make her suffer. It was a sort of victory, the only one she could hope for.

Slowly, she withdrew the knife from under her shirt, holding it behind her. She was afraid the blade would catch the light and give her away, though there wasn't much light in the kitchen, only the dim glow of the bulbs in the canopies over the counters.

He still wasn't looking at her. He seemed fascinated by the gun. And still whistling. The tune was familiar, but she couldn't place it.

All that was left was for her to do it. She'd worked it out, choreographing it in her mind like a scene in the movie when she had to hit her marks.

But this scene would end with a cut to black.

She wished Kate were here. Not to help her, but just to tell her about God and heaven and all that stuff. She didn't buy into that stuff, but hearing about it—that would be good right now.

Well, Kate wasn't here. And who needed that bullshit, anyway? All she needed was the knife and the courage to take the first step. It was like stepping onstage before an audience. The first step was the hardest. After that, it was all instinct and training, and once she got going, she almost wouldn't hear the pounding of her heart.

She moved toward Swann. One step, then another, and she'd been right, it was like easing into a performance in front of the camera—her last performance, for an audience of one.

He still hadn't looked at her. A stupid thought surfaced—*you might really get away*—but instantly, she pushed it down. She wouldn't get away. That wasn't possible. Even to think about it was a distraction, a false hope. She had to stay focused.

She shambled closer to him. He popped the clip back into the gun and set the weapon down on the counter. He turned to her.

"Hey, sugarplum. Feeling ambulatory?"

He smiled. A strange smile of needs and wants.

She smiled back, and then the knife was out, flashing in the overhead light, the blade angled at his chest.

She drove it forward, aiming for his chest, but he was quick, so quick. He stepped aside, making it look easy, and grabbed her knife hand by the wrist. He held the weapon safely away from him.

"Stupid bitch," he said.

With a backhanded slap, he knocked her to her knees, and then he was on top of her on the tiled floor, the knife teasing her throat.

"We made a *deal*; we had an *agreement*. No more bullshit. No more games. And then you go pulling a stunt like this. God damn it, I ought to cut you. Cut you up good, like you wanted to cut me."

He let her think about that, then tossed the knife aside.

"But you wouldn't be so pretty after that. And I want you to stay pretty. For later."

His hand in his pocket, one of the syringes coming out.

"So I'll give you another dose. Just till you learn to mind your manners. After a while, you'll be docile as a lamb."

She thrashed and flailed. His knees ground into her hips, pinning her down.

Then her arm stiffened, pulled taut in his grasp, and he forced the needle in. A hot wire of pain seared her. She whipped her head from side to side, sobbing.

She didn't even notice when he pulled the needle free and flicked it away. He rose and left her on the floor. She pushed herself to a sitting position, supporting herself with one arm, and looked up at him.

"That'll hold you," he said.

Her elbow buckled and she fell sideways, sprawled on the floor. The tiles were glossy and cool. Her feet kicked.

"What's the matter, did it go to your head?"

She didn't answer, couldn't speak. It was as if she'd lost control of her body. She tried to flex her fingers. They didn't respond.

"Hey, what's wrong with you? Not going comatose on me, are you?"

He crouched, turned her onto her back. She felt his hand on her neck, taking her pulse.

"Christ. Think I topped off your tank a little too much."

Her feet wouldn't stop kicking. She still couldn't speak. But the words reached her.

Overdose, she thought.

Of course that was it. She always knew she would die of an OD. Like Mila.

But she didn't expect it to be like this.

"All right, sugarplum, stay with me." He fumbled in his pocket, took out a new syringe. "I've got the antidote right here. It worked before. It'll work again."

His words strange and echoey and far away.

"You're not going anywhere," Swann said, fiddling with the syringe, his fingers trembly, frantic.

But she *was* going somewhere. She was going away. Falling down a steep incline into a warm and comforting blackness.

"You hear me, kiddo? You hang the fuck on!"

She did hear him. But she wasn't listening, not anymore.

His shouts pursued her into the dark.

42

SAM took his time getting to San Fernando Road. He was in no hurry to meet up with Swann. And his phone hadn't rung yet, so he guessed Swann wasn't in much of a hurry himself.

Once or twice, he'd tested the rig worked up by that faggoty kid who worked for Malick. It functioned fine. He figured they were listening right now—Malick, the pair of techie queers, and Vicki—listening to the shallow in-out of his breathing.

The two bodyguards, he was told, had left a few minutes after he took off. They were behind him somewhere, at least a mile back. No use to him if he got in a scrape. But nobody cared about him. The only thing they cared about was their precious movie star.

It had always been like that, ever since his daughter's acting career took off. She was the money machine, the cash cow. She was important, and he was just some mooching piece of shit sucking on her momma's tit. Vicki kept him around out of habit, but she didn't love him. No one loved him. They all loved Chelsea, the whole world did, but no one gave a crap about him.

He wondered how much he really felt for his daughter. He knew he was supposed to feel all kinds of tender shit for her. Was supposed to be willing to take a bullet for her. And now maybe that was what he was doing.

But it didn't mean he had to like it.

The truth was, he sort of hated the little bitch. She'd been a pain in the ass her whole life, a deadweight dragging him down. He tried to get away from her by moving to Colorado, but she followed him there, showing up at his trailer one afternoon, smelly and disheveled after two days of thumbing rides. He hadn't known what the hell to do with her. He wasn't set up to deal with a kid. And then Swann started coming by and things got even more complicated…

Swann. It always came back to Swann. How many times had he wished he'd never met that bastard? Only every single day for the last ten years.

Now he was going to meet him again. For the last time—one way or the other.

His cell phone burred.

"Fuck," he whispered, knowing that the people in the house could hear him, and not giving a shit.

He flipped open the phone and answered the call, putting it on speaker as he'd been advised.

"Hey, Jack," he said, trying to sound friendly and unworried.

"Hello, Sam. Good to hear your voice again."

"Yours too." He hoped the lie wasn't too obvious. "I'm on San Fernando Road. Just passed Roxford Street. Coming up on Sierra Highway."

"Took you long enough, didn't it?"

"I'm a slow driver."

"I'm guessing it took a while to fix up whatever tracking device they're using."

"There's no tracking device."

"Sure there is. Your car's a Lexus. They have GPS built in."

"Yeah, but only the company can track it."

"And with all the technical know-how Sister Kate has at her disposal, she couldn't jury-rig a workaround? Don't bullshit me, Sam."

"I'm not."

"It's okay. Your baby girl's life is on the line. I expected you to play it safe. And I've got a little workaround of my own."

"Do you?"

"Get on Sierra Highway and go north for eight miles to Solemint Junction. That's where the highway crosses Soledad Canyon Road. A quarter mile past that intersection, you'll see a '97 Ford Mustang parked on the shoulder. The keys are under the floor mat of the driver's seat, but you'll have to crack a window with a rock or something to get in. I couldn't risk it being stolen. Okay?"

Sam listened, his mind running through the implications.

"You're going to park your Lexus and get out and take the Ford. Bring your phone and the valise. Turn around, get on Soledad Canyon Road, and head west into Canyon Country. I'll call again to tell you where to go from there. You got all that?"

"I got it," Sam said, licking his lips, which were suddenly too dry.

"Look forward to seeing you soon, old friend."

Swann clicked off. His last words—*old friend*—resonated in Sam's memory. There was nothing amiable about those words. They sounded like an epitaph.

He knows, Sam thought. *He knows I ratted on him. He has to know.*

"Sam"—Kate's voice, calm and soothing—"we heard all that. You're doing fine. Now, listen, this isn't a problem. We can still track you. We'll use your cell phone signal. Alan already set it up."

"Right," Sam said, barely listening.

Without the Lexus, they could track him only by the phone. And without the phone...

They couldn't track him at all.

He had two million dollars in jewelry in the valise, and in a few minutes, he would have an untraceable car. He could go anywhere. Start over. Buy himself a new life.

And Chelsea...well, Chelsea was shit out of luck. But since when was that his problem?

Fuck, it wasn't like he'd ever been in the running for Father of the Year.

———

Skip looked at Kate as they watched the moving blip that was Sam Brewer's Lexus. "You think he'll rabbit on us?"

"I don't know."

"Swann's just given him a way out. If he wants to take it..."

Kate looked at Victoria, sitting next to her at the computer. "You know him best. How will he play it?"

Victoria sat unmoving for a long moment, then closed her eyes. "He'll run," she whispered.

Kate got on the phone to Di Milo. "We think Sam's gone rogue. Swann's left him a second car, a Ford Mustang, and we're afraid he'll use it to take the ransom and go. He's making the switch just past the intersection of Sierra Highway and Soledad Canyon Road."

"On it," Di Milo said laconically.

Kate wanted to stand, to scream, to do anything, but she remained seated at the computer console. "There's no way to track him if he doesn't take his phone," she said, not really asking, since the answer was obvious.

Skip and Alan both shook their heads. "He'll be in the wind," Alan said, "unless Vince and Alfonse can intercept him in time."

"How far behind are they?"

"Last time I checked their position, they were hanging back by a mile and a half."

"I thought we said one mile, no more."

"San Fernando's a long, straight road. I guess they were playing it safe."

On the screen, the blip froze.

"He's parked," Alan said. "Just past Solemint Junction."

Kate tried reaching Sam on his set headset. "Sam, you there? Sam?"

No answer.

"How can he do this?" Victoria asked the silence. "How can he be like this?"

He had always been like this, Kate knew. Until now, Victoria hadn't allowed herself to see it. Denial—Sam had told her about that. *This is how she deals*, he'd said.

She resisted the urge to yell into the phone, demanding to know where the chase car was. She knew Di Milo was speeding to the site. He would be pushing the Skylark as fast as it would go.

But not fast enough. That was what terrified her. Not fast enough.

The speaker crackled with Di Milo's voice. "We're at the location. The Lexus is here and the cell phone's inside."

"And the Ford?" Kate asked helplessly.

"The Ford's gone. Brewer could have stayed on Sierra Highway, or taken Soledad Canyon, or the Antelope Valley Freeway, or any side street."

"We lost him," Alan said, sagging.

Kate shut her eyes. Yes, they'd lost him. And lost Chelsea, too.

43

VICTORIA fled from the room, retreating to the rear of the house. Kate heard a door slam.

Someone ought to console the woman, but there was no time. The situation wasn't hopeless, not yet.

"Vince, search the routes Sam could've taken. Try them one at a time. Look for the Ford. You could get lucky."

"Right," Di Milo said. If he thought it was a fool's errand, he kept his opinion to himself.

"Swann will call me when he realizes Sam is incommunicado," Kate was thinking aloud. "We'll have to renegotiate."

"Think he'll be open to that?" Alan sounded dubious.

"He has to be. He still wants his payment."

"Yeah, but there *is* no payment. Brewer took off with it."

"We can get more. Victoria can go back to the Rodeo Drive store, Étagère. She can replace all the items Sam stole."

"You think the store will let her run up that kind of tab? She's already in the hole for two mil."

"We'll find a way to convince them. If we can get Swann to agree to a new exchange."

"Who'll do that drop this time?"

"I will," Kate said firmly.

"That's not safe, chief. He hates you. He won't let you walk away."

"Vince and Alfonse will just have to get there fast enough to stop him."

She knew she was being reckless. But she couldn't give up now. They still had a chance to get Chelsea back. It had to work out. To lose her now, lose her for good…it would be like…would feel like…

Like the second time she'd lost a child.

Yes, she was still punishing herself for that. Maybe she always would.

We've all done things we're ashamed of, Victoria had said. *Some of us, a lot more recently.*

A curious thing to say. Still, whatever she was referring to, it couldn't have anything to do with the situation at hand. Could it?

She wondered. The tone of Victoria's voice when she made that comment…almost as if she'd been ready to share a secret of her own…

An irrelevant secret? Or one that mattered?

Kate decided to find out.

"Stay by the phone," she told Skip and Alan. "Let me know if the chase car spots the Ford."

She left the room and went down the hall to the rear of the house. Victoria had slammed a door, but none of the doors was closed. The woman seemed to have simply vanished, until Kate thought of looking on the deck.

Victoria was there, leaning on the railing, smoking a cigarette.

"Bad habit," she said as Kate came up to her. "I've tried to break it, but it doesn't matter now."

Kate stood next to her, looking out over the dark canyon that descended into a pit of gloom.

"He was never any good," Victoria went on. "I don't know why I stayed with him. It wasn't love." She drew another long drag on the cigarette. "Just another bad habit I couldn't break."

Kate decided to be direct. "You told me before that you'd done some things you aren't proud of. I had the impression you wanted to say something more about that."

"It's not important."

"Anything could be important. Is there something you've been hiding?"

"We all hide things." Her voice was hollow and flat.

She tried a different approach. "Swann got the list of jewelry from your insurance agent. How did he know who your insurance agent was?"

"What difference does that make?"

"And Swann knew Sam's cell phone number," Kate pressed. "That number has got to be unlisted."

"Yes. Yes, it is."

"How did Swann get that information?"

"I don't know."

"You must have household help."

"We have a housekeeper who comes in during the day."

"Have you ever seen her looking through your things? Maybe flipping through your address book or your mail or—"

"My address book."

"What is it?"

"No, nothing."

She moved away from the railing and made a slow circuit around the deck, circling the Jacuzzi.

"Victoria…"

"It can't be anything."

"Whatever it is, tell me."

"It's personal."

"Is it the thing you said you weren't proud of?"

"Yes."

"You have to tell me. It's for your daughter."

"Chelsea's lost. We'll never get her back."

Kate closed the distance between them and placed a hand on Victoria's arm. "We don't know that. Now, tell me. You *have* to tell me."

"Oh, all right. It's a trivial thing, really. I mean, everybody does it." She met Kate's gaze. "I've been seeing someone. For the past few months."

"All right," Kate said carefully.

"Sam doesn't know. Not that he would have cared, or would have any right to. We're not married anymore. He only stayed with me for the money. And the spotlight. He loves being photographed by the paparazzi. I can't stand them…"

"Victoria…" Trying to get her back on track.

"I met someone, and we started…sneaking around, I guess you could say. Meeting at a cheap motel, a real dive, the kind of place I would never go."

"What does this have to do with the address book?"

"Well, it does have Sam's cell number, of course. And my insurance agent's name and address."

"And?"

She pulled in more smoke from the cigarette, then expelled it in a rush of words. "One time in the motel, I used the john, and when I came out, I caught him by surprise. He'd taken the address book out of my handbag, and he was looking through it."

"I see."

"He said he was just checking to be sure his name wasn't listed there, since Sam might see it. I told him of course I wouldn't be that foolish. I was peeved at him. But that couldn't have anything to do with…anything. Could it?"

"Who is this man?"

"He couldn't possibly be involved. He's not a criminal, for God's sake."

"Who is he?"

Victoria almost took another drag, then impulsively stamped out the cigarette. "Oh, hell, I can tell you. It's Carson Banning. The movie star," she added, with a note of pride.

The deck seemed suddenly slippery. Kate felt herself losing her balance. She retreated to the railing and placed a hand there, holding on with a tight grip.

"Kate? What's the matter?"

Too many thoughts crowded in on her. His insistence on keeping their liaisons secret—for fear of the paparazzi, he said. But it was never about the paps. He didn't want Victoria to find out he'd been two-timing her.

Banning knew Daniel Farris. He'd bought a plane from him. The two had become friends. That was how Banning knew about Mila—information he'd passed on to Kate, because the Brewers hadn't wanted her, or anyone, to know.

And when he met her…

He'd just happened to be at the gun range she used for target practice. He struck up a conversation, charmed her. He was a pretty good actor. He made it seem casual and spontaneous, but it must have been planned.

He'd wanted to get close to her. To have an inside source of information on Chelsea's security.

What had she told him? In their brief, hurried liaisons, they'd chatted about work, and she'd said things—the guns her bodyguards carried, their procedure for checking in with home base…

Tonight, when she visited him at home and got Skip's phone call, he must have heard enough of her end of the conversation to know they were closing in on Swann.

Swann had left the church just before she arrived. Had Banning warned him she was on her way? Called him on his cell and told him to clear out?

"Kate?"

There was more, much more, but she couldn't think about it now.

"The motel where you met him," she asked, "where is it?"

"In Hollywood."

"What's the address?"

"The corner of Santa Monica and Vermont. It was easy to find. There's a billboard for Chelsea's last movie right across the street. Her last movie—God, I didn't mean it that way."

Kate remembered Swann's voice in her ear: *Have you seen the billboard for her last movie?*

"I have to go there," she said.

"But why? You don't really think…?"

"I think Banning and Swann are in it together. I don't know how it happened, or why. But Banning gave him inside information on you. And I'm guessing Swann has been to that same motel. Maybe he stayed there himself."

And saw the billboard every time he came and went.

I've looked at it plenty of times…

"Even if he did stay there," Victoria objected, "he's not there now."

"He could be, if he kept the room. He needs to hold Chelsea someplace, and with the church off-limits, he might have returned to the motel. Maybe that's why he's got her drugged—to keep her quiet."

It was a long shot, but it was also her only shot.

"Then I'll come with you," Victoria said.

"No."

"If there's any chance of finding her—"

"There's a chance of finding Swann, too."

"I'm not afraid of him."

Aren't you? Kate thought. *I am. Almost as afraid as Sam is—only, I'm not running away.*

44

SAM sped north on Sierra Highway, now a two-lane road coiling between rising escarpments. A warm, dry wind blew through the passenger window, which he'd shattered with a rock to unlock the door. Housing developments dotted the canyons and mountainsides, scattered lights in the darkness before dawn.

It goddamn floored him that he'd pulled it off. Even as he'd approached the abandoned Ford on the gravel shoulder, he had been sure it was a trap. Down on his belly, he'd peered under the car, half expecting Swann to be concealed beneath the chassis. After breaking the window, he'd inspected the interior, thinking Swann might be lying on the floor of the backseat. Keys in one hand, gun in the other, he'd even opened the trunk to be sure Swann wasn't curled up inside.

But the car had been clean. The engine had started on the first try. Since he'd left, his rearview mirror had showed no lights behind him.

Everything had worked out, and now he was racing past patches of desert scrub and rare stands of thirsty-looking trees, through a night so black he had to use his brights to pick his way through the sinuous curves.

He had no particular destination in mind. Vaguely, he thought about going to Vegas or losing himself in the mountains of Colorado, as he'd tried to do once before. In the longer run, he'd need to get out of the country. Mexico or Canada…or if he cashed in some of the jewels, maybe he could buy a plane ticket to some Caribbean paradise.

Of course, the law would be looking for him. He would need a fake ID, a new name, a change of appearance. But he could arrange all that. With money, he could arrange anything.

That was what people didn't understand. They wondered why he stayed with Vicki when she gave him no love and hardly any kindness. He was pretty sure that, lately, she'd been sneaking around with some other guy. Which made sense, because she sure wasn't getting any from him. It had been a year since he banged her—a quick, impulsive throw down after a drunken party. Neither of them spoke of it afterward.

So people looked at him and he could read the unstated question in their eyes. Why was he with her? Why didn't he up and get away?

It all came down to money. Without a steady stream of cash, he would be reduced to seeking employment, when he hadn't held an honest job in fifteen years. With his record and his lack of skills, he'd be lucky to find work as a dishwasher in a greasy spoon.

He could be rinsing the crud off people's plates—or hanging with his ex-wife in a mansion. The choice wasn't hard. Hell, it wasn't a choice at all.

But now he had money of his own. He was free and clear. He had outsmarted Swann and saved his own skin.

And Chelsea…

Fuck Chelsea. Even the nun said Swann wasn't going to give her back. And that half-assed plan to intercept Swann never would have worked. A couple of bodyguards would be no match for him in a gunfight. They would have been cut down like dogs in the street, and Sam with them, and Chelsea would have been no better off.

Besides, let's face it, Chelsea'd never been much of a daughter, anyway. Spoiled and headstrong, rebellious and smug. Now she would be Swann's plaything until he tired of her. Then he would cut her throat or put a bullet in her brain, and that would be that.

He supposed he ought to feel something about that outcome. The girl was his flesh, after all. He'd never loved her or even liked her much, but she was his progeny. There were blood ties. But there was no point in dwelling on it. She was finished, and he was free, and the rising road was carrying him to a new life.

He had left the developed area behind. The highway was climbing higher into the mountains, a tunnel of blackness, unrelieved by any light anywhere except his headlights, twin cones piercing the dark.

The Ford began to falter. The steering wheel tugged to the left, gently at first, then more insistently. The car was bumping even though the road surface was smooth.

Flat tire, he thought. *Shit.*

He eased the Ford to a stop on the shoulder. He stepped into the empty road to inspect the tires on the driver's side. As he suspected, the rear was losing air. He ran his hand over the treads and felt a nub of metal.

The tire had picked up a nail.

He opened the trunk, wrestled out the jack and the spare, and knelt by the car. He had most of the lug nuts off when he caught a glimmer of light on the road behind him.

A car, heading north.

It could be the bodyguards, looking for him.

He watched the car as it approached. Gradually, he relaxed. It wasn't the Buick Skylark the two Guardian Angel guys had been driving. It was some boxy foreign job. A Hyundai, it looked like.

Not a problem.

He loosened the last of the lugs. The Hyundai was drawing near; its high beams were brightening, erasing his night vision. Everything around him was turning bright white in the glare. It was like one of those sci-fi movies where the hero is caught in a nuclear blast and the screen goes white...

Too late, he realized the beams were targeted at him.

He spun in his crouch, trying to bring up the gun, but the car was already on top of him, the headlights in his face and the front end impacting his chest as the Hyundai sideswiped the parked Ford.

It all happened so slowly. He was flung up in the air, weightless, floating, his gun flying away in unreal slow motion, and then he descended, the pavement hard against his back as he hit the ground.

Abruptly, time sped up, the dream sequence over, and the car was barreling back toward him, but swerved at the last moment, mostly missing him, just catching his legs with one rear wheel and crushing the bones to powder.

The sudden crunch was the worst pain he'd known in his life. He tried to scream, but no sound would come.

A few yards away, the Hyundai rolled to a stop. It creaked, shifting on its shocks, and the driver's door opened, and Swann stepped out.

Of course it was Swann. That was no surprise.

Swann walked up to him, limping, one leg stiff. He had a pistol in his hand but showed no interest in using it.

Sam gritted his teeth and tried to lift himself to a sitting position, thinking dimly that he could retrieve his lost gun, make a fight of it, but his body wouldn't respond. His legs were ruined, and his chest felt caved in, and when he coughed, something warm and dark, like chocolate sauce, bubbled down his chin.

He gave up and lay on his back, breathing hard, shivering with pain, and looking up at the night sky, the swirl of stars.

Then Swann was there, looming over him, bigger than the constellations.

"Hey, buddy," Swann said.

Sam thought he should say something, but his mouth didn't work anymore.

"I know you fucked me over." Swann leaned closer. His voice was quiet, almost gentle. "Found out a while back that the feds had new intel on me. The stuff they knew—it had to come from someone I ran with in the old days. You or Bob or Giovanni. I thought it was Giovanni. I really didn't think it was you. We were always so close, you know?" He put his fingers together. "Simpatico."

Sam exhaled a bloody breath.

"So, not long ago, I went to Giovanni and got him talking. He told me about Bob, and where to find him. But I knew Bob hadn't snitched on me. Bob's a fucking retard. And Giovanni...well, he didn't snitch, either. The things I did to him...he would have told me if he had. He would have told me anything I wanted to know. Eventually, I let him die. He might not have snitched, but he was still a loose end that needed tying."

Swann moved out of sight, back up the road toward the Ford.

"So if it wasn't Bob and it wasn't Giovanni," he called back to Sam, "then bingo, it had to be you."

With effort, Sam turned his head sideways to see what Swann was doing. It was painful—every effort was painful—but he had to know.

Swann was crouched by the Ford, penknife in hand, digging the nail out of the tire.

"Remember this nail, Sammy boy? I pulled it out of Bob's skull just a little while ago. It's just itching to find a new home."

Then Sam found his voice, or a remnant of it, and he made a strange sound.

"Aww…"

A soft, pitiful sound, the sound a kid would make when the ice cream dropped out of his cone.

"Aww…"

He didn't know why he was making that goddamn sound. He wished he would stop.

Swann had worked the nail free. He returned to Sam, whistling. He knelt beside him, and he smiled.

"The thing is, Sam, I'm always three steps ahead. People keep forgetting that."

Sam shut his eyes. He didn't want to hear any more. He wanted to go away, just go away forever, anywhere—to hell, even—anywhere, as long as it was far away from Swann.

Then he felt a hand on his face, and against his will, his eyes opened. Swann was still there, crouched by his side, twirling the nail between his fingertips. It was rusty and dark with old blood.

"I went easy on Bob," Swann said. "He only stole a sandwich. But you, old friend…I'm not going easy on you at all."

45

WITH effort, Kate made Victoria understand she wasn't invited to the motel. But that left a problem. She didn't have a car of her own. To get there, she asked to borrow Skip's Mazda RX-8.

"No one drives my car except me," Skip said obstinately.

"So will you drive me someplace right now?"

"Is it dangerous?"

It could be, but Skip didn't need to know that. "No."

"Then I'm your man."

She left Alan at the house to monitor the chase car's progress. So far they'd seen no sign of the Ford.

She said nothing to Skip during the fast trip from the Brewers' house to Hollywood. She felt antsy, uncomfortable without her Glock, especially knowing James was still out there. He'd managed to follow her even to the church. He could be following her now.

She frowned. *How* had he tailed her to the church, anyway? She'd gone there after the car crash. She hadn't noticed any pursuit, and she was looking for it.

And if he'd been shadowing her, why hadn't he tried to take her out when she was wounded and unconscious or when she was walking alone in the deserted streets?

It seemed more likely that he'd been scared off by the police after the episode beneath the overpass. That he hadn't followed her immediately afterward.

Yet he must have, or he couldn't have known she would end up at the church. No one knew she was going there, except the people she was working with.

No. Wrong. There was one other person who knew, if her suspicions were correct.

Carson Banning might have overheard enough of her conversation to warn Swann. If so, Banning knew she was headed to Swann's hideout.

Banning could have gone to the church after she left his house. Could have waited in the alley, hoping she would show up alone.

She thought back to their conversation in his house. He hadn't pressed her for the location of the overpass. Maybe because he didn't need to. Because he already knew. Because he'd been there.

Closing in on her from the shadows. Laughing at her in the dark.

She shut her eyes. She let it sink in slowly—the truth, the obviousness of it, and how wrong she'd been.

Banning had been her stalker all along. Not James. Never James.

It was no coincidence that he had chosen tonight of all nights to go into killing mode. He'd picked tonight because he couldn't wait any longer. He had to be worried that Kate would learn of his affair with Victoria; in combination with his friendship with

Farris, it was all she needed to start putting it together. But if she were out of the way, his worries would be over.

He'd covered his trail as best he could. Disguising his voice in phone messages so she wouldn't identify him. Setting up the storyline of an anonymous stalker so her murder investigation would be on the wrong track from the start.

But why not kill her in the limo tonight, or in his house? He must have wanted to do the job in the streets, where there could be no possible connection to him. Shadowing her as she navigated the city, he expected to have his chance before long.

She'd called his home number after leaving the overpass. The call must have been forwarded to his cell. The caller ID would have shown him who was on the line. He'd faked grogginess and surprise, then sped home to throw on a robe before she arrived.

But when she'd showed him Amber's charm bracelet, his reaction had been real. He'd been genuinely moved. She had seen it in his face, and he wasn't *that* good an actor.

After being scared off at the church, he'd switched his focus to his daughter. He didn't expect Kate to go out alone again tonight, and the bracelet gave him his first solid lead to Amber's whereabouts. Amber became his priority. After all, he couldn't know Victoria would reveal their affair tonight. He expected to have more time.

He had no idea his cover had been blown.

He still thought he could get away with killing her.

Suddenly, she wanted to talk to him. Not to let him know she was on to him. If he knew, he might run for it, and she wanted him caught.

No, she just wanted to hear his voice. His lying words.

She called Banning's cell. She wasn't surprised when he answered, wide awake, on the first ring.

"I hear you're out looking for her," Kate said.

There was a beat of hesitation. Then he gave in. "How'd you know?"

"Georgia."

"Right. I couldn't very well ask her to keep it secret from you, since I had told her you sent me there."

"I should have realized you wouldn't leave it alone."

"It's her bracelet. She's close. I can find her."

"How, Carson, if she doesn't want to be found?"

"I'm handing out bribes to everyone on the street. Getting some info."

"That's not very safe. They could jump you for the money."

"I'm armed."

Of course you are, she thought. "You're still taking an awful chance."

"She's my kid."

"I understand. Good luck. I hope you find her."

She meant it. There would be time to deal with Carson Banning later. For now, she wanted him to rescue Amber. His daughter was an innocent. She deserved to survive.

She ended the call and put the phone away, feeling unsatisfied. Part of her had wanted a confrontation, a demand for information. But there was nothing he could tell her. Though he'd known about the church, it was unlikely he knew where Swann had relocated. Even if he did know, he couldn't say anything without incriminating himself.

They neared the motel. Kate looked at Skip, who had said nothing throughout the drive. "You're quiet."

"Just thinking."

"About Chelsea?"

"No. Well, yeah. I guess I am. What will happen to her?"

"We'll get her back."

"Yeah, but if we don't…"

"He'll keep her doped up until he's established full control over her. Once she's thoroughly brainwashed, he'll take her off the drugs. And she'll be his slave."

"But she's famous. It's not like he can hide her anywhere."

"He's got a place in mind. Even in today's world, there are places where no one has heard of Chelsea Brewer." She frowned. "What's it to you, anyway? She's just another contestant in the game you run. Just pixels on a screen."

"You're doing your best to make me feel bad about myself, aren't you?"

"You bet."

"Good job," Skip said softly.

He pulled up at the motel and got out when Kate did.

"So you think Swann was staying here?"

Kate glanced at the billboard looming over the street, Chelsea's face huge and luminous. The sign would be visible from any of the front rooms. "Yes."

"But he's not here now?"

"Probably not."

"Probably? I thought you said this wasn't dangerous."

"I lied. Wait in the car if you're scared."

"Didn't say I was scared. I'd just appreciate a little heads-up, is all. So how are we going to know what room he was in?"

"Bribery." She entered the small, rancid office and rang the bell until a sleepy-eyed desk clerk stumbled out of a back room. His hair was matted and askew, and his breath was foul.

"What can I do you for?" he asked with a yawn.

"Have you seen this man?"

Alan had transferred the memory card from her old phone to her new one. Swann's photo was on it. She showed the clerk the picture. Skip took a look, too, craning his neck over her shoulder.

The clerk's face closed up. "Nope."

"He's lying," Skip said.

Kate already knew that. "This man kidnapped a young woman earlier this evening. We believe he's been staying at this motel. Now, take another look and tell me if you've seen him."

"You cops?"

"We're private security operatives," Kate said, stretching the truth to include Skip.

"Well, I don't gotta cooperate with no private operatives." He put a contemptuous emphasis on the last word.

She flashed a fifty-dollar bill. "We can make it worth your while."

"Lady, I'm not for sale."

Sure he wasn't. "How about if I double the price? A hundred bucks if you tell me what room he took."

"Make it two hundred."

She would have paid a thousand, but it seemed important to establish herself as a tough negotiator. "A hundred's my top offer. I can pay you, or I can bring in the police and you'll answer their questions for free."

"Okay. Lemme have it."

"First, give me his room number."

"He ain't here no more. He checked out around eight. Start of my shift."

"You work all night?"

"Twelve hours. Eight to eight."

Sleeping through most of it, Kate thought. "I still want to know which room he used. And I want to search it."

"It's already occupied. By someone new."

"They paying by the day or by the hour?"

"Hey, this ain't that kind of establishment."

"When did the new people check in?"

"Not long ago," the clerk admitted.

"After four in the morning? So it's by the hour, then."

"I don't ask questions."

"Just tell us the room number. We'll handle the rest."

"The money." He extended a hand.

Kate lifted it almost within his reach but hung on to the cash. It was a childish contest of wills, but one she intended to win.

"Oh, hell. It was room seventeen B. He had it for like a month, maybe more."

She gave up the money. He snatched it out of her hand and stuffed it into his pants pocket in guilty haste.

Kate moved toward the office door, then stopped. "Did he ever give you a name?" Knowing his alias might be useful in tracking him down.

"It's not like we keep a registry."

"He didn't use a credit card or write a check?"

"Cash only. That's how he paid. Regular as clockwork. Scared the shit outta me," he added as an afterthought.

"Did he? Why?"

His thin shoulders lifted. "Some guys, they just give off that vibe, you know. That stone-cold killer vibe."

"Yes," Kate said. "I know."

She left with Skip and hurried down the outside walkway. Along the way, Skip asked what was the point of entering the room when Swann was already gone.

"People leave things behind," Kate said. "People make mistakes."

"Not this guy."

"Yes. Even him."

Through the thin door of 17B, groans and laughter could be heard—a man's groans, a woman's laughter. Kate banged on the door and kept pounding until it eased open, a pale man in disheveled clothes glaring out. "What the fuck's going on out here?"

"You need to vacate the premises."

"I paid for this room."

"It's a crime scene. I was sent ahead to secure it. In about five minutes SID is going to be here along with two dozen officers. If you're still hanging around, they'll have questions for you. And"— Kate glanced past him at a naked brunette who appeared to be fifteen years old—"for your *wife.*"

The man swallowed. "I don't think we want to get involved in that."

"Then clear out."

The two of them were gone within thirty seconds, leaving Skip and Kate alone in the room.

"That was awesome," Skip said. "You totally socially engineered his ass."

"Search the drawers, the closet, and wastebaskets. Look for anything Swann might have left behind."

"You don't think the maid would have cleaned it up?"

"I'm guessing this place doesn't put a high priority on maid service."

She pulled open the drawers of a bureau, starting with the bottom drawer and working upward, the most efficient approach. One of many things Barney had taught her.

There was nothing in the bureau or in the nightstand. She checked the pad by the phone, hoping to find a note left by Swann, or even an impression of his handwriting on the paper, but the pad was brand new and unused. She thought about trying redial on the phone, but the line was dead.

"Anything?" she asked Skip.

"Not even a Gideon Bible."

"Wastebaskets?"

"Empty except for a condom wrapper. The bathroom looks pretty spic 'n' span. Unless Swann is the ultimate neat freak, I think a maid *was* here."

Kate glanced into the bathroom and saw that the sink and toilet had been wiped down.

"You're right. The maid came in after Swann checked out. She gave the place a once-over and emptied the wastebaskets." Bending, she picked up a hank of hair under the sink. "Must have swept up, too. Swann shaved himself bald and probably left hair all over the floor, so they had to clean the room."

"Then we're shit out of luck."

"Not necessarily."

Kate left the room and went around to the trash bins at the back of the motel.

"Dumpster diving?" Skip said dubiously. "Really?"

"It might be our only shot."

"How will we even know which trash is from seventeen B?"

"We won't. We'll have to look through it all."

She was about to hoist herself into the nearest bin when a small voice said, "Excuse me."

Kate looked over and saw a slender, dark-haired figure at the entrance to the alley. The underage hooker from the motel room. Her face was scared and serious, and her small hands fidgeted with her oversized handbag.

"Yes?" Kate said, her voice gentle, as if she were facing a frightened fawn and didn't want to scare it away.

"You're the *policia*, no?"

"That's right." Kate hoped the girl wouldn't ask to see her ID.

"You're here about the man who was in there."

"Yes." Kate showed her the photo. "This man."

The girl drew back with a flinch of recognition. "I knew it must be about him. That one, he is crazy. He made me…do things."

"What things?"

"He made me cut him. He had this razor blade. He has scars all over. He likes to be cut. He likes the blood."

"Shit," Skip murmured.

"When was this?" Kate asked.

"About…um…six o'clock. He scared me. When I tried to leave, he stopped me and I thought he would cut me then. But he only wanted to pay me extra. He said I was a good girl and I helped him stay awake."

"Stay awake?"

"That's what he said. It was a funny thing to say because it was still early. Nobody gets sleepy at six o'clock at night."

"So he paid you extra?"

She nodded. "He pulled on his pants and grabbed some money out of the pocket and put it into my hand." She reached into her handbag. "Mixed in with the money…I found this."

She took out a small, creased scrap of paper, worn and curling at the edges. A telephone number with a 213 code was written in pencil in a neat, careful hand.

"He didn't mean to give it to me. Maybe it can help you?"

"Maybe it can. Thank you."

"This man—he should not be on the street. He should be locked up. Like an animal."

"We'll see that he is," Kate promised.

She called Alan and had him run the number through an online reverse directory. "Will do, chief," he said in a low voice.

"Why are you whispering?"

"Because the police are here."

"What?"

"They pegged you as the owner of a smashed-up Jaguar involved in a hit-and-run. Guess they found the car at the diner where you dumped it. They linked it to the crash somehow. They know you were here at the Brewer house earlier, because those other cops saw you and filed a report. Now there's a bunch of new guys here, plainclothes and uniform, and they are *very* eager to talk to you."

"I don't have time to talk."

"Mrs. Brewer's got them distracted, but I don't know how long she can keep it up. We haven't told them what's going on, but I think they're starting to figure it out. They're talking about putting out a BOLO or an APB or whatever it is."

"On me?"

"You fled the scene. That's a crime. One guy was shot in his apartment and another guy was shot in the street. It's kind of a big deal."

"What's the condition of the victims?"

"The carjack vic is dead. The apartment guy is expected to pull through. What do I say to the police?"

"Hell, just stall them. You have no idea where I am or how to reach me."

"I told them that. They're not buying it."

"Then tell them I went to the motel. I won't be here much longer, and they won't be able to trace me from this location."

"That could buy some time, but…you're getting in pretty deep, chief."

"I was already in deep. Have you run the number?"

"Yeah, it comes back to Giovanni's Trattoria. Italian restaurant downtown. Maybe Swann just liked the food there."

Kate shook her head. "Sam said one of their former associates was named Giovanni. Give me the address."

Alan rattled it off. The restaurant was on Crocker in downtown LA, south of Little Tokyo. "If you think Swann's holed up there," Alan said, "you can't go in alone."

"I'm not alone. I'm with Mr. Slater."

"That doesn't count."

"Point taken. But if Swann was ever there, he's probably not hanging around now. Anyway, I've got to check it out. Any word from the chase car?"

"They're still looking. Uh-oh, the cops are coming my way. Gotta go."

Kate ran for the car, Skip jogging after her. "So now we're breaking into some restaurant?" he asked when she filled him in.

"Just me. I'll go in, and you wait outside in the car and watch the place."

"Sounds kind of pussy."

"I'll need a lookout. If Swann ever was using this location, he might come back."

"Okay." He slipped behind the wheel. "Do I understand the police are after you? So, basically, we're on the run from the law?"

She slid in beside him. "As an anarchist, you should have no problem with that."

"Anarcho-libertarian," Skip said morosely as he shifted the Mazda into drive and tore away from the curb.

46

SWANN sped east on the Antelope Valley Freeway, the valise on the Ford's passenger seat rattling softly. It was the sound of money, and he liked it.

He'd given Sam Brewer a good death. The injuries sustained in the collision had killed him a little faster than Swann had hoped, but not before the nail went into his temple, shorting out whatever part of the brain was hooked up to the optic nerves. Sam died blind, his eyes rolling in panic, his hands waving at the darkness around him.

To make his last moments extra special, Swann broke his fingers one at a time and snapped his wrists. He was setting to work on Sam's privates when the man expired with a moan.

He lay there now on the side of the road, near the abandoned Hyundai. The Ford was safer to drive. There was probably an APB out on the Hyundai, but no one would be looking for the Ford except Kate Malick's people, and Swann would soon be far outside their range.

He was smarter than the nun. He was smarter than everybody. He had no problem acknowledging it. Humility was for sheep, not wolves.

His strategy, multilayered and complex, had come off with barely a hitch. He had worked it all out like a chess match. People were easy to manipulate, as easy to move as pawns on a board.

Chelsea's life wasn't the only one he held in his hands. He was God. He had the whole world in his hands.

From Sierra Highway, he had cut east, hooking up with the freeway, which would take him to Palmdale. There, he would shoot due east, eventually connecting with Interstate 15, which would take him south to San Diego. He would cross the border off-road in the desert, and then he would be in Mexico.

With the girl.

He glanced behind him at the Ford's backseat, where she lay unconscious. He had transferred her from the Hyundai to the Ford before taking off.

He worried about the girl. Her condition remained dicey. In the restaurant, he'd given her some of the GHB antagonist, and it had roused her a little, but maybe not enough. He was reluctant to give her more. He couldn't have her fully awake, or she would be too hard to control. Her stunt with the kitchen knife had proved that much.

It was a balancing act—he wanted her alive but not alert, unconscious but not comatose. He would have to monitor her throughout the drive.

She was causing him a lot of trouble, more than he'd anticipated, but he wasn't giving up on her. He wanted her to live. He had plans for her. In the small town in Mexico where no one would know them, she would become his bride. They would spend months together, even years. And when he tired of her—he always tired of women, eventually—then he would market her to the highest bidder. A movie star would be worth big bucks to qualified buyers. The price he'd get would ensure a pleasant retirement.

Meanwhile, they would have good times, the two of them. She would serve him, slave for him, cook and clean and tend to his physical needs. And sing. Yes.

He liked to hear her sing…

Swann grinned, contemplating his future, but the grin faded when he caught headlights in his rearview mirror, closing fast.

———

Grange and Di Milo had spent the past half hour prowling the roads that branched out from Solemint Junction. Now they were eastbound on the Antelope Valley Freeway, bearing down on a Ford Mustang.

"Think it's him?" Grange asked, holding the Glock that belonged to his boss.

Di Milo, economical with speech as always, merely shrugged.

If it was Sam Brewer, he hadn't made very good time. He should have been miles farther away. But things could happen. Car trouble, second thoughts, or simply getting lost on unfamiliar roads.

"It could be him," Grange said. "Fucking asshole abandons his own kid."

Di Milo still had no comment. He kept his foot on the gas, the Skylark narrowing the distance to its quarry.

"He won't want to pull over." Grange rolled down his window, letting in the cool predawn air. "We may have to persuade him."

Di Milo drew his weapon.

"He was armed when he went to the drop-off," Grange added. Kate had told him so.

Di Milo nodded.

Grange leaned forward as the Skylark eased into the fast lane, pulling up on the driver's side of the Ford. He strained for a view of the figure behind the wheel.

Then the two cars were side by side, and the man in the Ford turned to them, a bald man with a hard face, the man who'd taunted Grange at the bar and beaten him unconscious in the restroom.

"It's *Swann*!" Grange shouted, and purple muzzle flashes flared as the Ford's driver opened fire.

Grange took a round in the face and felt the sting in his cheek and grinding pain in the jaw. He shot back wildly, unable to aim because his vision had gone double.

Di Milo shoved him back against the headrest, out of the way, and squeezed off four rounds in quick succession, and the Ford slewed, the driver hit but not killed, still firing back, a drumroll of bullets punching through the Skylark's door, crumbling the windshield, blowing the side mirror apart.

The Skylark lost speed, drifting behind the Ford and veering toward the shoulder. Grange tried to focus his eyes. He saw Di Milo slumped forward in his seat, blood all over him, the car driverless. Grange grabbed the wheel and tried to steer, but not in time to prevent the car from plowing into a utility pole that smashed the front end and left the engine smoking under the hood.

The Ford had passed them now. Grange looked at the taillights, seeing four of them, two Fords. As he watched, both cars slowed, easing onto the shoulder, then reversed, coming back.

He had to defend himself, but his gun—Kate's Glock—was gone. It had fallen out of his hand and was lost somewhere, maybe out the window, maybe under his seat. But Di Milo's Beretta was still in his hand, clutched tight in a death grip. Grange pried it loose.

The Ford pulled to a stop a few yards away, the taillights red like devil's eyes, burning holes in Grange's vision. His eyes watered. His mouth was on fire. He thought his jaw must have been dislocated or broken. The gun shook as he raised it in both hands, aiming through the glassless windshield.

Fuck you, Swann, he thought. He would have screamed the words if he'd been able to open his mouth.

The Ford's door swung open and Swann stepped out. He stood there, an easy target if there had been only one of him.

There were two. Grange fired at the man on the right. Three shots, snapped off fast and sure, but the man didn't go down.

The one on the left, then. That was the real Swann.

He fired two more shots and the Beretta was empty, and still Swann hadn't fallen.

He needed to reload. Kate had given him a spare magazine for the Glock. It wasn't compatible with the Beretta, but both guns shot the same ammunition. He could transfer the rounds from the Glock's clip to the Beretta's.

If he could find the clip. It was in his pocket, but which pocket? He couldn't remember. He patted himself down, searching.

He'd rehearsed this situation a thousand times. He'd lived it in his dreams. Now the real test was here, and he was flunking.

Swann approached the car, walking slowly, his steps unsteady. He looked hurt.

Grange found the Glock's twelve-round magazine in the left pocket of his jacket. He ejected the used clip from the Beretta, then thumbed the insert on the Glock's mag and dumped the fresh cartridges into his lap. He needed them in the Beretta's clip, but he couldn't seem to load the damn things. His fingers were trembling and slippery with blood. He didn't even know where the blood had come from. He hadn't been shot in the hand, only in the face, but he must have touched his face without realizing it, and now the rounds kept sliding out of his grasp as he tried to feed them into the mag.

Swann's footsteps slapped the asphalt. Almost there.

Forget the clip. Just put one round in the chamber. One round would be enough. He needed only one shot at this range.

He locked back the Beretta's slide and tried to insert a single cartridge. It squirted out of his hand and into his lap. He tried to pick it up and succeeded only in spilling all the rounds onto the floor between his feet.

God *damn* it.

He groped on the floor, searching for a cartridge, found one, picked it up.

Then Swann was at the window, leaning in, his gun against the bandage that wrapped Grange's skull.

"Should've stayed out on sick leave, asshole," Swann said, and he pulled the trigger.

———

Swann made it back to his car without falling, but just barely. He dropped into the driver's seat and pulled up his shirt to assess the damage.

He'd been hit twice in the upper body. One bullet had gone clean through the flesh of his armpit on the left side; he found an exit wound. The second had caught him in the ribs, and it was still in him. It had fractured a rib, definitely. If it had tumbled or fragmented, it might have done other harm as well.

He felt numbness in his right calf and lifted his pants leg. He'd been struck there, too. His sock was soggy and dark, and he could feel his shoe filling with blood.

"Shit," he muttered. Maybe he'd spent a little too much time killing Sam. But he hadn't expected Malick's apes to catch up with him. The saving grace was that they weren't expecting him in the car. He'd seen the surprise on their faces when they'd pulled alongside. They must have thought he was Sam. It was the only reason he'd been able to get the jump on them.

The armpit and the leg didn't matter. Both were bleeding badly, but pressure would close up the wounds. The round in his rib cage was a different story. No telling where that fucker had ended up. It could be a half inch from his heart, ready to nick the aorta if it shifted a fraction.

Even so, he'd have to risk leaving the bullet inside him until he got to Cabo San Lucas. He knew a doctor there who would patch him up.

But he sure as shit wasn't driving all way to Cabo in this condition. He needed to clean out the bullet holes, pour on some disinfectant, apply bandages.

Giovanni's restaurant had all that first aid shit. He'd seen it in the supply closet. And no one would be there, not even the cleaning staff; the place had been closed since its owner's tragic demise. He could wash himself in the sink, then repair the damage on a temporary basis. After that, head south to Mexico with...

Chelsea.

In sudden alarm, he turned in his seat, ignoring a new shout of pain from his ribs, and reached out to the girl. She was still unconscious. He ran his hands over her body, checking for damage.

There was none. No shots had penetrated the Ford's rear compartment.

"You're okay," Swann breathed in relief. "You're just fine, sugarplum."

She stirred briefly, murmuring, but her eyes stayed shut.

If Malick's goons had killed the girl, he would have hunted down the nun and tortured her slowly, done worse things to her than he'd done to Sam. Hell, he'd like to do it anyway. He would, if he was ever lucky enough to run into her again.

Swann slipped behind the wheel and racked the gearshift into drive. He sped back onto the freeway, looking for the next exit, one that would take him back to LA and Giovanni's.

47

EN ROUTE to Giovanni's Trattoria, Kate got a call from Alan. The police had left for the motel. "You need to be gone from there."

"Already am."

"Good. Look, there's another problem."

How could there be? It seemed impossible that anything else could go wrong. "What problem?"

"I've lost touch with the chase car. Di Milo's not answering his cell. I don't know where the hell they are or what's happened to them."

"Maybe his phone conked out. Or they're in a no-coverage zone."

"Yeah. Maybe."

"If you hear from them, let me know."

"Right, chief."

She closed the phone. Skip looked at her. "It's all falling apart, isn't it?" he asked simply.

She wanted to deliver some brave reply, but she didn't have the strength. "Looks that way." She rallied. "But we can still make it work. When I hear from Swann—"

"What makes you think you'll hear from him? He's gotta know Sam's incommunicado by now. If he was going to call, he would've done it already."

"He may be planning his next move."

"I have a feeling he already planned all his moves."

"Meaning?"

"This guy's sharp, right? He *knows* Sam. And he made sure we knew his identity. He didn't use an alias or anything. He came right out and said he was Jack Swann."

"So?"

"So don't you think he could anticipate how Sam would react? We thought Sam might cut and run. I'm guessing Swann thought so, too."

"You're saying he wanted Sam to take off? But then he…"

He wouldn't get his payment, she almost said, but the words died unspoken. Because of course he would get his payment. He had it all worked out.

"It was a trick," she whispered. "He knew we'd be tracking Sam, so he got him to lose his pursuit."

"That's what I'm thinking. Of course, he might not be that smart."

"He is, though." Kate felt a great heaviness settle inside her, the beginning of a long and fruitless grief. "He won't call. He's already got the money and Chelsea, and he's probably killed Sam, too. He's got everything he wanted. He's won. And we"—tears misted her field of vision—"we've lost Chelsea for good."

Skip said nothing. Neither did she.

It was over.

There was nothing left to do except go through the motions. But she would do that much. And keep hoping for a miracle, even if she didn't believe in miracles and never had.

Half a block from Giovanni's, she had Skip pull over at the curb. The spot gave him a good vantage point on the location.

"How are you going to get in?" he asked.

She hadn't thought about it. It didn't seem to matter. "I'll improvise."

She approached the front of the restaurant. A CLOSED sign sat in the window, held in place by a curtain. The street was dark, but a pale glimmer to the east hinted at dawn. Or maybe it was only the glow of the city lights. Maybe there would be no dawn today.

No lights were lit inside Giovanni's. The front door was locked, and all the windows were shut.

An alley led around the side of the building to a back door. Near the door was a high window. In a pile of trash, she found an apple crate. She dragged it to the window, stood it on its side, mounted the crate, and punched a hole in the window with her elbow, the jacket protecting her arm. It felt good to smash something.

With her sleeve tucked over her hand, she brushed away the shards clinging to the frame, then climbed through, dropping to the floor. Her eyesight took a moment to adjust to the darkness. She was in the kitchen. A white countertop gleamed like bone in the faint ambient light. Pots and saucepans hung from hooks.

She made a quick pass through the kitchen, glancing into the main dining area. Rows of tables, upended chairs stacked on top.

No one was here. She returned to the kitchen, found a wall switch, and turned on the lights.

On the floor were two syringes like the one she'd found at the church.

Swann had been here, then. With Chelsea.

She looked around hopelessly for some clue to where he might have taken her from here. There was nothing, of course.

Dead end. Swann was gone and he'd taken Chelsea, and she would never see either of them again.

Her phone rang, startling her. The ringtone was still "Lady Madonna." Alan had taken the time to program it into her replacement phone. She wished he hadn't. The song was too cheerful, and she wasn't in the mood.

"Yes?" she said wearily, expecting an update from Alan, but it was Skip's voice she heard.

"Ford Mustang just pulled into the alley and I think Swann's driving!"

Her heart kicked, and she heard the slam of a car door outside the kitchen.

She reached for her Glock, then remembered Grange had it.

Footsteps crunched, moving fast. He must have seen the crate, the broken window. He knew someone had entered.

A key turned in the lock. He was coming in, and she was trapped in the restaurant—and unarmed.

48

SWANN saw the busted window and the crate beneath it as soon as he pulled up. Before leaving the car, he ejected the clip from his handgun and heeled in a fresh one, another eight rounds. He left the unconscious girl in the back of the car and the valise stuffed with jewels on the passenger seat. He would return for both items after the nun was dead.

Because of course it was the nun. Who else could it be? She'd been dogging his tracks all night. She'd traced him to the church and now here. He only hoped she was still inside.

She would be armed, and he could be walking into a trap, but his blood was up and he wasn't in the mood for caution. He unlocked the kitchen door and threw it wide and entered shooting. He squeezed off four rounds in quick succession, laying down a field of fire as he spun out of the doorway and crouched down.

She wasn't there. The kitchen was empty, but the double doors to the main dining room were flapping gently. She'd gone through there a moment before he entered.

He pursued, moving fast, his gun leading him. It was a 9mm Makarov, East German made, a good no-nonsense firearm. It had killed Daniel Farris and the two Guardian Angel goons, and the Hyundai's driver and maybe the old man in the apartment near Seventh Street as well.

Funny how pain and exhaustion bled away from him, vanishing like an illusion. He was on the hunt, seeking prey, no distractions.

He kicked open the double doors and stepped back, expecting the noise to draw her fire, but nothing happened. She was playing it cool. All right, then. He blew through the doors, snapping off four more rounds that lit up the gloom, then pivoted and sunk into a crouch by the long bar that ran along the rear of the room. He dumped the empty magazine and rammed in a new one.

He doubted he'd hit her, but the racket and muzzle flashes had to have her rattled. She'd never been in a firefight. He wanted her shaky, wanted her to make a mistake.

He let his eyes adjust to the darkness. A big room, carpeted, filled with a checkerboard array of tables. She'd be under one of them. Probably along the right-hand wall, the one nearest to the double doors. She would have wanted to take cover fast.

Silently, he made his way to the left side of the room. He would circle around, close in on her from behind. It was a move she wouldn't expect. The key was to move without sound, camouflaged by darkness. He knew how it was done. He'd crept up on people better armed and more battle-tested than Kate Malick, and they never heard a thing.

He reached the front wall of the room, where heavy curtains blotted out the windows. Outside, there was a faint stir of traffic as the city woke up. Nearly daybreak of his last day in Los Angeles, and Kate Malick's last day anywhere.

He'd told her not to fuck with him. He'd *ordered* her. She'd taken a vow of obedience as a nun. So why wouldn't she obey? He was her god now. He'd made that clear. Still she insisted on breaking the rules, hunting him down, playing her stupid games. She had to die for it, and die slowly.

He saw her.

She knelt behind a table by the far wall, her head darting in quick, nervous jerks as she watched the room. She was studying the area around the bar, obviously having lost sight of him there.

She wasn't looking behind her. She had no idea where he was.

He settled into a half crouch, leveling the gun as he centered her shoulders above the sights. He was applying gentle pressure to the trigger when she shifted her position, her back suddenly hidden behind a table leg.

He could still take her out with a head shot, but he wanted a nonfatal hit. Wanted her down but not out so he could take his time finishing her. There were knives and other implements in the kitchen. Many ways to inflict pain.

He took a long sliding step to bring the target into view.

A floorboard creaked under his shoe.

She heard the noise, and suddenly, she wasn't there anymore. She snapped forward, diving deeper under the table and scrambling out the other side, and she was gone. It happened so fast he had no time to take a shot.

He ducked low and covered a few yards of floor space in case she decided to shoot at his position.

She didn't. He began to wonder why she hadn't fired. She could have tried to nail him when he came in from the alley or when he entered the dining room. She'd had another opportunity just now. Maybe she had inhuman patience, or maybe, just maybe, she didn't have a gun at all.

Though he'd missed his chance at an easy shot, he still had an edge. He'd killed before. He knew how it was done.

She couldn't have scampered far. She was still on this side of the room, huddled under one of the tables. Eight tables in all. Eight hiding places. He would scope out each one in turn, while maintaining concealment so she couldn't pick him off.

If she was armed. If not, she was all done anyway.

He prowled past the table she'd abandoned and took a long look at the next two in line. When he was satisfied she wasn't there, he moved on to the next pair, and the next. He worked his way to the rear of the room, finding nothing.

Where was she, then? Behind the bar. She had to be.

It was a smart move. She could hunker down, lie in wait for him. She would have the advantage of cover and concealment in a defensive position, while he would have to risk showing himself.

Clever—but there was a flaw in her plan. The back of the bar was stacked with bottles. All he had to do was open fire and blow a storm of glass onto her, then close in while she was dazed and bleeding. With luck, he could take her alive, and then the real fun would start.

He took a step forward, and there was music.

A cell phone ringtone. Behind him.

He didn't know how in hell she'd backtracked to that part of the room, but he spun, pinpointing the source of the noise—a table three rows back—and his finger jerked the trigger again and again, splintering the table legs until the flat surface listed sideways and hit the floor.

Bent double, he advanced on what was left of the table. His ears were ringing and his night vision had been compromised by muzzle flares, but he could function well enough. Better than the nun, who had to be wounded or dead.

He reached the table and scanned the area, looking for a body. There was none. And that goddamned phone kept chirping—he could hear it over the chiming in his ears.

He found it on the floor and snatched it up. The LCD showed the name of the caller: Giovanni's Trattoria.

It took him a second to process the information. Then he understood that she'd done more than hunker down behind the bar. She'd found a phone back there, a landline, and she'd called her own cell, which she'd left behind on the floor.

A ruse. And while he was chasing shadows...

He turned. Ran. Plowed through the kitchen doors, heedless of an ambush.

The kitchen was empty. The door to the alley hung open.

Outside, the rumble of an engine.

The keys—he'd left the goddamn keys in the Ford.

Along with the valise and the girl.

"Bitch," he breathed. "Fucking bitch."

He staggered into the alley just as the Ford whizzed past him in reverse, the nun at the wheel.

He snapped off three shots, starring the windshield, but her head was down and he missed her, God damn it.

The car skidded onto Crocker, accelerated, speeding away, gone, and Swann screamed.

It was a scream of rage, a sound of madness, and it echoed on the alley's brick walls and came back at him in hiccups of broken noise like mocking laughter.

And why shouldn't there be laughter? He'd *lost*.

At the very end, when everything was over and he was set for life, he'd lost it all.

He was back in the kitchen now. He lashed out, jerking open drawers, spilling their contents on the floor. He stumbled into the dining room and raged among the tables, overturning them, hurling chairs against the walls, and screaming, always screaming.

Lost. Lost it all.

The biggest play of his life, his final score, and it was gone and the nun had beaten him, the nun with her cell phone and its piping singsong ringtone…he could almost hear it…hear it right now…

He *did* hear it. The phone, jammed into his pocket, was ringing again.

It was her. Had to be. Calling to laugh at him.

He whipped out the phone and flipped it open.

"What?" he rasped.

"Oh, I'm sorry." A soft female voice with a Southern lilt, not the nun's voice. "I hope I haven't called the wrong number. Is this Kate Malick's phone?"

Swann almost clicked off, but some quality of urgency of the woman's tone made him hold on. "Yeah," he said more slowly. "I'm Kate's assistant."

"I see. Well, I'm sorry to disturb you so early, but she did say to call anytime."

"And you are?"

"My name is Georgia. I work at Teen Alliance, the shelter for runaways. And I have news. I've found Amber. I'm sure of it this time…Did you hear me? I found the girl Kate's looking for."

"I heard you," Swann said, and he smiled.

49

KATE sped two blocks from the restaurant and around a corner, then pulled to the curb and looked in the backseat, where Chelsea lay unmoving. Reaching between the seats, she pressed her fingers to the carotid artery and felt a throb of life.

"Chelsea?" She slapped the girl lightly on the cheek—the second time she'd slapped her in the past twelve hours. No response. Not even a murmur or groan. Her breathing was so slow and faint as to be nearly undetectable.

She was alive but deeply unconscious, maybe comatose, and in respiratory distress. Swann had overdone it with whatever drugs he'd injected.

Get her to a hospital. Call for an ambulance—

She'd forgotten all about Skip until the bleating of a horn made her turn to her left. Skip was there, double-parked alongside her, his side window rolled down. "You okay?" he shouted.

"Where's the nearest hospital?" She didn't know this neighborhood and didn't have her phone. "No, wait—that's where Swann might go. The *second* nearest."

"Let me check." He typed on his cell with thumb and forefinger, accessing the information online. "Good Samaritan. Corner of Sixth and Lucas. Follow me."

He accelerated, blowing through a yellow stoplight. Kate followed, running a red. She kept casting anxious glances at Chelsea's reflection in the rearview mirror. It would be so cruelly unfair if the girl died now, when she'd been rescued and her ordeal was over.

She hadn't even been sure Chelsea was in the car when she'd left the kitchen. Hadn't known the keys were in the ignition, either. She'd been prepared to hotwire the engine—another skill passed on to her by Barney, her mentor—but fortunately, there was no need.

The Ford was in bad shape, pockmarked with bullet holes and scraped along the driver's side. Swann had been in a shootout; expended shell casings littered the front compartment, and there was blood on the seat. Kate remembered that Grange and Di Milo were incommunicado, and feared she knew why.

The Ford was the car Sam had been directed to take. Obviously, Swann had caught up with him. It didn't take much imagination to guess what had happened after that.

Distantly, she was aware of the valise on the passenger seat. She hadn't bothered to check its contents. Two million dollars in jewels, not to mention the artwork, but none of it mattered if Chelsea didn't survive.

She sped west, over the Harbor Freeway. Skip guided her to the hospital in under three minutes. As they pulled up to the ER entrance, the sun broke the eastern horizon. She hoped it was a good omen.

She parked the car and opened the rear door while Skip disappeared inside the ER, emerging with a nurse and two orderlies.

The orderlies snapped open a gurney and loaded Chelsea onto it, then toted her inside, through the waiting room already crowded with the sick and hurt. The people in the chairs stared at Chelsea as she was carried past, and her name ran through the crowd in a ripple of astonished whispers.

Kate and Skip followed Chelsea into the ER but were stopped at the door to her room. The nurse who'd accompanied them said they had to stay out and let the doctors work.

Through the doorway, Kate could see another nurse already fitting Chelsea with an IV. As she watched, a doctor in green scrubs flew past her, into the room, and began examining the girl.

"What do we do now?" Skip asked, sounding lost.

"Did you call the police?"

"Huh? No. I thought we were keeping them out of it."

"It doesn't matter anymore. Call them and have them go to the restaurant." She shrugged. "Swann will have left by now, but maybe they can pick up his trail."

"He can't get far. You stole his ride."

"A man like that can always get transportation."

Skip looked uneasy. "Maybe you call the cops. I don't like to interact with the authorities."

"Just do it. I'm going to move the Ford away from the entrance. I left it sitting there."

With a couple million dollars of jewelry and art inside, she added silently. *Better secure that.*

She headed back toward the waiting room but was sidetracked when she spotted a pay phone. She could spare a minute to bring Alan up to date and see if there was any word on the chase car. She pumped in some coins and dialed his cell.

"Alan, what's up? You hear from Vince and Alfonse?"

There was a pause that scared her. "Chief, we've got some bad news in that department. Just got a call from the state police. They found our guys in a wrecked car on Sierra Highway. They were both shot. Shot dead."

It wasn't a surprise, not after what she'd seen of Swann's car. Still, she took it hard. For some reason, she thought of Grange petting Chanticleer, the small shivering dog in the big man's hands. And of that arrogant asshole Sal French, crowing about how many death threats he got, insulting Di Milo to his face while Di Milo just stood there, taciturn as always.

"Chief?" Alan asked, worried by her silence.

"I'm still here. Just…processing it." But she knew she couldn't process it. Not this soon. Not until the funerals, or afterward. "You said the police called you?"

"They found Guardian Angel ID on both…uh"—*bodies*, she knew he'd been about to say—"both men, so they gave us a call. Office calls are forwarded to my cell when I'm away from my desk."

She knew that, and he knew she knew it. It was just something to say, a small detail of normality to keep them both grounded.

"What about you?" he asked. "Any luck at the restaurant?"

It came back to her, then. He didn't know. Quickly, she ran through a summary of the events, ending with Chelsea in the ER and Skip calling the police. "Oh, and I got the valise back," she added indifferently.

"Is Chelsea going to make it?"

"She has to," Kate said firmly. "Get her mother down here."

"Will do. I—hold it, another call." Click, a few beats of silence as Kate shifted her weight restlessly, and then Alan was back. "Chief, got the lady from Teen Alliance on the line. She wants to talk to you."

"Can you patch her through?"

"No sweat."

A moment later, she heard Georgia's mellifluous Southern accent. "Miss Malick?"

"Yes, I'm here."

"I'm probably being awfully paranoid, but something about my earlier call didn't sit right with me."

"What earlier call?"

A beat of loaded silence. "The one I placed to your personal number. I talked to your assistant."

"When was this?"

"Why, just five or ten minutes ago."

"You say you talked to someone? Who?"

"Well, he *said* he was your assistant. But I don't know, I got a funny feeling about him. I thought I'd call your office and make certain—"

"What did you call about? What did you tell him?"

Again, Georgia hesitated. "That man *wasn't* your assistant, was he?"

"No. What did you tell him?"

"Where Amber is."

"You found her?"

"I'm quite sure of it. I've been showing the flyer to everyone who comes in. One girl knew her. She'd been with the gang when the police rousted them. She knew where Amber was headed."

"What makes you think she told the truth?"

"She wants Amber off the street. Says she's not cut out for it. Thinks she won't last much longer if she doesn't get help."

"Where's Amber crashing?"

"The Monroe Towers. It's this old low-income high-rise at Monroe and Normandie, just north of the 101. Condemned, but kids break in and squat. Amber and her set usually take a room on the top floor."

"You told all this to the man who answered my phone?"

"Well, not all of it. He wasn't interested in the details—"

"But you told him where to find Amber? The building? The room?"

"Yes. He *said* he was your assistant," she added defensively, miserably.

"I'm not blaming you, Georgia. Did you call Carson Banning?"

"No. You asked me not to."

"Good. Keep him out of this."

"Miss Malick, what is it? What's happening?"

"I have to go." She set the handset on the cradle and stood there for a long moment, leaning forward, her hand on the phone.

Then she dug out more coins and dialed her cell number.

Two rings, three, four.

He was making her wait, just as she'd made him wait when he called.

On the fifth ring, he answered. "Hello, Sister Kate. So who is this Amber, anyway?"

"She's no one. She's not important."

"She's important enough for you to tell that social services bitch to call you anytime. Anytime, even at five fucking thirty in the morning. So I'd say she's plenty important. I'd say she's important as hell."

"Swann—"

"I told you to *call me Jack*. But you can't follow simple fucking instructions. You don't know how to *behave*. That's your goddamn problem. *You don't take orders.*"

He was shouting into the phone. Losing whatever was left of his mind.

"I'm sorry, Jack."

"You're *not* sorry. You're trying to fuck with me in a whole new way. But not this time, Sister Kate. This time you do what you're fucking *told*."

"What you want me to do?"

"Bring me Chelsea."

She shut her eyes. "Jack, you know I can't do that."

"You can find a way. You have to. We'll make a swap. Amber for Chelsea."

"It can't happen."

"But I want her back. I just want her back." He was frantic, almost pleading.

"Chelsea is safe. You'll never get her again."

"So you want this other girl to die? Is that it?"

"I'm not trading one life for another. I'm not playing God, Jack. Not like you."

"You sanctimonious cunt." A long silence ticked past. "All right. All right, God damn it, then I want my reward. The bag with the jewelry. And the paintings. Bring that. It's my money. I earned it. I deserve it."

"Bring it where?"

"Where Amber is. You've got the same info I do. You know the building and even the room."

"You'll get it."

"And *you* have to bring it. No one else. No one comes with you, and no one comes instead of you."

"It'll be me. Just me."

"We'll finally get to spend some quality time together, Sister Kate. Looking forward to it."

Click.

Oh yes, he was looking forward to it, all right. She knew that, just as she knew why the delivery had to be made by her and no one else.

Swann was going to kill her, of course. And do it slowly, make her suffer. That was what he meant by quality time.

But she would go anyway.

50

THE Monroe Towers was a cement monolith rising next to a vacant lot. The building and the lot were hemmed in by a security fence, but gaps showed through the fence, marked by scattered leavings and trails of footprints.

Kate parked the Ford near the building's entrance and got out, lifting the valise. The bag, she noticed, was stained with Swann's blood.

She looped the strap of the valise over her left shoulder, leaving her right hand free.

Ducking, she slipped through a break in the fence, catching the sleeve of her jacket on a loose wire. She pulled it free, tearing the leather, not giving a damn.

The day was brightening, but the tower cast a long rectangle of shadow over its front walk. She left the sunlight and headed to the lobby doors in a deep drift of shade.

The doors were padlocked, but someone had broken the boarded-up windows on either side. The glassless frames were the new entryways. She stepped into a cavernous room cut off from sun and sky.

Power in the building had long since been extinguished. She drew her flashlight and let it guide her to the stairwell, a shaft of concrete threaded with an echoing metal staircase. She started climbing, aware that death waited for her on the top floor.

She had to watch her step. The stairs were strewn with castoff items. Syringes, condoms, pocket litter. Some of the treads were slick with dried vomit or feces. She caught the strong ammonia smell of urine. People had relieved themselves here, crouching in the stairwell like animals.

The building was a temporary home to many people, stirring awake. She saw them in the hallways as she passed each landing—huddled groups of three or four, drawing warmth from trashcan fires.

Most of them were children. Runaways like Amber, but unlike Amber, most had probably come from far away, riding a bus to reach Los Angeles, a city they knew from movies and TV shows. A city of dreams, they thought—and they ended up here, in this cinder block purgatory, starved and shivering, wearing unwashed clothes that clung to their unwashed skin, having quick, furtive sex in dark corners, picking up diseases and addictions, and dying young.

The city was a killer, and they were its victims, and this maze of concrete corridors was their burial ground.

She reached the top floor. She looked down the hall in both directions. An ambush was possible. Swann could be lying in wait.

But he wasn't. She heard his voice, desperate, crazed, from the far end of the hall.

"I don't give a shit. You're wasting your breath, asshole."

Another voice spoke in hushed, urgent tones, but Kate couldn't make out the words.

She advanced down the hall. The rooms lining the corridor were doorless—all the doors must have been removed for reuse when the building was condemned—and through each doorway came a glow of morning. She put away her flashlight and drew the gun.

Daniel Farris's gun.

En route to the towers, she'd detoured to the church and recovered it from the floor where it lay by the dead man.

She had checked the Sig Sauer's clip. Five rounds fired, nine left. The gun had been meant to kill her, earlier tonight. Now it just might save her life.

Swann was talking again. "You were never my friend. You were someone I could use."

She was a yard from the last doorway. There was only one door into the room. Just one way in or out. Every room was identical, and from passing the others, she knew this one would be small. A concrete cage. No space to maneuver.

Near the door she hesitated, listening.

The other voice was clearer now. A rasping, plaintive voice.

Carson Banning's voice.

He'd found his daughter—at the worst possible time.

"For Christ's sake, Jack," Banning said, "I'm your partner in this."

She risked a look inside, hoping Banning had Swann distracted, offering her a shot. No luck. Swann had one arm around Amber's waist and a gun to her head. Banning stood a couple of feet away, his hands open, palms up, pleading.

She didn't understand why he was so passive. He had to be armed. He'd been carrying a gun when he went after her, and he must still have it.

"I set it up," Banning went on in the same cajoling tone. "I was the go-between for you and Farris. It was practically my idea. God damn it, I'm as much a part of this as you are."

Kate stepped into the doorway. "Interesting confession."

The words came out louder than she'd expected, clanging against the bare walls.

Banning turned to her but didn't seem to see her. His whole focus was on Swann, and on the gun in Swann's hand, a gun aimed at his little girl.

The three of them—father, daughter, Swann—stood in a haze of pink light from the rising sun. There was nothing holy in that light. It was febrile, sickly, the color of hell.

Swann didn't bother to look in her direction. He held Amber tight, pressing her to his body, a human shield blocking any shot Kate might have had.

"Glad you could make it, Sister Kate. Bring the valise?"

"I've got it."

"Toss it my way."

"And then what? You'll shoot us all?"

"Jesus, Kate," Banning said, "do what he says."

"Shut up, Carson. I told you not to come looking for Amber."

"I had to find her—"

"Did you have to help Swann with his kidnapping plans, too?"

"I had my reasons."

"Everybody has their reasons," she said.

Swann glanced at her for the first time. The sun through the window burned on his bald scalp, reddening his face. He could have been a demon. "You giving up the bag or not?"

"First, you give me Amber."

"I don't think so."

She glanced at Banning, still wondering why he didn't draw and fire. Swann wasn't watching him. He had his chance.

Swann caught her look and smiled. "You hoping this asshole will shoot me?" He shook his head. "I already disarmed him. Came up from behind while he and his kid were enjoying a tender reunion."

That was it, then. One hope gone.

"You didn't mention she was a movie star's daughter," Swann added. "No wonder you were so keen to find her."

"You didn't mention you were working with a movie star, either. So I guess we both left out some details."

"Well, we're all coming clean now. Me and you and the guy you were fucking."

Banning had told him about that. She remembered Swann saying, *So you weren't a virgin? You were a fucking whore even way back then?*

She tried again to negotiate. "Why don't you let the girl go and hold on to her father as a bargaining chip?"

"Doesn't seem like he's worth much to you." Swann's gaze glittered, and Kate thought of rodents with their small, bright eyes. "Not worth much to anyone."

She didn't trust her marksmanship enough to take a shot at Swann with Amber in the way.

"Just give me the girl," she said, "and I'll throw you the bag. All the jewelry's here. Paintings, too. It's what you wanted."

Swann stared at her, a long stare throbbing with hate. "Then why don't I just shoot you and take it?"

"You're not the only one who's armed."

"I like my chances against you." He smiled, a brief, vicious smile. "But I'd rather not end things between us so impersonally. So here's the deal. You throw away your gun, then toss me the bag."

"Or?"

"Or I shoot this little bitch." He prodded Amber with the gun. She whimpered, eyes shut tight.

"Kate, God damn it"—Banning's voice was hoarse—"just give him what he fucking wants."

"If I do, he'll shoot her anyway."

"He won't. Tell her, Jack. You won't shoot anybody."

"Of course I will," Swann said, and he shifted the gun and fired once, into Carson Banning's chest.

Amber shrieked. Her father stared down at his shirt, blankly astonished.

"Why'd you do that?" he asked, the question oddly casual. His mouth twitched into an ingratiating smile, a movie-star smile. "We're friends."

"No one's my friend," Swann said.

He fired again.

Banning's head snapped back. He collapsed on the floor in an undignified sprawl.

Down the hall, there were muffled cries, stamping footfalls. People spooked by the gunfire, running away.

The noises faded, and then there was only the silence of death in the room.

Slowly, Kate stepped forward, out of the doorway, into plain view, offering herself as a target if Swann wanted to shoot. She didn't know why she did it. She only knew she wouldn't hide from this man.

"The bag," Swann said.

He hadn't shot her yet, and she realized there was still doubt in his mind, doubt that the valuables were really with her. She could have cleaned out the valise, could be carrying the bag empty, as a ruse.

"I'll leave it in the hallway," she said, "after I get Amber."

"You're fucking trying to negotiate, you stupid bitch? Didn't you see what I just *did*?"

"I saw it. That's why I'm not going to trust you, Jack."

"It's not about trust. It's about power. The power I have. I can kill this little shit." He cupped his hand over Amber's chin and lifted her head. "I can kill her, and you too. I can do *anything*. Now hand it over. *Hand it over!*"

If she did, Amber would die. And if she didn't…

Same outcome.

There was no way out. She couldn't talk him down, couldn't bargain, couldn't even get off a shot with the girl in the way.

"Hand it the fuck over," Swann breathed. "I'm telling you for the last time. Lose the gun. Toss the bag. Do it now."

She had no choice. Barney, her mentor, had taught her years ago never to surrender her weapon. But he wasn't here.

She threw her gun aside. It clattered on the concrete floor and skidded into a corner.

Carefully, she unshouldered the bag, then threw it across the room, where it landed at Swann's feet.

Still holding the girl, he stooped and opened the valise, looking inside. Something flickered in his face. Relief, elation, vindication.

"So I got it," he said, his voice hushed. "I won, after all."

"But you didn't get Chelsea."

He looked up, his eyes brighter than before. "I got you, Sister Kate. You're my consolation prize." He waved the gun. "Come here. Come on. Don't be shy."

She took a step toward him, and another, until she was close enough to see the blind panic in Amber's eyes and the tears on her cheeks.

"Kneel to me, Sister Kate. Kneel and worship. Pray to me."

His gun loomed, the muzzle a black hole of death.

She knelt.

"Repeat after me." His voice rang in the concrete vault. "Jack Swann is my shepherd, I shall not want."

"Jack Swann is my shepherd, I shall not want."

"He leadeth me beside still waters. He maketh me lie down in green pastures. Jack Swann restoreth my soul."

She said the words, the stupid, blasphemous words. "Jack Swann restoreth my soul."

"Though I walk through the valley of the shadow of death, I will fear no evil because Jack Swann is with me. His rod and his staff, they comfort me."

"They comfort me."

"Now, say, 'Jack Swann—into your hands I commend my spirit.'"

It would be her epitaph. She saw it in his eyes.

"No," she said.

"Say it."

"No."

Swann pressed the gun to Amber's temple. "I'll shoot her."

"You will, no matter what I do."

He let out a shout of laughter. "You're right about that, Sister Kate. I'm leaving three corpses behind when I get out of here. Now say the words."

"Why should I, Jack?"

"Say what I want, and I'll make it easy on the girl. I'll put her lights out with one shot. Deal?"

"No."

"That's the best offer you're going to get."

"It's not good enough."

"God damn it. Do what I say."

"No."

"You don't obey. You *never* obey!"

He would shoot her now, she knew he would, and Amber next. And there was nothing she could do. It was over.

She saw his finger tighten on the trigger.

And then he froze, his head cocked at an odd angle.

Listening.

"Sugarplum?" he whispered. "Is that you?"

51

SWANN'S ears still rang like cymbals from the gun's reports when he'd shot Banning, but over their constant chiming, he heard a new sound.

It was Chelsea, and she was singing the willow song.

He smiled, because it was so perfect, so right.

The nun had brought the girl, after all. Or the girl had come on her own, to be with him, as she was meant to be.

"It's okay," he said. "You can show yourself. I won't hurt you, sugarplum. You know I won't."

The song flowed through the room like the flood of morning sun, blinding him.

The poor soul sat sighing by a sycamore tree,
Sing all a green willow…

For a moment, he wondered if he could be imagining it. No, it was real, as real as it had been in the church when she sang for him.

"Come on out," he called. "Where are you hiding?"

He looked around the room, but the only place of concealment was a closet without a door, and there was no one inside.

She wasn't in this room, anyway. She was in the hall. That was where the music came from. The hall.

He started forward, forgetting the girl in his grasp until her deadweight slowed him down.

"Move!" he ordered, waving the gun at her.

The girl walked with him, dragging her feet. They brushed past the nun, kneeling on the floor. The nun didn't matter. Only the song mattered. It drew him forward.

Her hand on her bosom, her head on her knee,
Sing willow, willow, willow...

The hall was empty. He moved on, in pursuit of Chelsea's voice. He passed room after room. She wasn't in any of them.

It was impossible to tell where the song originated. It seemed to come from everywhere, the notes reverberating off the bare walls, a storm of echoes.

The fresh streams ran by her, and murmured her moans;
Sing willow, willow, willow...

Then he understood. It was the stairwell. That was where she was. The stairwell acted like a megaphone, amplifying sounds and scattering them throughout the building. She was singing to him from the stairs.

"Chelsea? Come to me, baby." He reached the landing. "Chelsea!"

The girl in his arms pulled free. She simply slipped loose, supple as a ferret, and he was holding empty air.

He let her go. She didn't matter.

He leaned over the railing. Flights of metal stairs dropped into darkness. There were no windows here; the daylight from the corridors barely touched the shaft.

In the shifting gloom, he saw a pale, thin figure.

Her salt tears fell from her, and softened the stones;
Sing willow, willow, willow...

It was her.

He descended the stairs, taking them two at a time. Distantly, he was aware of the complaint of his fractured ribs, the electric arcs of pain running up his side.

The song faded out. Halfway down the first flight of stairs, suspended between two floors, he saw her again, clearly this time. She had gone lower, staying below him. Silent now, she gazed up at him with her shining eyes.

There was no love in those eyes, and no anger, only contempt. He knew then that she was taunting him, mocking him. She had come back only to show him what he'd lost.

But he'd lost nothing. She was the one who'd lost.

He lifted his gun, centered the figure over the sights, and fired twice, the double report raising a clangor of new echoes.

It made no difference. She was still there. And his gun was empty. But he had Banning's gun, confiscated, tucked into the waistband of his pants. He threw aside his weapon and pulled out Banning's 9mm and drew a bead on Chelsea again.

He fired. He couldn't miss this time, but somehow he did.

"You fucking *bitch!*" he screamed.

She answered with laughter, light and musical.

He blasted at the sound. Chips of concrete flew off the walls. Sparks sizzled on the metal banister, the metal treads.

And still she was laughing. Laughing as he pulled the trigger again and again.

And then she was gone. Just gone.

He must've taken her out. It was the only explanation. She'd fallen.

"Got you!" he howled down the shaft. "*I got you*, you little shit!"

Flushed with triumph, he lifted his head, and there above him, on the landing, was the nun.

Resting both elbows on the railing, she trained her gun on him.

"Drop your weapon, Jack."

He stared at her, and in that moment, he came back to himself. He understood that Chelsea Brewer had never been there, that the song had been only in his head, that he'd fired at a shadow or a ghost. He'd given the nun an opportunity to recover her weapon. He'd surrendered his hostage. He'd emptied and discarded one firearm. He'd left himself open to attack from above.

It had been a temporary madness, and now, too late, he was sane.

"Drop it," she said.

Banning's gun wasn't empty yet. He stared up at her, taking her measure.

"You won't shoot me," he said slowly. "You're a nun."

She lifted her gun just a little. Her eyes never left his. "Not anymore."

It was her eyes that did it, her eyes and the unnatural calmness of her voice.

He knew then that he would never have a chance to get off a shot at her. She would gun him down where he stood.

Slowly, he spread his fingers and let the pistol fall. It hit the stairs and bounced down, clattering like a child's toy, disappearing into the dark.

Swann raised his hands in surrender.

52

THE police arrived just ahead of the ambulance, summoned by Kate after Swann gave back her cell phone. She saw Swann submit to handcuffs, his face unreadable. The paramedics had loaded Banning onto a stretcher by the time she got back to him. His face was sheeted, and no one was in any hurry to move his remains. Amber sat against a wall, draped in a blanket, protection against shock. Kate knelt by her and told her it would be okay.

Amber shook her head, refusing comfort. "So my dad was mixed up in this shit? He was, like, that crazy guy's accomplice or something?"

"We can talk about that later."

Kate expected a protest, but the girl seemed too exhausted to argue. "Who are you, anyway?"

"My name's Kate. I've been looking for you."

"Why?"

"To help."

Cynicism darkened her gaze. "Right. Saving lost girls—that's just what you do, right?"

Kate squeezed her arm. "It is, tonight."

―――――

Kate spent two hours with the police. She told them everything, withholding only Victoria's relationship with Banning. It wasn't her place to tell that part of the story.

At the end, she asked if she was under arrest. She wasn't.

At Good Samaritan Hospital, she found Victoria sitting with Skip and Alan in a room in the ICU. Chelsea lay in bed, unconscious, amid a tangle of tubes and wires. Blood tests showed she had overdosed on GHB. The overdose had brought on respiratory depression and bradycardia. She had been intubated and given atropine and activated charcoal, as well as a continuous saline drip to combat hypotension. No one was using the word *coma*.

"For now," Victoria said, "all we can do is wait."

And pray, Kate thought, remembering Mrs. Farris and her shrine to Mila. But Victoria didn't ask for a prayer, and Kate didn't offer one.

"You were right," Victoria spoke up abruptly, more than an hour after Kate's arrival. She was looking directly at Kate. "When you said I could replace any material thing, but I could never replace…You were right."

True to his word, Barry Larrison broke the story at seven a.m. on *Good Morning America*. Hospital security kept the media out. From the window, Kate could see a line of TV vans with satellite uplinks, reporters doing live stand-ups outside the ER. Carrion feeders gathering to gnash their beaks and caw. She hated them.

"Goddamn vultures," Skip said, following her gaze.

She looked at him, surprised to hear her thoughts echoed by Skip, of all people. He glanced away, but not before she caught the guilty, self-conscious flicker in his eyes.

An hour later, Victoria spoke again, this time without looking at anyone. "They found Sam."

Kate glanced at Alan. "Did they?"

Alan nodded. "Forgot to mention it, chief. We got the call on the way over."

"He was left by the side of the road," Victoria said. "He'd been… mutilated. He's dead, of course," she added as an afterthought.

"I'm sorry," Kate said, though the news was no surprise.

"Are you?" Victoria's mouth puckered. "I'm not."

At noon, Kate took a walk through the ICU. She couldn't stand the bedside vigil any longer. She had to move, walk, think, or she would go crazy.

She wondered if Swann was somewhere in the ICU. More likely, he was in surgery. He had been wounded in his encounter with Grange and Di Milo. Shot three times, she'd heard. Her men had drawn blood, at least.

She looked down at the street, where the TV people seemed to be hastily setting up for new live reports. By now the coverage would be wall-to-wall, every channel, a whole nation fascinated by the death of Carson Banning and speculating about Chelsea's fate.

But as for Grange, Di Milo—no one cared about them. No one cared about the driver of the Hyundai shot to death in the street, a man whose name Kate didn't even know. No one cared about Mila Farris, dead of an overdose, her story hushed up. No one cared about the children of the Monroe Towers or the vagrant named Lazarus by the railroad tracks.

The sisters used to comfort themselves by saying God cared. God watched out for all the forgotten ones. But where was God tonight? Was he there for Chelsea? For Amber? For anyone?

God was nowhere. There was nothing but pain, nothing but grief. Children dying in graffiti-streaked corridors or in the sterile confines of the ICU.

She walked back to Chelsea's room, feeling empty. It took her a moment to realize that Victoria was seated on the bed, holding her daughter's hand, and Chelsea's eyes were open.

Kate caught Alan's eye. "How long ago?" she asked softly.

"Couple minutes. She just opened her eyes and smiled, like nothing had happened."

No wonder the reporters had been preparing to go back on the air. They'd heard the news even before Kate had.

A nurse came, then a doctor, and after some consultation, the endotracheal tube was removed. Chelsea coughed hard for thirty seconds, then motioned for a glass of water.

"Kate," she said when she could speak.

She approached the bed and leaned in, avoiding the IV lines and the ECG leads, and gave Chelsea a quick, fierce hug.

"They said"—the girl's voice was rough as sandpaper—"you rescued me. They said Swann came after you with a gun…"

"Don't worry about Swann. He's in custody."

"I know. Mom told me." Chelsea frowned. "I wish he'd been killed."

"He'll be locked up for life."

"You never know. This is California." She took a closer look at the people around her. "Do I know you?" she asked Skip.

"I was just…um…freelancing for Kate tonight."

"Skip was very helpful," Kate said. "He supplied some major technical expertise."

"Atoning for past sins," Skip said uncomfortably.

Chelsea giggled, a pleasingly girlish sound. "What sins?"

"Exploitation of my fellow humans for fun and profit."

"That's not a sin. That's just, you know, the business. So I guess the TV assholes are all over this, huh?"

"Like stink on a monkey," Skip said.

"Well, fuck 'em." Chelsea sounded cheerful. "I don't care."

"You'll have to make a statement," Victoria said cautiously. "They'll be expecting it."

"Fuck 'em. That's my statement."

Victoria folded her hands. "I'll come up with something more appropriate."

"Whatever. Hey, did Gabrielle get out of Panic Room all right?"

"I saw her," Kate said, pleased that Chelsea would ask about her friend. "She was fine. Worried about you, though."

"Yeah, when she sees this on the news, she'll freak." Chelsea seemed to enjoy the prospect, but then her face turned serious. "You're *sure* he can't get out?"

"He'll never get out," Kate said. "He'll never hurt you again."

She nodded, not quite believing it. "How long was I unconscious, anyway?"

Victoria estimated six hours or longer.

"He gave me way too much of that stuff. I had the funkiest dreams. Really vivid." Chelsea stared at the ceiling. "About *him*, of course. Who else, right?"

"It's best not to think about him now," Victoria said.

"Yeah, okay. But…it was weird. I mean, I could swear I was really there with him. Singing that stupid song."

Kate let a moment pass. "What song?"

"It's from Shakespeare. An audition piece I learned a million years ago. Swann made me act it out for him. I was Desdemona, and I sang about the willow tree…"

"This was your dream?"

"No, that part really happened. In that old church where he was holding me. Where he killed Mr. Farris. You know about that, right?"

Kate nodded.

"And Chanticleer. He got killed, too." Moisture glimmered in her eyes, but she went on resolutely. "The dream was different. I was singing, but he couldn't see me, which was weird 'cause I was right there. And it was driving him crazy. He was looking for me everywhere and calling for me and then…then he started shooting at me. But I wasn't scared. I knew he couldn't hurt me. I thought it was funny. I was laughing at him."

"You dreamed all that?" Kate asked quietly.

"Yeah." Chelsea closed her eyes. "Really vivid. Trippy, you know?"

"It was only a dream," Victoria said.

Maybe it was, Kate thought. But Victoria hadn't been there. Hadn't seen how Swann had looked, his eyes wild, his head darting, as if seeking the source of an elusive, maddening sound. Calling Chelsea's name. Chasing her—chasing something—on the stairs. Firing into the darkness.

And all the while, Chelsea had been unconscious in this hospital, near death, and dreaming her dream.

Coincidence, possibly. But in a night with so much suffering and loss, could there have been a miracle—just one small miracle—to help balance the scales?

And did that mean God was watching, after all?

She didn't know. Her uncertainty was new and unfamiliar. Frightening, almost, because she didn't know what it meant or where it might lead.

"You should rest now," Victoria told her daughter. "You don't want to wear yourself out."

"Yeah, okay." She was already drifting off.

As Kate was leaving the room with the others, Chelsea surprised her by saying, "Tell Mr. Grange I'm sorry I treated him so, you know, shabbily. I was pretty much a bitch."

"I'll tell him," Kate said firmly.

She meant it, too. Later, with eyes closed and hands folded, she would tell Grange.

And maybe, somehow, he would hear.

53

SWANN lounged for six days in the Men's Central Jail in a single-man cell in the High Power block, the ward reserved for the most serious offenders. That was the theory, anyway. In practice, High Power was reserved for the offenders who'd garnered the most media attention. In LA, you really weren't anybody unless you'd been on TV.

He had been all over TV. He knew it, even though there was no TV in his cell. He knew it from the mob of reporters stationed outside the courthouse on the day of his arraignment, and the standing-room-only status of the courtroom. He knew it because the camera people tailed him back to jail, shooting video of the sheriff's department van. He knew it because one of the deputies in the jail surreptitiously asked for his autograph.

His *autograph*. Swann could hardly believe it. Fucking thing would probably wind up on eBay. But he signed. He signed with a goddamned flourish and handed back his signature with a smile.

So far he had met no other cons. He was isolated from the general population and even from the other heavy hitters in the High Power wing. But he hadn't been lonely. Some DEA narcs dropped by to talk to him about his activities in Miami some years ago. LAPD detectives asked him to clarify some details in the Brewer case, and they inquired about Bob Ellis, recently deceased, and his old pal Giovanni, who had gone missing.

To all questions, Swann had one response, and only one.

"After I talk to the nun."

At first they told him it was impossible. Then they told him it would be too difficult to arrange. Then they told him it might be doable, if he gave them some preliminary cooperation.

He didn't cooperate. He didn't give them anything. He had time, nothing but time, and he was a patient man. Once he talked to the nun, in person, in the same room, not on a video hookup, not through a sheet of glass…once he sat down with her, face-to-face, and they had their little chat, then and only then would he talk to the DEA and the LAPD and, hell, the YMCA, if necessary. Until then, he would say nothing to anybody.

He waited.

And finally they came for him.

They took him out of the cell, his wrists cuffed to a chain around his waist, his legs shackled. They marched him through the labyrinth of long white hallways, into an elevator that went down three floors, then through more corridors, and into a small, windowless room with a big metal table and two chairs. They sat him in one of the chairs and cuffed his hands to the table. One of the deputies stayed behind, standing against the wall and eyeballing him, while the other went to fetch someone.

They provided no explanation, but he knew. He'd broken them. They had brought him the one he wanted. They'd brought the nun.

He glanced around the room, noting a glint of light in an upper corner near the ceiling, which was probably a miniature camera. He had no doubt his conversation would be recorded. That was fine. He'd already waived his right to an attorney. At the arraignment, he'd pled guilty, sparing himself the inconvenience of a trial. All that was left was his formal sentencing, sometime next week.

The door opened, and she came in. She wore a black shirt and matching slacks, an outfit severe as a habit. Her hair was pinned back, bringing out the strong lines of her cheeks and jaw.

"Hey, Sister Kate," Swann said amiably.

She took the chair on the opposite side of the table. The deputy at the wall didn't move. They weren't leaving him alone with her, even when he was cuffed to the table, immobilized. They respected him, and he was pleased about that.

"I'm told you want to speak to me," Kate Malick said.

"How's Chelsea?"

"She'll be fine."

"Tell her I said hi."

"Chelsea will never know I was here."

"You're awfully serious, Sister Kate. You got a crucifix up your ass or something? Or maybe you keep it in a different hidey-hole."

The deputy snapped, "Watch it."

"The gentleman's defending your honor," Swann remarked. "Your girlish virtue."

Kate Malick just stared at him. He found her gaze somehow unsettling. It was the same gaze he'd faced in the stairwell.

"You know, you're supposed to be all about redemption. But be honest—you don't want redemption for a man like me. You want me burning in that lake of fire."

She said nothing.

"When it comes down to it, you're all about revenge, not redemption. And so's your God. He's licking his chops waiting to get hold of me."

"You don't believe in God."

"Neither do you."

"You don't know what I believe."

"How can you be sure?"

"Because I don't know, either."

Swann frowned. "So you're coming home to Jesus, are you? Too bad. Last thing the world needs is another deluded true believer."

"Is this why you asked for me? To have a theological discussion?"

"I asked for you because you earned it. Why should some lazy-ass cops get all the glory? You took me down. And you were nice enough not to pull the trigger when you had the chance."

"I'm surprised I didn't have to. Sam told me you'd never let yourself be taken alive."

"Sam didn't know me as well as he thought."

"Why *did* you surrender?"

"Simple. Something beats nothing."

"Meaning?"

"Life in a cell isn't much, but it beats no life at all. Dead is dead, and I'm not inclined to be dead just yet."

"And maybe you hope you'll break out of here?"

Swann shook his head. "I'm a realist. This is it for me. Before long, they'll ship me upstate to Corcoran or Pelican Bay. A different set of walls. And that's where I'll stay. Twenty-three-hour lockdown. Zero contact with the other inmates. Two showers a week. A toilet in my cell that I have to scrub myself. Corn flakes for breakfast, turkey bologna for lunch, beef stew for dinner. Lights out at ten thirty. Wake up at five and do it all over again. Every day for the rest of my life. I'll get old and I'll die."

He drummed his fingers on the tabletop, a hard staccato sound.

"But until I'm dead, I'll have food in my belly and a blanket at night. Maybe I'll smile now and then. Maybe I'll even get some sun in the exercise yard, eventually, when I'm old enough to pose no threat, or when everyone's forgotten who I was. I'll have breath in my lungs, going in and out."

"It's not a lot."

"No, it isn't. But it beats what Sam's got, doesn't it? And Banning."

"Let's talk about Banning."

"How he fits into all this? Sure. Must've been a real kick in the privates to find out he was working with me, huh? I mean, considering your special relationship."

"It was a betrayal. I'll get over it."

"Never trust anybody, Sister Kate. Then you'll never be disappointed."

"Tell me about Banning."

"His career was on the skids. Nothing but flops lately. Lots of expenses, red ink. His finances were shot to hell—he told me so. Took a major hit when the stock market tumbled. Had his money tied up with some fancy-ass wheeler-dealer who lost it all. He was strapped for cash in a big way, and he wasn't the sort of guy who would cut back on his lifestyle. That's why he started banging Mrs. Brewer. It wasn't love. It was a business move."

"How did you come into the picture?"

"I found out somebody was talking about me out of school. It had to be Sam or Giovanni. So I came out here and had a talk with Giovanni. Ruled him out. That left Sam. I was watching his house when the black Lexus left. I knew it was his vehicle, and I assumed he was driving, so I followed. But that day, Victoria took the Lexus. Maybe she didn't like using her own car when she went on a booty run."

"She visited Banning?"

"Right. I watched him meet her at the motel. Recognized him right off. Guy was a fucking movie star, after all. Even with a hat on and wraparound shades, he couldn't hide his famous face. They were in his room about an hour. After she left, I knocked on the door. Introduced myself. We had a chat. At first he thought I wanted to blackmail him. But I've never been into blackmail. Too complicated. I just wanted to know if he was interested in having Sam Brewer out of the picture. I said I could arrange it, for a fee. I knew I was going to do the job anyway, and I didn't mind making some money on it, as a sort of fringe benefit."

"And?"

"Banning said he couldn't get involved in anything like that. Not directly. But he knew a guy who might be able to make use of my services."

"Daniel Farris," she said.

"Give the lady a prize. Yeah, Banning had bought a plane from Farris, and they'd gotten pretty tight. Especially after Farris's kid died. Farris leaned on Banning for support. Confessed all kinds of shit to him. That's how Banning knew about Farris's betting problem. Farris fessed up, told him how he was putting down money on the next celeb to die. And then he started making these jokes. Only, they weren't jokes. You know, how if he had Chelsea killed, he could avenge his little girl and win back some of his losses at the same time. A twofer. Laughing it up. But you can't lie to an actor, I guess. Banning knew Farris meant it. And when Banning met me, he saw a way to work things so Sam Brewer would be out of the way, with no risk of implicating himself."

"Why did he care so much about Victoria? Carson Banning could have had lots of women. Pretty much any woman he wanted."

"Including you, Sister Kate. But I guess that part of the story hasn't gotten out. Don't worry, it'll be our little secret, unless some lowlife from the DA's office spills the beans. Anyway, Banning didn't want just any woman. He wanted a woman who was rich and in the media spotlight and in tight with every producer and studio exec in town. He wanted Victoria Brewer. But he knew she'd never marry him as long as her ex was in the picture. She didn't love Sam, but she was, you know, dependent on him. Mentally, emotionally. Whatever—I'm not really up on that psychological crap. Bottom line, Banning wanted Sam out of the way."

"How about Chelsea? Did Banning care about her?"

"Not a bit. I'm the one who cared. I really did save her. She's alive because of me."

Kate said nothing, just waited for him to go on.

"Banning set up a meet for the three of us. By then him and me were pretty close. I took a room in the same motel he used for his extracurricular activities. There was a billboard right across the street with Chelsea's picture on it. I could see it from my room. Just a coincidence, but it felt like fate. At the meeting, Farris paid me half the money up front. For a hit on Chelsea, to avenge his dead daughter. But all along, Banning and I planned to screw him over. I was going to kidnap Chelsea and kill Sam. And instead of the balloon payment on my fee, I would get two million dollars in Victoria's jewels."

"Whose idea was it to go for the jewelry?"

"Banning's. Victoria talked up her jewelry collection to him. He had no problem with Victoria being ripped off. The jewels were insured, so it wasn't like she'd lose any of her money—money being the principal reason he was involved with her in the first place. By the way, Banning told me about the paintings, too. Victoria liked to brag about her art."

"And once Sam was dead…"

"Banning would marry Victoria, and she could keep him in the lifestyle he was accustomed to. Private planes don't come cheap, you know. If Chelsea was dead, he'd share in the public sympathy. If she was alive, he'd be the stepdaddy of Hollywood's biggest star.

Either way, he'd be back on top, which was just where he wanted to be."

"Wasn't Banning worried there would be blowback from Farris after you double-crossed him?"

"What could Farris do? He wouldn't blame Banning. All the heat would be on me."

"Not all of it. You implicated Farris when you called in the anonymous tip to my office."

"Yeah, that's true. But Banning didn't know about that part of it."

"So it was a *double* double cross? Betray both of them?"

Swann shrugged. "Sure."

"And through all this, Banning trusted you? I didn't think he was that naive."

"These Hollywood types always think they're smarter than they are. But I don't think he trusted me entirely. He picked up an extra bodyguard after we started working together. I'm pretty sure the additional protection was on my account."

Kate remembered Sal French, in the restaurant on the night of Chelsea's abduction, complaining about Banning's two security escorts. "Did you have any plans to kill him?"

"Nah. I liked his movies—well, some of them."

"Yet you shot him in the towers."

"He was getting on my nerves. All that crybaby crap about his kid."

"Did you know Amber was his daughter?"

"Not a clue, till I showed up and found him there." Swann smiled. "Small world, huh?"

"Did you kill Giovanni?"

"What's it to you?"

"Did you kill him?"

"I can't see any advantage to answering that question."

"How about Bob Ellis?"

"Bob who?"

"Don't play games, Jack."

"Didn't Chelsea tell you what happened?"

"She has no memory of that part of it."

"Funny thing. Neither do I."

She nodded, seeming to accept the fact that she would get no more out of him on that subject. She leaned forward, and he had the sense that now she was getting to the heart of the interview, the thing she really wanted to know.

"When you fired the gun in the stairwell, you thought were shooting at Chelsea, didn't you?"

He frowned. The question both surprised and irritated him. That was the one part of the whole episode he'd done his best to forget.

"Yeah," he said reluctantly.

"What made you think she was there?"

"I thought I saw her. And…heard her."

"You thought she was talking to you?"

"Singing to me."

"Singing?"

He shifted in his seat. "I don't know, I guess I'd lost more blood than I thought. It sure as hell cost me, didn't it? Christ, sometimes I can still hear it—that goddamn Shakespeare song about the willow tree."

The nun's eyes showed something, but he couldn't tell what. Then it was gone and she was rising, pushing her chair back, the metal legs scraping the floor.

"So at the end," she said, "you wanted her dead."

"Just for that moment."

"If you had to do it over again, would you still keep her alive?"

"Sure I would. I never had it in for her. There's just one thing I'd do differently."

She waited, standing by the table.

"Remember how you were hunting for me in Stiletto, and I amscrayed out the window? I wouldn't play it that way. I'd wait for you in that back hallway and when you came looking…I'd snap your neck." He raised his manacled hands and pantomimed the movement. "Wouldn't be hard. It's a slender neck."

He studied her face, hoping for a reaction, something he could carry with him into the long dark tunnel of his future. She gave him nothing. She merely turned to go.

"How about you, Sister Kate? Anything you'd do differently?"

She looked back, her hand on the door.

"On the landing," she said, "I'd pull the trigger."

Swann watched the door swing shut with an echoing clang. Then he leaned back in his chair and laughed.

54

A week after meeting with Swann, Kate drove to Victoria Brewer's house.

The sun had set by the time she powered the Jag to the crest of Beverly Glen and turned onto Mulholland Drive. After ten days in the shop, the car was running smoothly again, the engine purring like a panther as the car prowled the night.

She took the curves fast, glimpsing flashes of the city past a scrim of dark foliage. The evening was warm and windless, the world hushed.

She appreciated the quiet, the privacy. Since the story had broken she'd had little of either. Media attention had been unrelenting for the first week. The police had endless questions. The office phone rang with requests for personal protection. It seemed no one in LA could afford to be without the services of Guardian Angel. And there were the funerals for Grange and Di Milo, the painful hugs shared with Di Milo's family, and more painful still, the absence of any family at Grange's burial. No wife or children. He'd been alone.

She was gratified that Skip Slater attended both services. The publicity had been good to Celebrity Whack-A-Mole. The site was more reviled and detested than ever, which, of course, only made it more popular. But Skip didn't seem happy. There were rumors that he was negotiating a sale, that he wanted nothing more to do with the site. She didn't know if the rumors were true. She would find out, in time.

The low driveway that descended to the Brewer house came up. She slowed the car and pulled in. No one was watching the house now. Swann's camera, wired into a utility pole, was taken as evidence. For days, the media people camped out on this street, until police harassment and declining public interest drove them away.

She parked near the steps and got out, leaving her Glock in the glove compartment. She wouldn't need it here. A pair of Guardian Angel bodyguards, assigned to deter publicity-seeking copycats, were on twenty-four-hour duty at the house. One of them waved from the front window, and she lifted her hand in reply.

What she had to do next was hard. As hard, in its own way, as anything she had done on the night when Chelsea had been taken.

She heard Banning's voice in her memory:

You'll handle it. You always do.

It was one of the few things he hadn't lied to her about.

She walked to the front door. Through the window, Chelsea was visible, seated with her mother on the divan, the two of them chatting like friends. Chelsea had spent two days in the hospital before coming here to stay with her mother. Her recuperation was nearly complete. She looked rested and healthy. Almost ready to move back to her own place, resume her life, start going out again. More parties, more wild nights. Or maybe not.

That was why Kate was here. To talk with Chelsea about her future. About choices, and mistakes, and the high price those mistakes could carry.

If the girl would listen. If she would learn.

Before going in, Kate said a little prayer.

ACKNOWLEDGMENTS

As always, I invite readers to visit me at michaelprescott.net, where you'll find news about upcoming or rereleased books, a bibliography, contact info, and more.

Many people contributed to *Grave of Angels*. In particular, I would like to thank David Downing for his sensitive and adept editing of the final draft; Deborah Schneider for handling the sale of the novel to Amazon Publishing; Cathy Gleason, Deborah's assistant, who took care of the paperwork; Maria Gomez and Terry Goodman of Amazon, who brought me on board; Lorin Oberweger, Donald Maass, and Gary Heidt for their insights and encouragement; Diana Ross for proofreading the early versions; Deb Taber for copyediting the final draft; and Margaret Falk for her feedback and support.

—MP

ABOUT THE AUTHOR

Born and raised in New Jersey, Michael Prescott attended Wesleyan University, majoring in film studies, then pursued a career as a screenwriter in Los Angeles. In 1986 he wrote his first novel; published steadily since that time, he is now the author of twenty-two thrillers, one of which, *Shiver*, was recently made into a movie starring Danielle Harris and John Jarratt. Currently at work on a new book, Prescott is also republishing his older titles in e-book editions, which have found a wide new audience.